According to Yes

By the same author

Oh Dear Silvia

A Tiny Bit Marvellous

Dear Fatty

According to Yes

DAWN FRENCH

PENGUIN BOOKS

PENGUIN BOOKS

UK | USA | Canada | Ireland | Australia
India | New Zealand | South Africa

Penguin Books is part of the Penguin Random House group of companies
whose addresses can be found at global.penguinrandomhouse.com.

First published by Michael Joseph 2015
Published in Penguin Books 2016
001

Printed and bound in Great Britain by Clays Ltd, Elcograf S.p.A.

A CIP catalogue record for this book is available from the British Library

ISBN: 978-1-405-93838-9

www.greenpenguin.co.uk

Penguin Random House is committed to a
sustainable future for our business, our readers
and our planet. This book is made from Forest
Stewardship Council® certified paper.

Nom patrui mei Dr Michael O'Brien, qui delexit verba

and

for Dr Cassie Cooper, my beloved friend

I moved my chair into sun

I sat in the sun

the way hunger is moved when called fasting.

'I sat in the sun', Jane Hirshfield

ACT I

Tested

Fifty-seven

Fifty-eight

Fifty-nine . . . Fuck.

Yet again, Rosie Kitto's belly was empty. No baby. Why did they bother to wait the full three minutes? As much as she knew anything, she knew there was no chance, but his darling desperate face persuaded her to see it through. Along with that second thin blue line on the pregnancy test, all trace of hope for a future with him failed to show up.

Funny how a moment so anticipated can be so fleeting and mundane in its failure. There was no mighty crash when the hope toppled, only a quiet whimper.

That hope deserved a bigger send off.

Once, it had been giant.

Landed

As if tightly choreographed by Pina Bausch, every puffy face in every serried row on the British Airways 747 is obediently upturned, staring at the seatbelt sign overhead. An elastic moment where a random group of strangers are united, some don't even breathe so suspended are they. Bing bong. The familiar cue releases them from their airline aspic, and all at once the plane bursts into a chaotic scuffle of bodies racing to grab their belongings, rushing to be first to stand still in a queue to get off. Everyone is frazzled, perhaps it's the lack of fresh air that makes people so grumpy. They all seem to have somewhere very very important to be. Somewhere that just can't wait. So, come on, hurry up. Me first. Shuffle. Push. Jostle.

In 26A, Rosie is the only person who remains seated. She gazes calmly out of the window with her forehead tilted onto the glass. She has been sitting just like this for the best part of the journey, lost in thought. No, not lost. Found in thought.

Thinking such a lot, working out how she feels about flying away from everything and everyone that she knows and starting an impetuous new adventure like this. She feels strangely calm, accepting. She has surely surrendered to her future, whatever it might bring. So why is she the only one still sitting, whilst the others have filed off the plane in an impatient orderly line, exiting past the very polite, well-rehearsed air stewardesses?

'Thank you for flying British Airways.'

'Thank you.'

'Thank you for flying with us today.'

'Thank you.'

'Have a lovely day.'

'Thank you.'

'Goodbye.'

'You're welcome.'

'Thank you for flying British Airways.'

'Cheerio.'

'Thank you.'

'Thank you.'

'Yes, thank you, yes, get off, yes, go away, sod off, goodbye.'

Why isn't she moving?

You know that tiny fragment of time, just exactly before the point of no return? The golden moment where you might . . . could . . . just maybe COULD change your mind, and reverse it all? Take it all back, say no, don't jump, be safe, go home. That moment? That's where Rosie is. Part of her wants to remain on the plane and let it bounce her back home on its return journey with all the new crew that will come aboard, fresh faced, fresh make-up, fresh hairdo, fresh smell. Spit spot. Bound for home. For home. For lovely familiar drizzly comfy old England. Where, even if she knows it's wrong, at least she knows how to *be*. That's where Rosie Kitto, thirty-eight, primary school teacher, is assuredly grown up, reliable and emotionally tuned in. This new Rosie Kitto seems to be running away like a seriously immature selfish twit. Very ungrown up.

Who is she?

Well, she is the person who, a couple of weeks ago, said no to all the even keel, and yes to grabbing life by the throat, yes to jumping off the edge, yes to what the hell's it going to be like?, yes to being afraid. YES, YES, YES PLEASE!

That's right.

So, get out of your seat, Rosie, this is New York . . . here goes . . . COME ON!!

'Thank you for flying British Airways today, goodbye.'

Met

In a new round mirror is a reflection of an old oval face. Everything is in its place here, especially on this fading face, because subtle expensive surgery has helped it be so. Glenn Wilder-Bingham has applied her make-up this same way for sixty years. She could probably do it without the mirror, she could certainly do it without the actual make-up, because the brushes, the pads, the puffs and the pencils have enough residue on them for a week's worth of daily applications. It is nearly done, except for the very last part of the process, which is the concealer. She clicks the end of the expensive concealer pen and draws bold lines of creamy light-diffusing liquid under her eyes, around the base of her nose, over her frown wrinkles, and along the sagging lines of her jaw. The stripes are bold and her reflection shows her a reverse negative of her face. It's light where it was dark, it's seemingly tight where it was loose. She blends the concealer with her finger and after adroitly powdering it all down, only a trained eye would notice her renovations. Not bad for a seventy-eight-year-old Upper East Side dame.

There is a gentle knock on the bedroom door, and from outside, Glenn hears the soft voice of her maid, Iva, 'She is here, Mrs Wilder-Bingham. Where shall I put her?'

'The library.'

Glenn takes a deep breath and expels a huge irritated sigh, which clouds up her mirror. Yet another chore to eat up her valuable empty time. She doesn't move immediately, she's in no hurry. Glenn Wilder-Bingham is no stranger to keeping folks waiting.

Someone else looking at her reflection, in the panelled mirror of the elevator, is Rosie Kitto, but she sees something entirely different. She sees a drowned poodle of a woman. This wasn't the look she had planned for an important interview. Until five minutes ago, she was dry and fairly presentable. She doesn't ordinarily wear make-up much, but she has put a little bit on today and she has wrestled with a round brush and blow-dried her naughty hair so that it looks nearly tidy. This is the Upper East Side. People here care about this stuff, so she wants to appeal, to be what her Cornish mum always called ''andsome'. Typically, Rosie wears bright and bold clashing colours with great panache. She always has, and now that she's thirty-eight, she has found a vintagey way to wear them. She often wears a bright scarf in a big askew bow on her head and vibrant flowery blouses, with rolled-up jeans that might reveal orange socks in her winkle-picker shoes, like a cheerful 40's landgirl. She finds this style suits her curvy figure and makes her happy, because it gives her the chance to rootle about in vintage clothes shops, oh joy, her favourite pastime. The pleasure a hidden-at-the-back-of-the-rail treasure can bring, and the thrill of the bargaining to boot. But Rosie is not a fool. She knows instinctively she will have to introduce any new employer to this eccentricity in stages, slowly. So for today, she has really tried to tone it down, smart navy pleated-front slacks, a yellow blouse and a light blue linen jacket. The red brogues are a bit of a risk, but she wants to be at least a *tad* honest about who she is, to anchor herself somewhat in her own authenticity.

Rosie hasn't allowed for the changeable New York February weather. It was sunny and snappy when she set out to walk the fifty or so blocks from her cheap as chips but clean hotel near Times Square. Two blocks from the imposing Upper East Side building where the Wilder-Binghams live, the heavens opened and sploshed their contents onto the head of Rosie Kitto. She has darted into doorways for shelter, but not wanting to be late she pushed on, trying to avoid the rods of unrelenting wet that hammered onto her blown dry head and her coat-less shoulders.

So now, Rosie Kitto sees a drenched frizzy-headed poodle woman looking back at her from the mirror in the elevator.

This is who her potential employer is going to meet. Not a great first impression, but Rosie is a buoyant person, a great believer in 'find the funny side', 'keep yer perk up'. Surely Mrs Wilder-Bingham will see what's happened and raise a smile? It might even be the perfect ice-breaker? Who knows?

The elevator is posh, wood-panelled and slow. The dour doorman was quick to make her feel less than comfortable. His lofty manner is uncalled for, but effective if his aim is to make sure you know you are a visitor only. Yes, you are lucky to be visiting someone in this quiet, grand, supervised building. You won't be here long. You don't really fit. But in the very temporary meantime, welcome to the intimidating lift. He has told her to go to the twelfth floor. Now that she's in the elevator alone, she realizes that she doesn't know which apartment it is on the twelfth floor. She needn't have worried. As the doors open, she realizes she is in a private hallway, with just one door in front of her.

The Wilder-Binghams don't just live on the twelfth floor. They *are* the twelfth floor. Just as Rosie reaches for the doorbell, the door is opened and standing there is a short, stocky woman of massive immediate presence. Rosie is tempted to step back to make room for the substance of her, so singularly effective is she. She hasn't spoken yet, but already she is significant. Rosie knows this undoubtedly, because unlike anyone she's met before, Rosie wants to simultaneously lean back to take her all in, and lean forward to know her better. Who is this? She has a neat bun on the top of her head and is wearing a black dress with buttons from the neck to the knee all the way down the front, which is clearly a uniform. In an instant, she examines Rosie thoroughly from head to foot. Unlike the doorman though, Rosie doesn't feel disliked by her, she just feels scrutinized, which is actually . . . . . . OK. This could so easily be Mrs Danvers, but it is actually Iva.

'Come in,' she says. She is, what? Polish?

'Thank you. Sorry. Bit . . . wet.'

Rosie is aware that each step is a squelch, it would seem that her marvellous red brogues are functioning as sponges. Not only are they leaking water with each step, the red dye is also running, so she is leaving little bloody pools in her wake as she follows Iva up a long dark corridor.

This corridor wasn't intended to be as dark, requiring internal lighting at all times. It's the kind of space that is supposed to have light thrown into it by the leaving open of various doors all the way along. That doesn't happen in this apartment under the rule of Glenn Wilder-Bingham. No. All doors remain neatly shut, and all the corridors off the main hallway, of which there are four, remain gloomily dark. It's not that Glenn Wilder-Bingham is a vampire, it's that she is a consummate control freak. If she could she would control all the light and doors in the world. As it is, she has to satisfy herself with the light and doors in this vast apartment only. Until she takes over the world, this will have to suffice.

Squelch squelch, Rosie trudges behind Iva. The journey to the library takes longer than you would think it was possible to walk in an apartment, giving Rosie an inkling of its sheer size. Like most British people, she would regard a big flat as about the size of a house, but on one level. Twenty steps would more than cover it, walking from a hallway to a reception room. Not here. This place is huge and strange. Eventually Iva opens a door, and inside they go.

Three large windows dominate this daunting room of books, but even those don't let in enough light, because of the profusion of flowery curtainage obscuring it. The thick expensive drapes are each caught back on one side by a giant wrap-around gold tassel that the Lilliputians might have stolen from Gulliver. The three remaining sides are covered in austere dark wooden panelling with bookcases from floor to ceiling. In the centre of the room, there are two large sofas the colour of a faded daffodil sitting opposite each other, with a marble coffee table in between them, and several stuffy lamps. Was this arrangement supposed to be conducive to reading? Or, Rosie thinks, is this a room conducive to the appearance of reading?

She makes several valiant attempts to connect with Iva, mainly by repeatedly apologizing for leaking everywhere, and by over-giggling about it to curry her favour. Rosie tries to look at her, but Iva resolutely won't be seen.

'Wait here please,' she says and leaves the room. By 'here', Rosie is in no doubt that Iva means exactly where she was pointing to, a fixed point on the floor, next to one of the windows. Rosie obediently stands on her given mark, and waits. Drip, drip. Very soon, Iva bursts back into the room carrying a newspaper, which Rosie reaches out to accept, mistakenly thinking that this is some reading material to keep her occupied until the lady of the house is ready to see her. Just as Rosie's hand touches the paper, Iva bends over and lays it out in a neat square on the floor.

'Stand on here please.'

Rosie obeys, and Iva vacates the room once more, leaving the Englishwoman to drip her humiliation all over the *New York Times*. Rosie shivers. She is acutely aware of how quiet it all is. She hears Iva's footsteps retreating back up that awful dark corridor to ... where? ... the kitchen, maybe? Rosie strains to hear any other sound. Bat-like, she anticipates the footfall of Mrs Wilder-Bingham but no such sound comes. She can't even hear the noise of the street. Is this apartment hermetically sealed? There is something faint, a sound hardly perceptible, a hazy fizz ... it could almost be the sound of dust settling. How very *un*settling.

Glenn Wilder-Bingham closes the door of her bedroom behind her, and with a click sets off along the pleasingly dark corridor towards the front hall, where she will take a gentle left turn to pick up another artery of dark corridor, the slipstream to the library. She is dressed in wrinkle-free beige slacks, tan court shoes, a baby blue blouse. A beige cashmere cardi hangs off her shoulders, a perfectly placed cape of confidence. Around her neck is a gold chain with her tortoiseshell glasses hanging securely at the end. She strides past the gallery of well-placed black and white photographs of her family. This is a selection of photos that announces, 'we are successful, we are attractive, we are united'. It patently doesn't say, 'we are happy'. The images are all mounted on cream card and framed in lacquered black wood, giving them the air of a collection, of consolidated importance, and unquestionable class.

The first photo is almost sepia-tinted with age. It is of a rugged nineteen-year-old man in fifties American football gear, covered in dirt and proudly holding a trophy aloft, along with a few rufty tufty team mates. Their strip proudly displays the name of their college, YALE. This is the virile, young, triumphant Thomas Wilder-Bingham.

The next photo is of the same man, slightly older, and his fresh twenty-two-year-old wife Glenn, on board a wooden yacht, their hair blowing wild in the wind, their eyes squinting into the Nantucket sunshine, their faces creased up with laughter. Both of them wear shorts and shirts in watery colours, and they look like relaxed, entitled, happy Kennedy-people.

Next, a Madonna-like photo of a shell-shocked, milky twenty-eight-year-old Glenn in a green, green garden, holding a tiny new baby. This is her son, Kemble Wilder-Bingham. She is beaming at him as if he is a gift from God. Which for her, he is. Two pregnancies came before him, but neither had gone full term. Kemble took six years of hope and anguish to arrive. Try as they might, and they did, no other baby came after. Glenn keeps that particular sadness tucked well well away.

Here is the requisite professional photograph of a graduating young Kemble with his mortar-board hat and his robe, clutching a fake rolled-up parchment degree, flanked by his proud parents. A stilted rite of passage. A milestone. A young man who has done the right thing, for all to see.

Adjacent to this is a noticeable space, where a framed photo of a happy wedding day once was, but isn't any more.

Glenn has the recurring but fleeting thought she has every time she passes this open wound of empty wall, she really must look out a suitable replacement to plug that gap. A picture of her mother and father perhaps, when they were young?

Well, NO, not her mother.

Does she own a picture of her father alone? That might do. Except, in all the pictures she has of him, he is wearing his work overalls. Perhaps not . . .

The final photo is a black and white copy of the studio shot Glenn arranged last December of her family, to use on their most recent Christmas card. Here they all are, gathered around her. Her men.

In it she sits in a chair, front centre, cool and collected. Her husband Thomas and son Kemble stand behind her, and Thomas has his hand on her shoulder. She wishes Kemble had worn a better suit and stood more upright, but oh well. On the floor in front of her are her twin eight-year-old grandchildren, Kemble's sons, Thomas Wilder-Bingham the Third, also known as 'Three' and Kemble Wilder-Bingham Junior, also known as 'Red'. Kneeling awkwardly to the side of royal Glenn is Kemble's eldest son, the eighteen-year-old suit-begrudging photo-begrudging Edward Wilder-Bingham, also known as Teddy.

This is Glenn's kingdom. Her kith and kin. Queen Lear. Queen Herod. Queen Bee.

She sweeps past the well-edited, well-displayed gallery of her life with a great swoosh of assured click-clack.

Click. Clack. Rosie hears the approaching footsteps as she is hurriedly trying to wring out the rain from the cuffs of her sodden jacket. Her attempts to dribble only onto the *New York Times* are futile. The drops refuse to fall tidily, this is renegade rain, weather which just will not behave, even when it's debuting inside the library of a posh Upper East Side apartment.

With the immense confidence of only a White Anglo-Saxon Protestant, Glenn Wilder-Bingham enters the room. She is here. Rosie tries hard to remember that this would be a good time to heed her Nan's advice to her when she was young, namely that you really don't need to show every single tooth in your mouth when you smile. She can't help herself. She does it now, just like she did it then, to brighten matters when the moment could potentially be tricky. Rosie is a radiator, she will always risk an over-smile to channel some warmth into the room, even if it doesn't work. She is a megawatt optimist so now she *really* smiles, desperately showing lots of teeth. But Rosie has met her match in Glenn, an experienced smile withholder, who can snuff out Rosie's kind of bright joy in a millisecond.

'Hello!' beams Rosie, hopefully, smilefully. Glenn surveys the dripping Brit, nods almost imperceptibly and places herself on one of the faded daffodil sofas. Somehow, without any instruction, Rosie knows full well that she is not invited to sit down, so she remains awkwardly rooted to her square of newspaper. 'Lovely flat. Really . . . amazing . . . Lovely.'

'Yes,' confirms Glenn quietly, and adds, as a corrective footnote, 'apartment.'

'Of course, apartment, doh,' Rosie counters, generously indicating what a dolt she must appear to be.

Glenn calmly observes the apologetic display, allowing Rosie yards of rope by which to hang herself. Fortunately for Rosie, Iva interrupts the social hara-kiri by bringing in a tray of tea and placing it on the coffee table in front of Glenn, who assures her quietly, 'That's right, Iva.'

As Iva deferentially leaves the room, Glenn looks over to Rosie, 'Tea? I believe it's what you enjoy, English Breakfast.'

'Oooo yes, thank you . . . just what . . . the doctor ordered . . .'

Rosie increasingly loses faith in her own cheeriness . . . 'not that I need the doctor . . .'

For the next very long minute Glenn says nothing, and pours the tea exquisitely into the exquisite china cups. This is proper tea. No tea bag in sight. Glenn's hand is steady, and when the tea is poured and the milk is in (no sugar, wouldn't dream of it) Glenn rises and hands the cup and saucer to Rosie, who accepts it with gratitude and really *really* wishes it had sugar.

The rest of the conversation is conducted with Glenn on the sofa and Rosie remaining on the paper, as if she's in the cat-litter tray, juggling the cup and saucer and her handbag with some difficulty. Glenn holds her own teacup and saucer with no sign of nerves, utterly cool and collected. Rosie's cup shakes and rattles in its saucer throughout.

Rosie attempts an ice-breaker, 'Must be a big window cleaning bill,' she nods to the windows, 'Long ladders . . .'

No response. Jokes are not acceptable here. Glenn's teacup chinks on her saucer, 'You come highly recommended by the agency.'

'That's great, good. It's my first job with them.'

Glenn glances down at Rosie's C.V., which lies on the table.

'Fully qualified, experienced primary school teacher . . . Looe?'

'Yes. It's in Cornwall. Long pointy county at the bottom end of England . . . ?'

'I see. I have always believed 'loo' is British for bathroom?'

There's an uneasy pause, while Glenn continues to inspect the C.V. Rosie takes a welcome gulp of her tea, which unfortunately turns into a fairly audible slurp.

As if to make a point, Glenn sips her tea soundlessly. In every way she is superior. She decides to pry. 'So your parents live there?'

'They did, yes. Neither of my parents are alive any more, sadly,' says Rosie, honestly.

'I see.'

Rosie decides to grasp the bull by the horns, 'Are Thomas and Kemble your grandsons?'

'Yes.'

'Right. And they live with you?'

'No. They live with their mother, but we feel it's high time for them to come and live with their father, so they are moving in here for now . . .'

'I see.' Rosie reminds herself of the names, 'Thomas and Kemble, Thomas and Kemble . . .'

'Thomas Wilder-Bingham the Third, and Kemble Wilder-Bingham Junior.'

'Thomas and Kemble, Thomas and Kemble. It's that names thing about being a teacher, you have a year of looking at a whole new sea of faces, so I repeat them to get them in my head. Got a memory like a . . . like a . . . draining implement you use in the kitchen . . . with holes . . .'

Glenn ignores this renewed attempt at humour, and returns

to perusing the C.V. Rosie is hard-wired to fill the quiet with chirpy noise, but she resists, letting Glenn denote the tempo and the volume of this particularly stilted duet. She tries to sip her tea quietly, and gives Glenn all the time she wants. Which is a lot. Eventually, Glenn looks up at her. Is that a tiny disdainful smile on her face?

Rosie's inherent self-worth kicks in. Two can play at this game. The pause breadthens. No-one is giving in. At least, not overtly. But in the clod of that messy moment, a tiny shoot of mutual respect is planted. Yes, one of these women is potentially going to be in the employ of the other, but that's no reason for Rosie to surrender her backbone. Glenn is the first to cave . . . but only slightly.

'They arrive tonight. You are to acquaint yourself with them this weekend, then care for them before and after school, accompany them *to* and *from* school, and accompany them to activities on weekends and holidays, for which there is a nominal budget. You will take your meals here with the family and their father will join when his work permits.'

Rosie purposefully says nothing, just stares at Glenn, who seems a little unnerved. Eventually, Glenn asks, 'That is amenable to you?'

If you could count minute invisible molecules of power, this tiny shift might measure one out of a thousand on the status Richter scale. Minuscule, but potent, because Glenn doesn't ordinarily give away a single dot.

Rosie takes her place squarely in the centre of this rare opportunity. 'And where will *you* be?'

Glenn's face sours ever so slightly. A worthy blow. Who is this impertinent fat English upstart? The two women are locked in a game of who can be silentest longest. The cats are circling each other.

The orchids on the windowsill grow in the gap.

Then a big full pendulous waiting drip on the end of Rosie's sleeve gives up the ghost and hurtles to the floor in a sudden bid for freedom. It lands with an impressive splosh and breaks the moment. Now, Glenn has the edge, infinitesimally small though it may be . . .

Rosie says, 'I don't know what to call you.'

Glenn smirks, folds the C.V. and stands, 'Mrs Wilder-Bingham.'

'Right. Surnames. Got it.'

'Iva will show you your room and we will expect you at breakfast at seven thirty.'

And, just as assuredly as she arrived, Glenn Wilder-Bingham leaves.

Rosie remains, and drips in her right place.

Moved

Later that evening, Rosie is sitting on her single bed in her strange new home, with her suitcase and a bulging tote bag of clothes on the bed next to her. She can't believe how quickly everything has altered in her life. She is in a rather drab and dark suite of rooms which are set at the very centre of the apartment, so the window looks out, or rather in, onto the open stairwell of the entire block. All of the windows she can see on the other floors are small and dirty, and have air-conditioning units jutting out, just like hers. The only purpose of this well is to serve as a fire escape for all of the apartments, and to provide many window ledges for the pigeons to sit and shit on. Due to there being a further four levels above the Wilder-Binghams' floor, plus lots of structures on the roof, there is very little sky to be seen and precious little sunlight. The rooms consist of a small but cosy sitting room in which is crammed a large sofa, a coffee table and a desk against the wall. A bedroom with a slightly bigger than single bed, a bedside table, a

22

wardrobe, a chest of drawers and a mirror. And a small bathroom with a shower over a small half-sized bathtub the like of which she's not seen before. Especially made to fit into a small space. Although perfectly clean and comfortable, these rooms are distinctly unloved, the furniture clearly mismatched and obviously the least desired of anywhere else in the apartment. However, when it comes to the Wilder-Binghams even their rejects are still pretty classy, so Rosie feels that it can all work. Besides which, there are two Persian rugs on the floor, one in each room. She has always ALWAYS wanted to walk on a Persian rug in bare feet, she feels sure it would be the height of luxury.

So she reaches down and takes off her damp but still splendid red brogues and then peels off her soggy russet socks, and slowly stands up, savouring every step that puts the lavish dry carpet next to her pruney waterlogged feet. The carpet is surprisingly stiff, but it still feels heavenly. Rosie clenches her toes to gather up the pile and she feels the delight of having a long-term itch scratched. She wants more, so she swipes her feet alternately along the floor, like a dog smugly covering up an impressive poo. It feels utterly lovely and it grounds her properly, because it amuses her, and when you can laugh to yourself about something, about anything, it helps you to stave off any loneliness, doesn't it? Rosie knows that big pounding homesickness lurks naggingly somewhere deep but she is staunchly refusing to feel it. With a big deep breath she looks around her rooms and resolves to be good at this job. With that new courage as her fuel, she begins to unpack and settle into her nest.

The first item out of her case is the most beloved, a framed picture she took of a chough soaring above the cliffs at Bedruthan. Cornwall. The edge of her country, her county. Where the light is exquisite. Where there are moors and coves and cliffs and woods and raging surf and gentle pools and cream and endless skies. Where she is known. Home.

Twelve floors down, a shambolic fifty-year-old man in a good quality but crumpled city suit smokes out of the lobby door, nervously waiting. This is Kemble, a well-heeled, badly loved man. His glance darts up and down 90th St in its frozen February gloom. He finishes his cigarette, fidgets, paces and tucks his shirt in to try and make the best of himself.

Suddenly two boys appear from nowhere and bang on the glass, making him jump. He waves weakly, and sees behind them a small blonde, neat, well-put-together, smoky gamine woman, with startling green eyes, struggling with two large suitcases. The lofty doorman that Rosie experienced is completely different with these folk, who clearly have the right to be here, so he rushes to assist the woman. He knows her. She is Natalie, mother of the twins and soon to be ex-wife of Kemble.

It is immediately clear that this handover of the children is typical in its awkwardness. The boys dash into the revolving door and enjoy going round twice, and as they do, the man and the woman look at each other through the glass. She turns and walks back to the waiting car. Kemble remains watching her until he is jolted into the present by his two boys who finally tumble excitedly out of the revolving door and into the lobby with their father. All three of them get into the elevator with the suitcases. The boys are fizzing but they know to rein it in a bit when they come here. Dad isn't as lighthearted as Mum. And Granma Glenn isn't any fun at all, but Granpop Thomas is game, and anyway none of it matters too much at the moment, because they're with Dad. Yes, they want lots of Dad. Three is a more cautious lad than Red, who is a washing machine of continuous energy cycles. Three is also slightly smaller than Red, and he's a clever, sensitive anxious soul who, despite his slighter stature, is looked up to by the more robust Red. Three is a tidy blond with a touch of red. Red is red. In every way. He's fiery and fearless and funny, and has a flame of proud sticky-up red hair to announce it.

These twin chaps are magnets for each other. They are especially close, but when they do fall out, a rarity, the repell is cataclysmic and cruel. Then, just as quickly as they tear apart, they suddenly inexplicably mend again and all seems instantly, genuinely forgiven. These demolitions and repairs happen in twin-time, to the exclusion of others. They truly belong together in a way that ordinary siblings don't quite, and it's this phenomenal connection that has kept them both strong in the last year when the split between their parents could have been devastating. They are perplexed by it, and Three especially worries about it, but because each parent is behaving well in front of them, like a lot of decent divorces, the boys are shielded from the worst hurts. Those are reserved for private meetings with lawyers and shockingly clinical letters that fire off several times a week between the two parties. That's where the vicious greedy battles are fought.

The negotiations have recently collapsed entirely, prompting Queen Glenn to bully Kemble into insisting that the twins move in with them for a few revengeful months, thereby stoking the fire of Natalie's pain into a raging furnace of frustration. Glenn has stopped loving Natalie altogether, if indeed she ever did. It wasn't part of her plan for Kemble to marry a Frenchwoman. She would have preferred a less continental choice. A non-smoker. Someone more waspy, perhaps? Glenn now regards Natalie as a threat, and has closed ranks against her. Natalie knows of old that Glenn is not someone you want as your enemy, but it's her boys at stake, so 'little' 'fragile' Natalie has butched up for the fight of her life. This concession, letting the boys spend time with the Wilder-Binghams, is only because Natalie knows how desperately her beloved boys want time with their father. It's heartbreaking for Natalie but she knows she must do the right thing by them, so that's why she has delivered them up to the East Side. It's not forever, it's just for now.

Inside the lift, Red is gabbling away about the gadget he wants most in the world, which is a junior metal detector, 'It's, like, so cool, Dad, because you could get one too, the big one will fit over your arm. The one I want, like, fits over my arm. You can like find gold an' stuff . . . pirate coins . . .'

Three stands quietly next to his father. He looks at Kemble's hands in his pockets, and he reaches his own little hand up to link into his father's wrist. Kemble removes his hand from his pocket and holds Three's hand. Red clocks this and grabs Kemble's other hand, and so they travel upwards, the little men holding on for dear life to the big man they so want, and they so want to be near, and they so want to be.

Up

Inside Glenn and Thomas's bedroom there is silence save for the odd grunt and sigh as the octogenarian and the septuagenarian wake up their ageing bodies and clamber into their clothes. Morning is such a creaky time these days. Sleep is an anaesthetic that renders the body alien and stiff. Glenn has accepted the changes with a certain reluctance, she stretches and yawns and slowly goes about her morning ritual. She looks out of her bedroom window, where she has a view into Central Park and she notes that the snow from three weeks ago still remains in clumps here and there where the most shade is. It's cold, and that's just how she feels, cold. The apartment is heated and all the radiators are warm. Glenn's skin isn't cold, her skeleton is. She knows it will warm up as she goes about her day and begins to move, but at the moment she is very cold on the invisible inside.

Thomas is unwilling to concede that time is stealing up on him. If ever there were a Canute of time, this is he. Old age is lapping around his ankles, but still he insists his feet are dry. Although his bones ache, he likes to be brisk right from the very off. His wife often tells him to take it easy and slow down, but that's just not his style. Consequently he often pulls a muscle or jerks a joint purely because he goes at life like a bull at a cape. Still a substantial man, Thomas stands to pull up his trousers and neatly tuck in his shirt. Glenn has selected both, as always. Once upon a time, he resisted her controls but he submits most of the time for the sake of a peaceful life. He doesn't like the fact that he wears bigger shirts now to fit round his expanding girth, that his belt is two holes further out, that half of the suits in his wardrobe are now defunct. It's handy that Glenn puts out his clothes, it means Thomas can avoid thinking about everything connected to them. He doesn't even like to look in the mirror if he can avoid it, but he can't manage his tie without, so that's the daily reality check moment. Yep, here he is. Tall, bit stooped, full head of silver hair, was reddy-blond once, silty blue eyes, pronounced features, with a landslide of sun-damaged liver-spot skin drooping off a strong, big-boned skull. A face to respect with the promise of fun lurking just behind his lovely lively eyes at all times. There was a time Glenn enjoyed that cheeky side of him, but more recently, she has little patience for any mischief, so it has left the building. He doesn't stop to consider when they last belly-laughed together because the harsh reality would trouble him too much. He has occasionally wondered with sadness, whether he will ever ever laugh again with her? Maybe that's it now. No wife-fun til death. What a shame.

How did they slide into this joyless way? It must have been a slow creep, he can't recall a particular moment, a landmark of despair or depression that would have been a clear indicator. Nothing actually *happened*. It just became this way. And it's not so terrible that he feels the need to get out. She is who she is and he is who he is, just . . . sort of less than they were. Tracing paper versions of their vibrant former selves. Less colourful, less lit, less everything. On the face of it, he has accepted that this diminished version of themselves is purely the ageing, but somewhere deep he knows that is baloney.

He has reserve tanks he hasn't tapped yet, and he's not done, he's just idling.

So, yes, here he is. Tie done up. Maroon silk on blue striped shirt. Good. He looks like a reputable businessman, that's right, because he is. There has been talk of retirement for him for at least twelve years, but he's not prepared to go yet. He founded the law firm that has his name in its title, he is a presiding partner, why should he shuffle off? He is still useful as a consultant and advisor. He's employed enough thrusting young bucks to convince folk of the firm's strong contemporary heartbeat. A bit of experienced old-school advice from the sidelines doesn't hurt. He ain't ready to go yet. He's productive. Besides which he enjoys the structure, the schedule, the office, the point. He wants it. He needs it.

Glenn pipes up, 'She's so fat.'

Glenn is folding Thomas's pyjamas and her nightdress, and placing them both under the pillows. She folds the sheet and blanket back so that the bed can air. Iva will make it later. Thomas notices that she retrieves the nightclothes from under the pillows and refolds them. She is clearly distracted and tense.

'Who is?' he asks, genuinely unsure.

'The British girl, the nanny. She asked me what she should call me . . . I mean, seriously. What? "Glennie?" Seriously . . . . . .'

Thomas knows it's best to head her off at the pass, 'It's Sharpe's memorial on Wednesday. I've been asked to say something.'

Glenn isn't listening. 'She's from somewhere in the UK that sounds like a toilet . . .'

'I have to choose a reading, and say something personal.'

'She's far from ideal. I've got my eye on her,' says Glenn as she starts to vigorously brush her hair, 'Tillman phoned again for you. Is Kemble underperforming?'

Thomas puffs, 'He's getting divorced for God's sake.'

'Is Tillman carrying him? I don't want us to have to feel obliged to Tillman in any way.'

Thomas shakes his head and walks away. Everything around Kemble is tricky at the moment, and Thomas is all for letting it blow over, rather than tackle it head on.

Glenn stares after him, so disappointed at his weakness. 'I guess that's subject over,' she mutters under her breath.

Thomas bobs back into her reflection, 'I think we should give her a chance . . . the Limey,' and off he heads to breakfast, interested to meet the incomer.

Was that Thomas asserting himself?

Fed

Rosie is first in the imposing dining room, where a large mahogany table is laid up for breakfast. It is set for six people, and she has absolutely no idea where she ought to sit. Luckily, Iva bustles into the room carrying a bowl of scrambled eggs, which she places on the side, on top of a plate warmer alongside other bowls of streaky bacon and waffles and chopped fruit and yoghurt.

Rosie feels awkward standing by and watching her, 'Morning Iva, can I help . . . ?'

As she exits, Iva flings over her shoulder, 'No, that is my job. You sit.'

'Right.'

But where? There're bound to be assigned places, surely? She certainly won't sit at the head of the table, perhaps the last chair, the one nearest her is the safest choice? Just as she is wrestling with this dilemma, the door bursts open and clattering in come the twins, in their school uniforms, boisterously arguing about who should be first through the door. Rosie is standing on the other side of the table from them. They stop in their tracks the moment they see her. She looks at them, they look at her, and then, in one shocking sudden motion, Rosie falls to the floor like a tree felled in the middle of the forest. From their side of the table, she simply drops out of view. They are small enough to be able to crouch down and see under the table. There she is, a crumpled heap. Today Rosie has chosen a red polka-dot dress with a black cardigan and black tights with her bright red brogues, and a big red ribbon wrapped around her head. It would seem that a giant Minnie Mouse has collapsed in the corner.

The boys look at each other, very concerned. Red gasps and whispers, 'Is she OK?'

'Dunno . . . Get Granpop?' his brother suggests, sensibly.

'Just . . . yeh . . . Maybe . . . ?'

'Wait, look, breathing . . .' Three is watching intently.

The boys tentatively walk round the end of the table and approach the pile that unbeknownst to them is to be their new nanny. Bravely, bravely, they creep up on her, Three first and Red closely behind. Their eyes are as wide as saucers and they hardly breathe while they listen carefully for any movement or noise. Closer, closer . . . They cling to each other . . . Closer . . .

Just as they approach, Rosie springs up like a jack-in-the-box and looks at them in amazement, mirroring their gobsmacked little faces. They hastily retreat to the nearest corner, grabbing on to each other for dear life.

'Wow!' Rosie shrieks. 'Amaaaayzing! You guys, your super-powers are SO strong – just knocked me right off my feet.'

'Eh?'

'What?'

'What d'you mean?' The boys are puzzled.

'You do know you have superpowers, don't you? You must. I felt them straight away, the second you came in that door. Overpowering. C'mon, tell me, what are they?'

Red is captivated, 'I don't think I have any. I never felt any powers . . .'

'Oh, you definitely have. I don't know for sure what they might be, but I reckon it's multiple abilities, something like infinite empathy along with the ability to influence events and maybe even some mimicry skills? Something like that?'

'Really? Have I? How do you know?!'

Red is the eager puppy. He so wants it to be true.

'Because mate, it radiates off you.'

'Seriously?'

'Seriously. Try it again now. Think hard and try to influence events in here right now . . .'

Three is quiet, but watching everything very closely. Who is she? Who is this odd woman with a strange accent? What is she doing in Granma and Granpop's apartment?

'Go on . . .' Rosie urges him.

'. . . Uh, OK . . .'

Red screws up his face and tries really hard. He desperately wants to influence events. Whatever that means . . .

Rosie gives it a couple of seconds, then falls to the floor again.

Red is incredulous.

'Dude,' he yells at his brother, 'it works!'

Three is astonished, and puzzled . . .

At that very moment the door bursts open and Thomas and Glenn enter. They don't see Rosie at first since she is on the floor, out of vision.

Thomas is first to speak, 'Hi there, lil' critters!'

The twins run to him, and there are cheers and hugs all round, even with Granma Glenn, who pats them both on the head and affects a smile.

'I influenced events, Granpop!' Three exclaims.

'Did you now?' Thomas replies.

'Yea, coz she fell down again!'

He points towards where Rosie lies, and slowly but terribly surely, she emerges from the other side of the table like a wakening hobo, with her red bow all askew.

'Hello there,' she attempts to normalize the situation with 'just . . . checking the floor . . . and yes, I can confirm it is . . . there, and . . . works . . . so that's . . . good.'

Glenn allows Rosie to sink a bit, and then throws a thread of a lifeline, 'Thomas, this is the . . . woman I told you about,

Miss Kitto. Miss Kitto, this is my husband, Thomas Wilder-Bingham.'

'Please, just Thomas,' he says as he walks around the table and shakes her hand. At last, someone has touched her. 'Rosie,' she offers. He is big, extremely twinkly and pleasant, but she can see the lemon-lipped Glenn hovering in the background, unhappy about the casual introduction and first name permission, so she decides not to languish in the warmth of his smile for too long. Besides, she hasn't properly met the boys yet, and that's the most pressing thing.

Thomas takes the bull by the horns: 'Clearly you've met these two fine young fellas?'

'Actually, no, we haven't been formally introduced . . .'

'OK, well this firebrand is Red, and this fine specimen is Three. Gentlemen, this is Rosie, and she is going to be your nanny while you're here . . . say hello properly.'

They were just reaching their hands out to shake when the word 'nanny' lands on them. Three immediately withdraws.

'Why are we having a nanny? I thought Dad was going to look after us?'

Glenn intervenes, 'He is, but Miss Kitto is going to help. Mind your manners please, Thomas.'

Three reaches out again and joins his brother in shaking Rosie's hand, albeit reluctantly.

'Good,' says Glenn. 'Now, please, let's have breakfast, it's nearly time for school. Take a plate and help yourself from the side,' and she directs the seating plan around the table. As the family shuffle in an orderly fashion around the delicious breakfast treats, Iva bobs in and out, attentively making sure everyone has coffee and juice and all they need. The boys know her well and especially look forward to her delicious cooking, except when she adds cabbage or sauerkraut or weird white sausage, which no-one ever eats. Iva calls these dishes 'extras'. They arrive on the table unheeded at mealtimes, and leave the table untouched. Glenn has asked Iva not to persist in this, but unusually, Iva has entirely ignored her and as time has slipped by, the family have grown used to it and frankly, ignore it. Rosie notices though, a large bowl of something green and stringy, and she tentatively takes a spoonful to put on her plate out of politeness. This seems to elicit some quizzical looks from the family, who are accustomed to rejecting all of these dishes. Rosie is ignorant of it, so helps herself, unawares. At which point, Iva pops in with a jug of water for the table and can barely hide how astounded she is. The new nanny appears to be about to eat the dish clearly intended for Iva's own breakfast later. This shouldn't be happening.

Just as all are taking their assigned places at the table, Kemble crashes in, pulling on his tie, hair unkempt. Three and Red are in unison, excited, 'Hi Dad!' Thomas looks up at him. 'Morning, son.'

'Yep. Morning. Everyone. Hurry up guys, need to get you to school, I'm late, c'mon.'

Glenn calmly announces, 'Miss Kitto will take the boys. She needs to learn where to go, and Iva can show her, you get off to work, Kemble.'

'Awww,' the twins mumble.

Rosie is politely and carefully inspecting the father of the twins, whom she is seeing for the first time. What a nervous, chaotic bundle of a chap he is. Heftier than he wants to be. Darkish, reddish hair. Puffy-faced and waxy looking. A hangover in human form.

Rosie gets up, 'Hello, I'm Rosie Kitto, I'll be taking care of the twins.'

'Right. Yes. OK, I'd better shoot . . .' he can't wait to be out of the door.

Rosie quickly jumps up to stop him before he rushes out, 'Um, perhaps we could grab five minutes to discuss the plans for the boys . . . ?'

Glenn interrupts sharpish, 'There's no need for that, Miss Kitto, I will outline the schedule with you. Kemble needs to be at work on time, please . . .'

'OK,' concedes Rosie, and then a parting marker across his bows, 'later then,' and with that Rosie tells mother *and* son that she intends to communicate with both. Again it seems, Rosie has, in a small but thoroughly decent way, countered Glenn's authority.

Kemble pats each of the boys on the head and bumbles out, without any breakfast. It's clear that the twins are disappointed, but they know it would be rude to express it too much.

Rosie's eyes dart around the table watching how grand-father, grandmother and grandchildren all relate to each other. There are two clear levels going on. The boys are respectful and behave in their grandmother's presence, but Granpop is always winking and making faces behind her back so that only the boys can see. He is prepared to risk a lot to amuse them, and they adore him for it, and make extra effort to keep straight faces so that he isn't discovered. It's a delicious collu-sion that Rosie is now part of, purely by dint of spectating. So far then, the font of fun for these young chaps is Thomas.

The twins check out that Rosie isn't going to ruin it, and interrupt this delicate balance. They watch her very closely when these naughty moments with Granpop are going on. Rosie, despite all her froth, is an expert poker-facer, and gives zilch away. Their lovely games are safe and the twins go a little step further to installing her as a member of their trusted inner sanctum. Very few are permitted. Although Rosie hasn't been told any of this, she just knows – she wasn't voted most popu-lar year two teacher four years in a row for nothing – and her heart responds accordingly. Rosie begins to tackle the strange green stuff on her plate. It isn't anything she's familiar with, it tastes like iron, so she politely leaves it to the side.

Eventually, after a tower of waffles has disappeared inside the twins, accompanied by a lecture about the perils of too many waffles from Glenn, it's time for all around the table to scatter to their various places. The boys put on their school coats against the wind. It's a quick flurry of gloves and hats and bags and fuss and they are out of the door.

Thomas also puts on his good thick wool camel coat, and after a perfunctory kiss on his wife's cheek, he heads off into the biting Manhattan cold.

All of a sudden Glenn is alone in the apartment. She sits back down at the breakfast table to finish her black coffee. She exhales. The quiet is a relief, it means no-one is requiring anything of her. In fact, this is a good day because aside from an optional drop in to her favourite coffee spot, The Colony Club, she has absolutely no other call on her time. The boys will be home around four p.m., but even then the Brit will look after them so she is entirely free until dinnertime at seven thirty this evening.

How marvellous. A whole day, a day of holes, an aimless day full of holes.

How dreadful.

Out

The independent day school where the twins go is right across the street from the apartment, housed in the beautiful vaults of a huge church. This was Natalie's choice for the boys, she wanted the kind of 'traditional curriculum but taught in a progressive way' approach. Glenn had to bite her tongue when the decision was made. Nothing could be further from her preference for the more staid old-school prep education of other 'better', more established boys' schools. However, this school is a three-minute walk from the Wilder-Binghams' building, so the convenient geography was definitely a persuasive factor.

This was only one of many occasions that Kemble has been trapped in between his mother and his wife concerning a big decision. Natalie dug her trotters into the mud on this one though. Not only did she genuinely believe that this enquiry-based learning would suit her babies better, but she had already made a big mistake when she conceded to Glenn's

42

wishes for Teddy, their oldest son. He went to the same prep school his father and grandfather had attended, and is now eighteen, and finishing his last year at a posh boarding school in Connecticut.

Natalie has always felt that his education has been too stuffy and academic, and that the artistic light that shines inside Teddy has been dimmed incrementally by neglect at every school he has attended. Teddy is a musician at heart, and although he has dabbled in various bands, mostly this has been in his vacation time and regarded as a silly hobby by Glenn. Natalie and Kemble don't object to any passions he has for music, and they would encourage him more if it weren't for all the study he has to do, especially in this last spurt of school, when his crucial exams are.

Natalie is aware that Teddy is under a lot of stress and she clings to the fact that it won't be long before school is over. Of course, the hell that can be college will start then, but at least Teddy can be part of that decision, he can choose where he wants to go and he has already eyed up the more liberal arts-loving institutions. Another thorn in Glenn's side. Teddy is supposed to follow his family to Yale. Natalie prays that he won't, and now that she is apart from the Wilder-Binghams, she can be more assertive. For now though, her two little chaps are happily enrolled at this good, kind school on 90th Street, and that is where Iva and Rosie drop them off. Iva hurries back to work, leaving Rosie with time to wander these few blocks of the Upper East Side and acquaint herself with her new environs.

Rosie pulls her scarf up around her mouth against the bitter wind, and sets off, firstly to look inside the huge church, the entrance of which is round the corner from where the school is. The imposing grey neo-gothic limestone façade of the Church of the Heavenly Rest towers above the corner of 90th Street and Fifth Avenue and as she enters, Rosie sees that this is a church that is housing a cathedral inside. She catches her breath when she sees the height, the light, the air in it. It is vast and properly holy and reminds her instantly of Truro Cathedral. A cheerful lady is taking a group on a tour, so Rosie sits quietly in the last pew and strains to hear the odd morsel of info: 'land sold by Carnegie's widow ... art deco details ... stars on the ceiling ... the reredos ... the empty cross with the Christ above ... Gloria Swanson's ashes interred ...'

As the group meander off up the nave, towards the altar, Rosie is left to her own company and her own noticings. The buildings that surround this church are low rise enough to allow the February sunlight to flood in through many stained-glass windows, including a particularly beautiful rose window high above the distant altar. The vaulted ceilings and the beautiful colourful light from the windows dancing around her root Rosie to her seat in utter awe. How wonderful to be in such a serene open shiny space right in the heart of a busy crowded city. How surreal. How wonderful. As she feels her breathing slow down, she allows some quiet thoughts to flood in to her mind. There is a low-lying sadness nagging away at her to feel it, which she successfully ignores most of the time. Her busy arrival in New York has so far prevented it from being too persistent, but sitting here suspended in time, she can hear it rumbling. Faintly. She could mistake it for simple homesickness, but she knows that's only the top note. The more profound bass line is ache. Heartache. What exactly for? Is it a why or a who or a what question? Why is she so wanting to *ask* herself questions? Is it being inside a church that promotes so much internal enquiry? Have these walls woken up some uncertainty in her, simply because the age-old love affair that happens regularly here between God and human is synonymous with question and doubt? Strange questions with no real clinical answers. No real conclusion, save that of knowing that for sure, despite no scientific proof, love exists, and actually matters more than anything else. Love is the supreme dominion. Fact. Perhaps being in church is what irrefutably verifies this. A giant house of love, isn't it? That's what Mum and Dad always believed. They all went to church together as a family. Then, church was for saying goodbye. First to Dad. Then to Mum.

Rosie sighs, gathers herself and takes her leave before any of her thinking overwhelms her too much. She slips back out of the front door after dropping a five-dollar note into the collection box. Right opposite the huge door is the open expanse of Central Park and she knows that in the distance, across the park, lies the notorious Dakota building. She gets a sickening lurch as she thinks of Lennon. In those moments just before he was shot, trusting his wild world, hoping he could be part of a change for the better for everyone. He was vital and creative. And alive.

Then.

He wasn't.

Rosie was only three years old at the time. She knew nothing of it til years later, but Lennon's music is the link between Rosie and her dad. Lennon and Marvin Gaye were what Rosie listened to when she was growing up. They were his passions, and then hers. And now, here she is today, a park away from where some of that vital music died. Rosie isn't ordinarily a squeamish person, but her whole body shivers momentarily at the proximity and the reality. Yes, she really is in New York, and it is just as frightening as it is wonderful . . .

She turns away from the park and walks back along 90th Street, past the Wilder-Binghams' building, and on to Madison Avenue. She tries to make sense of the area. What do the people who live here want to shop for? Well, there's a bookshop, a keycutter, a pharmacy and a pizza parlour, but there are also many shops that Rosie has no reference for. Nothing like this in Cornwall. Shops that offer nail/wax/mani/pedi services with big hefty leather barbers' chairs all in a row, people with their heads down, hard at work, all visible through the window, all alarmingly unprivate. The women doing the pedicures have face-masks on. Are the feet of the Upper East Side so very toxic?! Then there are a plethora of expensive-looking maternity shops, and fur coat shops, and even a pet shop which seems to specialize in crystal-encrusted dog collars and strange humiliating dog jumpers.

The most intriguing shops are the ones selling hugely expensive crumpled yoga gear. The windows are full of what appears to be grey and black unironed laundry. For a brief moment, Rosie stands and stares at the price tags, working out if this is some kind of elaborate joke. But no, she can see that the skeletal women who work in the shop are indeed proudly sporting the gear. Presumably the idea is to appear effortlessly casual, at the same time ensuring that other people know exactly how exorbitantly dear the crumpled shabby chic is. These clothes say, 'Yes, I'm off to the gym just as soon as I've dropped the kids at this top notch school and grabbed a skinny latte en route. Yes, these are my yoga sweats, coz I'm just about to really sweat. I'm young, I'm fit, I'm a Noo Yawk kinda busy woman . . .'

As Rosie looks into the shop, she catches a glimpse of her own reflection, and guffaws out loud at what a polar opposite she is, in her retro charity shop coat which was so clearly previously enjoyed. It is bright green with a wide collar and a belt and oversized tortoiseshell buttons. She found it in a hospice shop in Plymouth and she loves it. Quite a lot of change has fallen through the hole in the pocket lining. She had considered cutting it open to retrieve the change until she noticed that the weight of the coins helps the coat to hang really well, so she has regarded this as a happy accident and left it.

Rosie notes how red and drippy her nose is in the reflection and she decides to treat herself to a cappuccino. On the opposite corner is a café called Yura, so she crosses over and goes in. It's quite big, more than a café, there's a counter for takeaway cakes and salads, and what appears to be a mini-deli, but mostly it's a meeting place for the thin busy-mom women. Many of them sit at tables, in groups or alone, but all are wearing furs over their yoga sweats. They are huddled over the steaming fat-free hot liquids with their chiselled over-dieted hot red faces looking for all the world like Japanese Snow Monkeys enjoying the hot springs. The devil in Rosie persuades her to order a big frothy full-fat cappuccino with a jumbo meringue on the side. She sits proudly at a table in the window, and unashamedly scoffs the lot, with extra slurping. Plenty of eyes are upon her, but Rosie Kitto is Teflon when it comes to the judgement of others. Besides which, this meringue is just delish!

Sandwiches

It is part of Rosie's job to give the twins a snack when she has collected them from school, and it's only now, the first time she is doing this, that she realizes just how much the kitchen is Iva's territory and how very sensitive to this she needs to be. As she prepares their sandwiches and milk (almond, of course, Natalie's rule) she is aware of the under-breath Polish grumbling that is a constant accompaniment. Each plate and glass that Rosie chooses is replaced with a different one by Iva, who holds the key to the secret code of which crockery and cutlery is kid-friendly.

'Not that, this,' she repeats, 'for dining table, not kitchen table,' and 'for wash carefully, not in machine.'

Rosie gets the distinct impression that much of what she is hearing was once told to Iva by 'Mrs W.B.' as Iva calls her, but nevertheless, the kitchen is a tight ship, captained by Iva and Rosie doesn't want to be keel-hauled or have to walk the plank, so she is happy to take orders and concedes with no complaints.

As with everything Rosie tackles though, snack-time is anything but dull.

'OK guys,' she says as the boys clamber up onto the high stools by the breakfast counter, 'first of all, I need to make sure everything in this healthy café is hygienic please, so if you could just . . .' she squirts them both with hand sanitizer to rub in, which they do, without fuss. 'Yep, great, and socks off please.' Both of them start to obey, until it quickly dawns on them that this is an odd request.

Three is first to question it, 'Why do we have to take our socks off?'

Red backs him up, 'Yeh . . . why?'

Rosie clearly annunciates every word as though it is massively good sense that she's simply endorsing.

'To be sure to keep our feet sparkly, clean and fragrant, gentlemen, at all times if you please.'

They look quizzically at each other, but they do, in the end, gradually reach down and remove their socks. Rosie hums and busies herself in the kitchen, getting the bread ready and softening the butter.

When the socks are off, Rosie squirts their feet with the same sanitizer. She does it with vigour so some of the foam splashes on the floor. She rubs it in like an over-efficient nurse, and neither of the boys can resist laughing because it tickles so deliciously much. Even Three, who is still a bit suspicious of Rosie, understands that there's fun to be had here.

'Right. Now I know you usually have peanut butter and jelly, which I like to refer to as "jam" by the way, in the original Queen's English, for your after-school sandwiches, but today we are going for a different, unique option. We are going to partake of a Kitto special, known to the initiated as the Sandwich of the Gods. It consists of bread, butter and this secret ingredient.'

With that, Rosie produces a small jar of hundreds and thousands which she sprinkles onto the butter and closes up the sandwich. She cuts them into quarters, garnishes with a milk chocolate Hershey Kiss, and places them in front of her wards, who gleefully reach out for them.

'Ah ah ah. No. Wait,' she admonishes them. 'We always say Grace first.'

The twins sit back on their chairs and watch her.

'Hands together please.' She makes a praying motion. They copy.

'Grace,' she says.

'Grace!' they repeat, delighted.

They reach out for the food.

'Ah ah ah. Not yet. The Sandwich of the Gods is eaten in the way the Gods intended. Via the feet. The fragrant feet. And the Gods always fed each other. So, please, go ahead . . .'

Rosie is aware of muttered profanities in Polish as the boys attempt to pick up the sandwiches with their toes and aim for the other's mouth. Of course, they miss. A lot. And bread drops on the floor, and hundreds and thousands spill out and crumbs are everywhere.

Even Iva manages a few giggles through clenched teeth as she sees the twins lose themselves in the mischief of the moment. Heaven knows, she has seen them sit so quietly and well-behaved in this kitchen so often before. This kind of noisy kitchen reminds Iva of her own one at home in Olsztyn that she hasn't cooked in for nearly a year now . . .

Tidy Room

In the evening, Kemble takes advantage of the boys watching a movie with Rosie to scuttle off to his bedroom. He has noticed his mother's eye on him throughout dinner and he purposefully doesn't meet her gaze once. Glenn exists for him mostly in his peripheral vision. Not since he was a little boy has Kemble looked directly, unflinchingly, at her. It might be that, like many people who meet her, he doesn't want to see himself reflected in her disappointed eyes, or it might be that he would risk her seeing right through him and knowing that in his deep heart of hearts, he is raging. He resents all the control she has wrought over him, his marriage, his kids, his father, over their whole family, and of course he is too afraid of her to confront it. Too afraid of how he might feel and how he might fail if he had to function without it. Would he simply crumple to the floor if the strings were cut now? It's been fifty years of dominance, does he even have any usable legs left to stand on?

Certainly at the moment, he needs the support of his parents, not least because he would be genuinely homeless if it weren't for them. He has let Natalie remain at their marital home, but he begrudges it badly. He knows it's the right thing to do, it's where the boys live, the divorce is basically his fault, this is the price he pays. But how high the price? It feels wretched to be living back with your parents when you're fifty years old. Nothing reeks more of failure than the smell of your child-hood bedroom when you're an adult living in it. But here he is, in jogging pants, sitting up in his old teenage bed, with his laptop propped up on a pillow in front of him.

Glenn taps lightly on the door, and immediately enters with all the entitled deftness of a rude chambermaid. He doesn't even get to finish his sentence, 'Come . . .' before she is in the room and firmly plonked on the end of his bed. Kemble is instantly uncomfortable, he feels like a little boy caught read-ing rude mags under his covers. Glenn looks right at him. Kemble fidgets and avoids her gaze as usual. He puts his com-puter aside, and pulls his legs up towards his chest. The big man who throws his weight around in the boardroom and wears a Rolex watch is ten years old again.

Glenn kicks off with, 'This light can't be good for your eyes.' He has only heard that twenty thousand times before, and it catapults him back to eight years old.

'It's custody business, Ma . . . got to do it.'

'Hmm. How's that going?'

This is combustible stuff. He doesn't want to go there, it will ignite a big angry discussion. He wants to hide. Like a six-year-old.

She persists, 'Are you having problems?'

'Problems?'

'At work, Kemble. Problems.'

He shakes his head, avoiding anything difficult. Feeling four years old.

'Good,' Glenn says, 'my good little man.'

Two years old now.

'Don't let your father down, Kemble. Don't let anyone down.'

'I'll try.'

'I know you will, darling.'

With that, Glenn pats the bed. Not her son. The bed.

She gets up, smiles pitifully at him, and leaves, closing the door softly behind her. Just in time to narrowly avoid her baby son creeping back up into her uterus.

Straight

The twins are hypnotized by giant robots that change into . . . other kinds of robots in the *Transformers* movie they're watching, so Rosie slips out of the TV room and walks along the corridor until she comes to the door she thinks is Thomas's office. She can hear mumbling from inside. Thomas is sitting at his desk, drinking a whisky, and reading aloud from a book of John Donne poems.

'Death be not proud, though some have called thee

Mighty and dreadful, for thou art not so.'

He tries again, with a cough and a deeper voice

'Death be not proud . . .'

There is a gentle knock at the door which startles him.

'Yep? Come in!'

The door opens, and it's Rosie, who looks a bit apologetic. 'Sorry, hello, can I . . . sorry, is this a good time?'

'Uh, sure, come on in. Have a seat.'

Rosie sits in one of the big leather chairs opposite his big leather desk. She is suddenly aware of just what a big leather man he is.

'OK.' She summons her resolve, 'This is probably doing myself out of an amazing – let's face it, bloody fantastic – job, but I don't really think you need me here.'

'Excuse me?' Thomas says, putting his drink down. 'I think perhaps you should speak with Glenn . . . ?'

'Mmm, yes I know, but I just thought that I would mention it to you, because the boys seem to . . . well, I think they would rather spend time with their father, they genuinely believe that's what they're here for . . . to be with him?'

Thomas is uneasy, 'Well yes, but really . . . it's Glenn who organizes . . .'

'I'm wondering, would you, perhaps, be able to spend a little bit of time with them? It's just that if their parents are getting divorced, this is a strange time to be leaving them with me, someone they don't really know? Do you see what I mean . . . ? I'm very happy to support, but I can't seem to get a strong steer on it from their father . . . ?'

'Shall I get my wife . . . ?'

'Just wondering if I'm the best person for them right now . . .'

'I should get my wife . . .'

Rosie is determined. 'Well, yes, but what do *you* think? You're their granddad, and a free-thinking adult . . .'

Thomas looks towards the door, which Rosie has left open. There in the doorway is Glenn. Thomas is embarrassed and relieved in equal measure.

'Ah, honey, perfect timing. Miss Kitto here, um, Rosie, was just saying it might be good, if, uh, we had some time with the boys? Maybe a day trip or something . . . would be good?'

He peters out as he notices the black cloud hovering over Glenn's head. She is looking at Rosie as if she is the anti-Christ, but she employs full-tilt politeness when she opens her mouth:

'Thank you for your suggestion and your concern, Miss Kitto. We will certainly inform you of our decision. As and when. Now, if you would allow Mr Wilder-Bingham some privacy to prepare for a difficult occasion . . . ?'

'Of course,' Rosie replies, getting up to leave, 'I shall look forward to being informed. Might it be by carrier pigeon?'

Glenn stiffens at this insolence and looks to Thomas for support. Maddeningly for Glenn, Thomas appears to be showing distinct signs of amusement, there is the smallest smile on his face. Rosie also clocks this.

Glenn takes control, 'Now, if you'll excuse us?'

There is a panicked knock at the door and an out-of-breath Iva appears. 'Excuse me Mrs W.B., but Miss Natalie she is here . . . the porter, he let her up.'

'Oh for God's sake,' Glenn says 'very well, show her in . . .'

At which moment Natalie thunders unheeded into the room.

The speed of her whips Rosie's head around, as she witnesses for the first time the flash of French that is the diminutive, gutsy mother of Red, Three and Teddy. She smells fabulous. Of figs.

'Is he here?' she demands.

'Hello, Natty'Thomas attempts the-oil-on-water approach.

'Is he even *here*, Thomas?!' she persists.

'If you mean Kemble, Natalie, yes of course he's here. He's with the boys . . .' says Glenn, and she flicks a glance at Rosie, who is finding this situation awkward and outright lying even harder.

Natalie's fury overrides her long held fear of the matriarch, 'OK, Glenn, but please would you explain what's going on, please? Why did he make this big fuss about having the boys live here, if he's only going to dump them with some strange nanny?'

Rosie mutters under her breath, 'Less of the strange.'

Glenn powers on, 'We made an arrangement, Natalie. Kemble is their father, and it's his turn to have them. You know that. I know that, and the lawyers certainly know that.'

Natalie replies, 'Yes, it's his turn to have them. For *him* to have them, that's the whole point, not some English weirdo.'

Rosie responds quietly, 'Less of the weirdo.'

'I'd be interested in exactly how you know about the nanny,' says Glenn.

'That doesn't matter, Glenn! My boys are supposed to be

spending time with their father. They aren't just pawns in your little game.' She turns to Rosie, 'Are you the nanny?'

Glenn ignores the question to Rosie, and squares up to Natalie, 'They are here with us for a time, and what we do with them is our business.'

Thomas interjects, 'Come on now, surely we can settle this . . . ?'

Alerted by Iva, Kemble appears at the door. 'Nat, what's going on?'

'Natalie was just leaving, Kemble, it's fine, go back to your room,' says Glenn.

There is a pregnant pause as the study reverberates with the realization of how Glenn has just spoken to Kemble. Is this really going to be allowed to pass?

Rosie audibly sucks in her breath, 'Excuse me, I'm going to check on the chaps . . .' and she leaves.

Natalie is the one to name it, 'Really, Kemble? "Go back to your room?" Really?'

Kemble responds, 'It's not . . . like that . . .'

'It's exactly like that. That's the whole damn problem. When are you going to . . .'

Glenn interrupts, 'Allow me to remind you where you are, Natalie. *Our* family home. Perhaps right now would be the perfect time to re-acquaint you with the front door?'

'For Christsakes, Kemble, find your spine, before it's too late,' says the furious Natalie as she is swept from the room, 'and please spend some time with the boys . . .'

'Thank you. Goodnight,' Glenn firmly closes the door behind Natalie. Kemble hangs his head. Thomas takes a long slurp of his whisky, and Glenn turns to them both, for all the world as if nothing has happened. 'So, what are tomorrow's plans . . . ?'

Rosie has returned to the TV room to watch the end of the movie with the twins, who are blissfully unaware that their mother has just been and gone. They are so gripped by the film, they're frozen in time and sit on the sofa like statues, absolutely still and hardly breathing. Red even has a nub of popcorn in his hand held still, two inches from his mouth, exactly as he did when Rosie slipped out of the room twenty minutes before. Guns are firing, robots are exploding, baddies are annihilated, the planet is ending. This stuff requires concentration and commitment. Rosie looks at their lovely little faces in the glow of the Friday night TV light. Their utter naivety moves her. Suddenly, the film finishes, and they both jump in unison and bounce about on the furniture to celebrate the triumph of the Transformers, the saving of the world as we know it, and the general fabness of the movie. In amongst their unbridled excitement, and without thinking, Red even jumps into Rosie's clutches with his arms about her neck. They all shriek and scream until they collapse on the floor, exhausted, the small chests of the eight-year-olds panting, and the very much larger chest of Rosie heaving for breath.

Rosie gasps, 'Mercy! Save me, guys, save me from the Decepticons. Honestly. I'm terrified. Megatron could get in here any day . . .'

'OK, wait' says Three, jumping up, 'Red, get those cushions. We gotta build a repeller round her, quick, quick, quick!'

'OK, OK, OK,' agrees Red, racing round and gathering the big cushions from the sofa and all the small ones from everywhere else. Together, they construct a shelter around her. Somewhere in them they know this is play, but somehow it's also very urgent and important, so they take real care about how they do it. It must be safe and secure. Built properly.

When it is complete, and Rosie is utterly protected inside the hot fuggy cushion fortress, Three calls to her 'OK, Rosie! You're safe now!'

'Yeah,' says Red, 'we're gonna guard you from out here, OK?'

'Yeah,' says Three, 'eyes peeled for Megatron, Devastator, and Starscream.'

'Yeah, we got guns,' Red decides, and immediately they both carry invisible machine guns and patrol up and down. When they stand together, they are a serious multi-headed junior Cerberus, defying anyone to enter.

'Three?' Rosie muffles from inside her cocoon.

'Yes?' he replies.

'I've worked out your superpowers, y'know, they're so obvious, I don't know why I didn't get it straight away.'

'OK what are they?' Three is properly interested.

'Well, like Red, I'm pretty sure it's multiple abilities. Firstly, enhanced mental strength, plus intuitive telepathic aptitude, and also I *think* possible force-field projection, because look what you just did – you used *all* of those skills. And now I'm totally safe.'

'Yeah. Right. Yeah,' agrees the cautious Three. 'Good.'

'Awesome,' his brother chimes in.

Thomas has secretly watched the last few minutes of this through the slightly open door. He chuckles to himself at the fact that the ferocious, vigilant mini guards have failed to notice him, but he is so pleased that they are happy. He takes a moment to watch the scene, and he prays that this extraordinary woman doesn't leave.

Bed

Later, in their tidy clean bedroom, Thomas and Glenn prepare for bed. They have their familiar rituals, there's comfort in all of it. The way Glenn collects their respective nightclothes from under their respective pillows and places them on the bed on the sides where they respectively sleep. Although, on the face of it, Glenn infantilizes Thomas with this routine, Thomas chooses to experience it differently. He knows her need for order, her fear of chaos and consequently her love of habit, so he doesn't let her control land on him too heavily. He leaves her be, to do the routine things that help her feel secure, without minding too much. Of course, if Glenn oversteps the mark, or is rude to anyone, Thomas finds it less forgivable, but this customary bedroom stuff? No problem.

There is an intimacy and ease to all that goes on in the bedroom and en suite bathroom every night. Very little is said between the two of them, as they move around quietly, undressing, washing, brushing their teeth and climbing into bed.

Thomas is prone to humming barely audible jazz classics under his breath. Very often Frank Sinatra or Dean Martin or Ella Fitzgerald. No song ever finishes, it's only snippets and shards of fractured lines. This disjointed music is the soundtrack to their bedtime, and neither even notice it any more.

Thomas sits on his side of the bed, and ever since he was a young man, he has taken his clothes off in the same order, with his trousers and underpants coming off first, so that when he sits on the bed, it's his bare arse that whoofs down onto the counterpane. Glenn used to nag him about this, about how unhygienic and unattractive it was, about how easy it would be to choose a different option and take his shirt and vest off first, perhaps? He used to listen and nod in agreement. She was right, there was a different order, but the plain truth is that he will always ignore her on this, because one of life's small and infinitely achievable daily pleasures, as far as Thomas Wilder-Bingham is concerned, is the simple fleshy contact of bum on crisp bedlinen. It's nothing short of delightful. He is clean, what's the problem? So, he decided long ago that Glenn's request for underpants at all times would remain in his domestic inbox so to speak; acknowledged, but never really attended to. They seem to have both settled for this.

So here he is, naked arse on fresh bedspread, taking off the rest of his clothes and putting on his pyjamas, which is in itself a compromise because he would always rather sleep nude. This was a minor battle he lost, conceding that Glenn is right when she surmises that older bones need to be kept toasty. His only renegade gesture is that, before the pyjamas finally triumph, he has a little strut around naked as a jaybird. This is usually how he brushes his teeth, and so in front of his mirror he gets to inspect his ageing frame. As a former athlete this ever-increasing physical dwindle is difficult to witness, but he comforts himself with the fact that, compared to so many of his colleagues, he's in pretty good shape for his years. Of course, his body is a surrendering version of what it once was, but it's upright and still strong. He doesn't seem to have developed the manboobs he dreads, and although he is thicker in the girth, his flesh is still tight on his torso, he has no folds or overhanging stomach, he's just wider and sort of relaxed. He has a Sunday kind of a body, which is taking time off from exercise, and not giving a toss.

Like most men, Thomas spends most of his naked time cradling his balls and looking at his cock in the mirror. He likes it. He is fascinated by how his pubic hair has been the last hair on his body to turn white. Why is that, he wonders? Is it to do with daylight? Even his leg hair is paler, and other than a few Nantucket weeks in the summer, his legs rarely get the sun. He takes a certain pride in the fact that this private fuzz still shows signs of the reddy-blond he once was. He's still got the fire, even if no-one's stoked it recently, the embers are vaguely red. Well, he thinks as he flicks the bathroom lights off, he's the proud producer of an assured erection every morning, so frankly, that's the sign of a healthy functioning groin, what else does he really need to worry about? Sharpe hasn't got a boner when he wakes up, because he doesn't wake up any more, because Sharpe is dead. Yeah, yet another one of his close friends is dead. Damn, he must decide about that poem, he must do it tomorrow.

Glenn is sitting on her side of the bed, with her white cotton nightdress on, facing away from him. She is taking off her watch, her necklace, her large sapphire ring, and placing them in a porcelain dish on her bedside table. He stands on his side of the bed facing her and wishing she would turn and look at him, look at his available body. Look at him and smile and want him, beckon him into the bed in 'that' way. She doesn't, she hasn't for too long a while. He sighs and sings quietly as he climbs into the inevitable pyjamas, 'say "nightie night" and kiss me, just hold me tight and tell me you'll miss me . . .'

Up up up the service stairwell goes Rosie. She has found an internal staircase outside the back door of the kitchen, where Iva goes to put the garbage into a huge communal shute. The apartment is quiet, the boys are asleep, so she has slipped out. She has a need for fresh air and space, so she follows the steps up four floors til they turn into a narrow staircase, then into smaller wooden stairs which lead to a big clunky iron door.

She heaves the bolt back on it, then leaves it like that so that the door can't close behind her while she steps out onto the roof of the building.

Immediately, she takes a big gulp of the cold city air. It's not clean in her lungs, but it's certainly bracing. The cold tightens her face and she pulls her cardigan close around her. The roof has various blocked-off areas on it which she assumes are the back brick walls of a penthouse or perhaps a service area, and there is a huge looming mausoleum-type tower with green copper roofs on its various levels. The open arches reveal the outline of a giant water tower inside. Rosie walks towards the edge of the building and leans on the balustrade. The buildings next door are much lower and beyond that is a distant garden and then Fifth Avenue, and then the park, so dark at night. Everything else is lit by hundreds of tiny lights. Lights from thousands of windows, and millions of cars below and trillions of stars above. Rosie looks out over Manhattan and wonders, is she in the right place?

Four floors below, Thomas is doing the buttons up on his pyjamas and looking at the same slightly lower view. Is *he* in the right place?

Round and Round
the Garden

It's a Saturday breakfast, later and more casual than week-days. A just-so breakfast with no real fun in it except that no-one is in their office clothes or school uniforms. Even Thomas has his jogging pants on, demonstrating his eternal intention to run on the weekend. He hasn't done so for many years, but wearing the gear allows him to delude himself that he might, and that in itself makes him feel healthy.

The twins are flapping about like gannets around the raisin-toast and sliced melon on the side table.

Glenn attempts to calm them, 'Boys, shush please, don't squabble,' and she puts her hand on the back of the coffee pot. 'Iva, can we have *hot* coffee please?'

Iva scurries off.

Rosie is right next to the boys and is secretly initiating some of the push 'n' shove as she whispers under her breath only for their ears, 'Yeah, but this might be the last raisin-toast left in the universe, we need to stockpile.'

'Yeah,' they agree, grabbing many more slices. Red even slips one into his pocket.

Three is loading his plate high with melon, 'and dragons love this stuff, we could distract them with it.'

'Excellent work, number three, good precautionary thinking,' Rosie agrees.

'Do sit down boys.' Glenn punctures the muffled fun. As they take their seats around the table, Glenn surveys her domain, and her sparrow's portion of muesli. All is in correct order.

Then, Kemble shuffles in, still in his P.J. bottoms and the t-shirt he's obviously slept in. He is trying very hard to hide a monumental hangover. He yawns, dry-mouthed, scratches his head and heads for the coffee.

'Hey Dad,' the twins say, virtually in unison.

'Hey guys,' he yawn-speaks back to them.

'Are we with you today?' Three really wants to know.

'Um, I have to go into the office today, which is a bummer, but know what? – we could catch a movie tonight, how's that?'

'Great!'

'Yay!'

'Cool!'

'Awesome.'

'OK, deal,' Kemble says, 'I'll check out what's on.'

The boys' delight is palpable. The promise of time with their dad lifts them into a happy froth. It's going to be a good day.

Rosie notes the general optimism and chances a suggestion

to Kemble, 'About the various activities for the boys actually. I was wondering if, by any chance, we could make a little garden on the roof? I've been up there and it would be perfect.'

'A garden?' Red and Three are immediately excited.

Kemble looks straight at his mother for approval. Glenn says nothing initially, using the expectant silence as a chance to sip her freshly squeezed orange juice. She then ventures, 'It sounds like dirt, mess and noise.'

Red can't help himself. 'Hey, we could have a fountain . . . and other way cool stuff . . .'

'Like herbs and . . . growing stuff . . .' Three chimes in.

'Yeh, and a secret doorway . . . that leads to a secret place that . . . like . . . I'm the only one who knows where it is . . .'

'Yeh, 'cept you've told us now, dude!' his brother laughs.

'Oh yeh. Duh. Shoot myself!'

Glenn takes another important long slow sip.

'When I suggested activities, Miss Kitto, I was thinking more of museums, galleries and concerts. Perhaps I was mistaken, but I thought that a British nanny, of all people, would appreciate a cultural itinerary?'

Rosie is quick to respond, 'Well, this would certainly be a learning activity, and we would all benefit, not only from the . . . salad things we might grow, but the . . . flowers . . . and how lovely would it be to have cocktails at sunset up there?'

Glenn cuts through the crap, 'Do you know anything about gardening?'

Rosie assumes a confident face, and then, frankly, lies her bum off, 'Of course!'

Iva passes by with the new coffee and gives Rosie an 'oh really?' sly look with a raised eyebrow.

Rosie has the bit between her teeth now, 'and I could teach them the Latin names of the plants . . .'

Kemble avoids Rosie's pointed gaze. So she turns to Thomas, who is staring right at her.

'I really think it's too much mess,' says Glenn, firmly. The twins groan with disappointment. Thomas looks down at his newspaper. The subject, it seems, is closed.

Then, from behind the paper, Thomas's voice is heard loud and clear, 'Well, it gets my vote. Go ahead.'

Glenn stares at Thomas, or at least, at the newspaper behind which he is. He lowers the paper and resolutely looks only at Rosie and the boys, both of whom are punching the air like triumphant goal-scoring footballers.

'Miss Kitto, we'll discuss it and inform you,' Glenn says, in an attempt to regain control.

'No, we won't,' retorts Thomas. 'It's decision time now. I will talk to the janitor. A garden sounds great. Do it. And I'll pay.'

'Go, Granpop!'

'Yay, Granpop!' the boys shriek, and rush round the table to hug him and Rosie.

Kemble watches carefully as his mother puts her juice down and smiles tightly at the scene. She is trying to cover up the

72

fact that she has just been defeated. He wishes he had his father's courage.

Iva brings fresh milk into the room, 'Surprise guest at the door, Mrs W.B.'

'Oh God,' huffs Glenn under her breath, dreading that it might be Natalie again.

All eyes in the breakfast room swing round to the door as in marches Teddy, age eighteen, taller than both his father and grandfather, and feigning a bucketful of adolescent confidence. He drops his bag inside the door, flicks his shaggy hair and announces, 'Edward Wilder-Bingham is in the building! Stay back! No pictures!'

The twins race at him and jump up at their big brother like excited terriers. First on his feet amongst the grown ups is Thomas, who immediately goes to his eldest grandson and embraces him with a back-slapping manhug, 'Hello Teddy, great to see you.' Teddy grins unselfconsciously and hugs his grandfather, the only man in his life he considers to be a great role model. The marked difference in his perfunctory 'Hey Dad' greeting to his father and the equally awkward 'Hey Ted' back is telling.

Glenn goes to him, holds his shoulders and looks him up and down, drinking in how quickly he has grown and changed, and how much like her darling Kemble he is becoming, physically at least. Teddy fidgets under this attention. She kisses him lightly on both cheeks, 'My, you look more like a man every day, you are such a Wilder-Bingham, look at you,' she tells him, and instantly brands him. Teddy knows full well that whilst she might be stamping family ownership on him with such a comment, there is a subtext. She is simultaneously rejecting his mother Natalie, her family, and all they stand for. Glenn has assumed this stance ever since the divorce began and of course it places the boys in a difficult position. Especially Teddy, who is old enough to feel real empathy for his mum.

'It's study week,' he explains as he sits down and tucks into his breakfast, 'and Mom has to be in France from tomorrow, so I thought it would be great to hang with you guys.'

'And study, of course,' Glenn reminds him.

'And study, of course.' Teddy agrees. 'Oh, thanks Iva, yeah, I love . . . this stuff,' he says, as a bowl of something cabbagey is put in front of him. He shoots a knowing glance at Thomas and Kemble and the family share a brief clandestine old joke.

In these times of conflict, Teddy is grateful for any shared levity with his disappointing father. Humour used to be their thing. Their house was full of it once, and through that, Teddy felt safe and clever and part of his dad. Then, there were a weird few years when Kemble seemed to float away. He wasn't at home as often and when he was, there were serious rows with his mother, which would often leave her in tears. Teddy would try to comfort Natalie, but not really know how to. He didn't know what to say to fix it, he really wanted to find those magic words that would cheer her up. Natalie and Kemble talked behind closed doors in their apartment, sometimes voices were raised, but always there were cover-over-the-cracks smiles for the kids. Teddy learned not to trust those smiles, they felt different to the easy true smiles that accompany real laughs and jokes. He longs for those again, and he grabs any opportunity. Even cabbage. The approval Teddy feels in those reflected knowing looks from his father and grandfather is disproportionate to the joke, but it doesn't matter, he's grateful for a tiny slice of tribe.

Glenn surveys her breakfast table, and announces, 'I like this view very much, I get to have all my boys around me at the same time. Now . . .' She gets up, 'I have . . . many things to do . . .'

She doesn't.

'So if you will . . . excuse me, I will catch up with you all later . . .' and she calmly leaves the room, smiling carefully, off to endure another day of nothing much. As always, the room lightens when she leaves, they all relax a tiny bit more. Iva bustles about, clearing dishes and filling up the boys' glasses with fruit juice. Even Teddy's, which is old habit.

Rosie has been sitting quietly, watching all the interesting dynamics now that this new younger energy has entered the arena. Teddy is incredibly tall and lean, with the beginnings of a wispy beard sprouting Amish-like under and on his chin. He is so very definitely made of both his parents. He has Kemble's big hands and strong dark eyebrows, and he has Natalie's astonishing, unmistakable green eyes.

'Hello, by the way, I'm the nanny-type person.'

'Oh yes, hi, Mom told me about you, I was kinda imagining you as Swedish though?'

'Really? No, I'm resolutely English, no real plan to change that, sorry. I know what a hurdy-gurdy is, and I've eaten herring in my life, but that's about the extent of my Swedishness . . . I'm afraid.'

'Right . . .' He says, weighing her up, trying to decide if she's funny funny, merely funny, or just plain odd. She stands out as a bit odd in this apartment, she's chubby and cheerful and colourful and eccentric. He likes her immediately.

'Well, I'm Teddy. Eldest. Cleverest. And best looking. I'm the most damaged by the divorce, which translates as: you have to feel most sorry for me.'

Kemble rolls his eyes at this chutzpah.

'Get it,' replies Rosie. 'Well, I'm Rosie, sometimes referred to by beloveds as Rosie Big Boobs, but that would, of course, be utterly inappropriate to say out loud in this varied age and strongly male environment, so I won't. Blood group O. Best bribe: chocolate.'

She pretty much floors them all with this. They are silent and open-mouthed around the table.

'So,' she continues, 'wanna help us build a glorious garden?'

'Cool,' says Teddy, imagining that's exactly what it will be.

Three pipes up, 'Can he come on the surprise journey today too?'

'Hmmm,' she ruminates, 'us guys have made a pact to keep it secret, and I totally trust us guys, so whaddya reckon?'

'Hey, come on!' Teddy pleads.

The twins enjoy having the power over their older brother's fate, and chortle away to each other, pretending it's a big decision, 'Yeah, OK, we think he can do it. He will keep the secret,' they grandly bestow their permission.

'What actually *is* the secret?' asks Red.

'Wouldn't be a secret if I said . . .' she replies.

Teddy joins in, 'A lady with secrets. I like it.'

'Shhh,' she says, and taps the side of her nose as if she's a spy. 'Let the journey begin. Coats on, lads.'

'What if I don't like the secret?' Red says as they leave.

'I guarandamntee you will,' says Rosie.

And up they get, Rosie, Teddy and the twins, off for an adventure in the city, leaving Thomas and Kemble to drain their coffee cups and wish they could be part of the fun.

Trains

As the four intrepid explorers emerge from the subway at 59th Street and Lexington Avenue, Three is complaining, 'But you said the secret would be found on the train? It wasn't.'

'Yeh,' Red chimes in, 'How come we're up on the street again?'

Rosie answers the impatient twosome, 'I categorically didn't say it was on *the* train. I categorically did say it was to be found on *a* train.'

'Hmmm,' says Teddy, 'looks like you're gonna have to wriggle outta this one.'

'Have faith please, gentlemen, there's more to this than meets the eye. You are thinking far too literally. All your logic is too earth-bound.'

'Isn't a train a totally earth-bound phenomenon?' Teddy questions, clearly intrigued by the whole idea, 'I mean either on the ground or under it, surely . . . ?'

'Yeh,' says Three thinking fast, 'or it could be on a monorail, like those ones we went on in Disneyland?'

'Yeh,' Red agrees, 'but there's nothing like that here.'

Rosie is quick to refute this, 'Oh, isn't there?' and she sets off towards Third Avenue.

The other three have to walk pretty fast to keep up with her as she is setting a brisk old pace. They shout quickfire questions at her bright-green back, as they whisk along the cracked sidewalks, avoiding slow walkers and old compacted lumps of unmelted ice from the frozen weather. Rosie doesn't answer, she has her head down and is determined to lead with confidence even though this is their city, not hers.

As they round the corner on to Third Avenue, Teddy has a grim realization.

'Oh my God, she's brought us to Bloomies, guys, she wants to shop.'

'I hate Bloomingdales.'

'Oh no. Mercy.'

'Please, not shopping,' the boys plead.

She turns, 'Do you want to uncover the secret or not?'

Teddy looks at the twins. 'Yes. We do,' he answers on all of their behalves.

'Right. Well zip it and follow me. Stay close because frankly, m'laddios, this is combat inside those doors, and we need to have eyeballs on each other at all times to survive. Got it?'

'Yes sir,' says Red.

'Ma'am,' corrects Three.

She shakes their hands, 'For God, England and North America, good luck . . .' and with that, she flings open the giant art deco iron doors and dives into the slipstream of the pushy crowd coming and going. She feels the warmth of Three's small hand creep into hers and as she looks back, she sees that they have formed a daisy chain of brothers, linked together by hand and all following her intently. She is the mama duck.

Rosie finds the escalators in the middle of the store and stays on them, travelling up up up to the sixth floor, where she heads towards the kitchen appliance department. Past the liquidizers, the fat-free fryers, the high-speed whisks, the spotty mugs, to a surprising chrome stairway, which looks like the glamorous entrance to a cruise liner from the roaring twenties. Up they go until they come to a narrow corridor. Are they still in Bloomingdales? It's so surreal! Here in front of them all is the side of an old French train, pulled in at the platform they appear to be standing on. A sign points to an open carriage door, 'Le Train Bleu'. Rosie ushers the wide-eyed boys through the door into a vintage dining car, all laid up with crisp white table linen, gleaming silver cutlery and tinging glass goblets. It's a restaurant, in a train, on the sixth floor of Bloomingdales, which could, for all the world, be hurtling between Calais and the French Riviera in 1924! The walls are wood and mirror-panelled, with little table lights and cream shades on every table. The ceiling is padded with green fabric and wood struts and there are delicate French glass lights and subtle bistro chandeliers with chrome fans in between.

One whole side has windows looking out onto Manhattan.

Four or five elegant tables have elegant diners at them, and in the furthest corner there is one very special diner sitting alone at a table laid for four. She has her back to the boys, but it doesn't take long before they recognize the familiar compact frame and expensively highlighted blonde crop of their mum. All three boys rush to her and she gathers them into her arms and showers them with lots of silly little kisses. They pretend not to like it, but nobody resists too much.

She especially greets Teddy, who she hasn't seen for a month or so.

'Teds! *Mon Dieu*! You've gotten so thin!'

'S'one of the benefits of emotional turmoil, Mom.'

She laughs and looks hurt at the same time.

'JOKE,' he assures her.

Natalie touches his cheek and adores him. She turns to Rosie, 'Thank you Miss Kitto.'

'Rosie, please.'

'Rosie, thank you.'

'No problem. I'll have a wander and be back in an hour or so. I know you've got your flight.'

They both nod at each other, two women complicit in the same endeavour, to keep these young men well-loved. Rosie leaves them to their mother and heads out into Bloomingdales to see what chocolate and shoe treasures it might contain. She won't be disappointed.

Knob

That evening, the happiness that comes from seeing their mum is still swirling around the boys, even around Teddy who is too cool to let it show much. Being eighteen and being jolly don't sit too well together. He's happier in his customary morose mode, but even he can't hide his cheer completely.

Rosie whips up some quick pasta with a tomato and basil sauce for the boys to scoff before Kemble is due home to take them to the movies. Teddy knows that if the choice of film is down to the twins, he is in for an evening of earth-threatening superhero high action. Does he mind? Not at all. All boys like the chance to be junior whenever possible, even Kemble, even Granpops. The excited chat around the kitchen counter where Rosie is cooking is all about which film they might choose. Thomas and Glenn are out, and it's Iva's night off, so she is in her room in the back of the apartment, next to Rosie's, catching up with her favourite Polish soap operas and talent shows on TV Polonia and using Skype to talk to her beloved daughter back home.

Rosie is the first to realize that the minutes are ticking away and there is a worrying no show from Kemble. She brushes off the concern as pessimism and serves up Oreo-cookie ice-cream for pudding, in the hope that by the time the last delicious gulp is gone, Kemble will be through the door and rushing to go straight back out again with them. The boys are loud but it's even louder inside Rosie's head where the clock is ticking. Tick . . . Tock. Come on Kemble.

Teddy is the next to wonder where his father is. Rosie shrugs her shoulders. Teddy picks up his phone and calls his dad's number, which goes repeatedly straight to voicemail.

'Shit,' he whispers under his breath. He looks at the kitchen clock, it's just gone seven thirty p.m. They have missed most of the earlier movie start times. Rosie knows what he is thinking. He is damning his dad to hell. The twins are thankfully oblivious of time, assuming rightly that someone else is doing that thinking for them.

Rosie has an idea, 'Hey guys, help me out with this, OK? Someone has been really annoying me recently, a man, a self-ish thoughtless man, and I need to think of the appropriate swear words to call him when I next see him. Obviously I wouldn't EVER dream of using any demeaning words that pertain to women or women's bodies in my swearing so, avoid those at all costs, but almost anything about guys, their bits, poo, wee or anything else including f-words is fine. So, if we say the next five minutes is a total cussing amnesty, meaning you can say anything within those rules, what can I call him? Go!'

The chaps look at each other, a bit uncertain how to process this instruction but, with encouragement, Teddy is the first to draw his curse sword, 'Um, well I would call him . . . a dickhead . . . or maybe . . . a fucking douche?' he says hesitantly.

'Yeah, those are good, but what about if you got a little more creative? Like, say . . . moosecock?'

The twins giggle. They love the fact that the gloves are off, that it's somehow, inexplicably alright to be so naughtily vulgar in Granma's house.

As Teddy gets more juiced up, he offers 'OK, assmonger, prickface, fucktard . . .'

'Great. More,' says Rosie.

Three summons his courage, and enters the ring with 'Dicknose', which gets a round of applause.

Red tries next, 'Pissmonkey', which gets whoops of approval. Then, it's a free for all, with words tumbling out of them like a silage truck chute of pure filth.

Red, 'Fannycheese!'

Rosie allows this, because she thankfully remembers fanny means bum here, and bumcheese is infinitely preferable.

Three, 'Dumbdick.'

Teddy, 'Fuckerhead.'

Rosie gives it her best, 'Oinking great arse knob.'

Teddy follows verbose suit, 'Tit-faced cock end.'

84

The twins try more inventive words.

'Turdbreath!'

'Cockasaurus!'

'Tithead!'

'Nitshit!'

Teddy tries to trump them with 'Jizzbucket!'

Rosie attempts something left field, 'Republican!'

They fall apart laughing at the randomness of that, but the pleasure of the rude stuff is too tempting, so they return to it for a final volley.

Teddy, 'Asswrangler!'

Rosie, 'Bumdonkey!'

Then the twins collaborate to achieve the finale, 'You . . . ratsuck . . . sweaty . . . fat . . . ass . . . balls!'

'Yay!' Rosie cries, and holds their hands aloft like prizefighters, 'We have the champions, ladies and gentlemen!!'

All of them are on their feet, stamping and clapping. And now, Rosie continues, 'I declare the official end of the cussing competition, I have exactly what I need, so it has served its purpose. Just like the visit to the "Le Train Bleu" earlier today, I hereby consign both of these activities to a secret place where none, other than we select four, shall ever speak of them again. Understand?'

They all agree and she spits on her hand for them to follow suit and shake on it.

'Now, listen, I am guessing your dad's been held up with

something important,' Rosie shoots Teddy a 'don't say anything else' look, 'so let's head on out and find a movie, yes?!'

She doesn't give the twins time to stop and think about where Kemble is or why he isn't there on time, she bustles them out of the door with Teddy's help. Teddy, who is very, very angry with his dad. Again.

Goodbye

Inside the cavernous cathedral earlier that same day, the congregation for Bill Sharpe's memorial seems insultingly tiny. There are a respectful couple of hundred people, but it still feels scant. That's the problem when you're important enough to warrant a service inside St Patrick's cathedral, but old enough to mean that few of your peers have outlived you and are able to attend. What you might have imagined to be a grand, significant occasion when you are alive and planning ahead, turns out to pall into a nugatory, rather slight thing of a do. Not for the want of effort. For some of the congregants, it has taken a *mighty* effort to come, so old and feeble are they. Some of them don't get dressed often, never mind dressed up, as they are today, in honour of their friend, colleague, husband, uncle and (for the two youngest people attending, who are themselves in their sixties) father, Bill. All are in their funeral garb. None have worn it for the first time. Some have worn these smart, suitably black threads too often for comfort. One of those is Thomas.

He sits quietly next to some of his old chums, nervously awaiting his turn to read. He is without Glenn. As expected. Glenn doesn't do memorials. He has been inside this cathedral on many occasions, happy and sad, and always he has been in awe of its towering splendour. Today, however, he is experiencing it differently. Yes it's huge and majestic and hallowed, but it's also cold and unfriendly and open to the public who mill about noisily, nosily, on the fringes of this very private service. It might have been better for them to be in one of the smaller side chapels, but the hubris, and the great grief of Sharpe's widow Betty, denoted that the main aisle and big altar was the only right place. So here they sit in their drab blacks and greys, feeling puny. Thomas is aware that he is in an inevitable queue of helpless mortals, merely waiting his turn, there but for the Grace of God ...

Today is to celebrate Sharpe, his old college roommate, but like all things funereal, it reminds Thomas that he could be next, so he finds himself relieved at his reprieve and guilty for feeling so. Glad that Sharpe went first, that he has some more time himself. Then he looks around at the older ones, those in their nineties with the sallow cheeks, grey eyes, loose teeth and liver spots, and he wonders just what he's glad for? And he looks up at the soaring ceiling and the intricate design of the huge vaults supported by the colossal stone columns, suddenly aware that they are obediently seated in the belly of an immense stone carcass, with the blanched raw ribs ascending and enclosing above them, a mighty, gigantic cage, to remind them of how small and insignificant and temporary they all are. The renegade Canute in Thomas longs to resist it all. Then, he hears his name, and it's time for him to climb the spiral stairs into the pulpit to say his poem loud and clear, in memory of his late friend. He looks out at the almost dead, and begins.

'Holy Sonnet Number Ten by John Donne.

Death be not proud, though some have called thee

Mighty and dreadful, for thou art not so;

For those whom thou think'st thou dost overthrow

Die not, poor Death, nor yet canst thou kill me . . .'

Thomas is a good public speaker, that's why he's been asked, but today his voice is thinner than usual, he fears he might falter. Why? Because frankly, he's not sure he believes this poem. It sounds great, he's heard it at a thousand funerals, it works, but what really is Thomas saying? The poem seems to be insisting that death has no right to be proud, because apparently human beings don't die, they live eternally. Yeah. Right.

'From rest and sleep, which but thy pictures be,

Much pleasure; then from thee much more must flow,

And soonest our best men with thee do go.

Rest of their bones and soul's delivery.'

'And soonest our best men with thee do go'? Sharpe was one of those 'best men', and Sharpe was younger than Thomas.

'Bones and souls'? He doesn't want to be bones and souls, he wants to be flesh and heart and laugh and kiss and sing . . .

'Thou art slave to fate, chance, kings and desperate men.

And dost with poison, war, and sickness dwell;

And poppy or charms can make us sleep as well

And better than thy stroke, why swell'st thou then?'

So . . . What? . . . death is a cowardly slave who just depends on luck, accidents, decrees, murder, disease and war to kill men? OK, death may hide inside all of these, but it's still DEATH. Death is in charge, and it took Sharpe. In a long slow agonizingly cruel cancerous way. And it might come for Thomas next. It's horrific, and there's nothing he can do . . .

'One short sleep past, we wake eternally.

And death shall be no more: Death, thou shalt die.'

No! It's not a short sleep if you don't believe all that afterlife crap. That's it. FINITO.

Death doesn't die, John Donne, we do. All of us die, Thomas thinks: the clever, the lucky, the poor, the pretty, the ugly, the wealthy. Just the same as the ignorant, the greedy, the evil. We leave it all, good and bad, behind us. Thomas refuses to buy the notion that death is some kind of High Calling, will glorify us for all eternity. It's not, it's THE END.

Why the hell did he choose this poem? He apologizes to Sharpe in his deepest heart, and as he steps down from the pulpit, Thomas knows what he must do. He must escape from the carcass, and he must live whatever time he has left with significance. He wants to love, and as he strides straight back down the aisle and out of the huge bronze doors onto Fifth Avenue, he gulps in the dirty air of his wonderful messy city and he resolves to live properly, to the full, while he can.

Fuck off, death.

Meantime, at a corner table in the lounge of The Colony Club, on 62nd Street and Park Avenue, Glenn sits alone, purposely. She sips Lady Grey tea and feigns reading the paper so that none other should approach. She prefers it when there are no men in the vicinity; this is a women-only private social club, after all, but occasionally, men are admitted as guests. Of course, she could join various other tables if she so chose, Annie Catlin is sitting with her daughter, and the Morgans seem to have a clattery round of mah-jong on the go. Glenn knows she would be welcome at either table, but she chooses to sit alone and appear occupied. She likes people to think she is taking a breather from her otherwise massively demanding life. Thomas made sure she knew she was welcome to come to the memorial, but Glenn rejects more than she accepts in every part of her life, and it's this simple choice that defines so much of her. She is comfortable with plenty of NO. She pours more tea through the strainer, and for a brief moment, she considers how delicious it might be to allow herself even one mouthful of the mini lemon meringue tart which arrived alongside her tea as a little treat. But ... NO ... she decides against. Glenn's bouche remains strictly unamused.

Very much later that night, after the loud shooty film, after the fairly long walk home, after the late night peanut-butter-cup munchies, after warm face flannels and calming bedtime stories and after hot chocolate with Teddy, Rosie's day is finally over. Glenn and Thomas are home by the time the movie posse arrived back, and Rosie assumes they have already gone to bed. The twins have insisted on buying a swirl of red liquorice for Granpops when they were out, they know he LOVES that. Just as Rosie is turning out the lights in the kitchen, she sees it on the side and decides to pop it onto Thomas's desk as a surprise for the morning.

Although she feels sure he isn't in his office at – what is it? One fifteen a.m. – Rosie still knocks gently at the door. She's aware that actually, she probably shouldn't enter at all, but her desire to deposit this little gift overrides the rules. Of course there is no answer, so she opens the door quietly and pads bare-footed into the dark room. She then goes on tip-toe which is kind of ludicrous, since no-one is here. She knows the layout of the room well enough to find her way to his desk. As she moves carefully her eyes adjust to the darkness, and her senses are heightened. She is aware of the smell of Thomas in the room. Yes, there would be that, it's where he always is. The aroma is of oak and leather and whatever that citrus aftershave is that he uses. As she gets closer to his desk, she can see the outline of his big chair against the window, and out of the shadows, suddenly his deep, quiet voice, 'Come in, whydoncha.'

Rosie's blood stops still in her heart with shock, she gulps a roomful of air in, and freezes. 'God! Sorry. I'll come back later . . .' she backs away, clumsy and stunned, and bumps into a bookcase behind her, 'Ow.'

Thomas switches the desk light on, 'No it's OK, what did you want?'

Rosie sees his face in the light and notices that his eyes are red, he's been crying. He is making a half-hearted attempt to wipe his face like proud men do, almost slapping themselves in an effort to cover up their emotions. In the moment, Rosie forgets that there is an invisible line of professionalism between them, and she reaches out, human to human.

'Is there anything I can do?'

Thomas shakes his head. He can't quite speak for a moment, and while he is trying to compose himself, tears well in his eyes again. He laughs a little embarrassed laugh as one of them rolls down his cheek.

'Only if you can make me immortal?'

'You don't want that,' she says, as she takes a step nearer to him, 'think of the fortune you would spend at the barbers . . .'

He smiles. 'I went to the memorial service of a very close friend today. He was six months younger than me ...' Rosie takes another step closer, while he continues, 'So naturally, I'm sitting in the dark, feeling sorry for myself. It's completely selfish.' He stands up and goes to the window, where he is framed by the lights of the city outside. 'I've given up red meat, red wine, smoking. I go to the gym most days. Well, I don't, but I have the guilt, and that's punishment enough. I even go and sit silently at the shrink's regularly. And the Grim Reaper's still out to get me.'

There is a pause. Rosie walks over to the window and stands next to him. She gently touches his arm,

'Sod it then. If you're on your way, why not have the occasional glass of red wine and a ciggie?'

Thomas carefully pulls away, 'Being nice to me is making it worse, I fear.'

For an interesting moment or two, they stand there, sharing the promise of the city beyond. Two very different people, two very different ages, with no problem standing still, being connected.

Outside in the hall there is the sound of a drunken Kemble stumbling into the apartment and dropping his keys. For some reason, Thomas and Rosie both feel a fleeting moment of guilt.

Kemble is in a heap on the floor of the hall, just inside the front door. He has banged into the table and sent a porcelain lamp flying, so he is sitting amongst the debris when Thomas and Rosie arrive to try and pick him up.

'Hey, pops!' he slurs at his father, 'Why you still up? You should be in bed . . . with . . . Cruella . . .'

It's at this most inopportune of moments that Glenn rounds the corner in her neat dressing gown. With her blows a bitter wind, 'Thank you, Miss Kitto, that's quite enough, you may go to your rooms now.'

Thomas nods to indicate that may well be the best course of action. Rosie says goodnight and scootches off to bed, leaving Glenn and Thomas to pick up their broken son.

She doesn't dare look back, but she can hear Glenn admonishing him,

'Get up Kemble, get up you idiot!'

Breakfast Again

It's another Saturday morning, a few weeks later, but this time the twins are making the breakfast with Rosie and Iva, while Glenn and Thomas sit and wait to see what the junior chefs whip up. Pancakes are on the menu, which means that flour, baking powder, salt, sugar, milk, eggs and butter are on the floor. Some of the ingredients have survived and seem to have been sifted, whisked and fried, and with Iva's expert guidance, there is an unruly stack of blueberry pancakes in the centre of the breakfast table, along with a jug of hot maple syrup, some whipped cream and some chopped up fruit in a separate bowl. Red cut up the fruit, so it's his favourites of course, bananas and kiwi fruit only.

The boys and Rosie tumble into their seats around the table, covered in flour and egg, but mighty proud of their culinary prowess. 'TA-DA!' announces Rosie, 'Ladles and Jellyspoons, we give you . . .' and the twins complete it, 'The Tower of Power! Pancakes to rock your world!'

This is, of course, Glenn's absolute nightmare because now, she HAS to eat. They cooked it, and they are watching, so she must.

Thomas is first to lunge at the Tower, 'GUYS, Rosie, thanks for this, it looks darn delicious, here I go!' and he helps himself to a few. Glenn does some of her best fake happy smiling, pretends to lick her lips, and also sets about helping herself to a considerably smaller amount.

'Hey! The cocktail!' shouts Three, as he rushes out to bring in a huge jug of maroon goo he has made in the liquidizer. No one is quite sure just what his smoothie consists of, but Rosie saw some berries and beetroot and blue M & Ms go in there. Rosie takes extra pleasure from watching Glenn attempt a mouthful of this challenging mixture, without visibly retching. More calories are entering Glenn in five minutes than have whizzed around her skeletal physique in the last five years.

'Where's Dad?' asks Three.

Glenn answers, 'He's not feeling too good today, so we're going to leave him be. OK?'

'OK.' The twins agree, resigned to yet another day of no contact with him. Glenn and Thomas and Rosie all know the same thing, which they don't discuss, certainly not here and now. The fact is that Kemble hasn't been home for several days this week, and no-one, including his work colleagues, knows where he's been. They are all worried in the Wilder-Bingham household, but as per usual, no one mentions it.

'Granma, Granpops, can we ask you something?' says Red.

Thomas stiffens. Please don't let him have to lie to this little guy about his father. 'Sure.'

'D'you wanna have a look at the garden? We've started it.'

Rosie intervenes quickly. 'Guys, hang on. Wouldn't it be better if we wait til we've got it into better shape before we invite guests up there?!'

'Yes,' agrees Glenn, who clearly doesn't want another commitment beyond this very challenging smoothie/pancake combo today, 'wait til it's ready. I want to see it when it's all done.'

'OK,' says a disappointed Red.

'I'll come and check it out, fellas, just as soon as I've had another twenty of these big ol' boys . . .' says Thomas as he helps himself to more. He knows he'll feel sick, but so long as the little men are happy, so is he.

'Teddy would, like, so love these, can we make them again when he's back Rosie?' asks Three.

'Of course,' she replies.

Half an hour later, puffing, full and nauseous, Thomas climbs through the door at the top of the service steps, out onto the roof where, in one corner there is a three foot by three foot boxed-off planting container about eighteen inches high, full of new earth. There are bags of soil and spades and trowels everywhere and various small new plants in pots waiting to be dug in on the side. It's a holy mess, but the twins have all the plans bubbling away in their heads, and they excitedly chirrup it all to their grandfather, '. . . a fountain here . . . some tomatoes here . . . plants growing up a stick . . . chairs here . . . basil . . . roses for Granma . . .' on and on they go, running about.

Thomas whispers to Rosie, 'This is great, kid. Look at 'em, they're really into it.'

Rosie is delighted, 'There's nothing like a bit of planting to remind you of what matters, and, y'know . . . take your mind off stuff.'

'That's right, he says, 'and, er, I just wanted to give you this. He quietly hands her a small envelope. 'I hope I've . . . got it right . . . come on you guys, back downstairs . . .' and he wrangles the boys back through the door, glancing at her over his shoulder before he dips out of sight.

Thomas is suddenly gone, and Rosie is left holding the envelope, which she slowly starts to open. What is it? Is he giving her some money towards the garden? Why is he behaving so surreptitiously? Why did that last glance so interest her? What *is* this?

She slides her finger under the fold and rips it back carefully.

Not money, but a letter . . .

Rosie reads.

Goosebumps . . .

ACT II

St Paddy's Day

Rosie doesn't come down to this lower part of Manhattan very much, she's only just becoming familiar with the few blocks on the Upper East Side where the Wilder-Binghams live. She has visited Broadway and Soho a little bit, on days off, and she has come to know parts of Central Park, but Chinatown and, below that, the Financial District are unknown territory. This boutique hotel in Tribeca is unlike anywhere she has stayed. For a start, it's very dark. When she walks off the busy St Patrick's Day-crazy street, into the lobby, Rosie genuinely thinks they must surely be having a problem with their generator, she can hardly see a thing. Or perhaps she was having a brain haemorrhage? Then she notices that attractive people are sitting about in big purple velvet armchairs on flat animal skin rugs, in front of a roaring fire drinking green cocktails, regarding the very low light as perfectly alright. So it must be.

She makes her way to the dark lifts and exits at the sixth

floor, which is also very 'atmospheric'. Rosie feels she might be on the set of *Mad Men* – the whole vibe of the hotel is retro sixties with the odd modern twist, especially the art. Intriguing art, which you would never choose, and which intimidates you, and insists that you admire it, otherwise you're stupid, right?

And now here she is, at the door of room 610, her heart beating fast and her hands clammy. She is carrying a very heavy bag, full of gardening books, with all her senses on high alert and certain in the knowledge that a moment like this simultaneously carries you forward and offers you no way back, she . . . eventually . . . knocks.

A pause.

Oh God, a pause.

Is it OK?

The door opens . . . it's Thomas, with eighty-three years of hopefulness glowing on his concerned face. They smile nervously at each other, and he stands back to let her in. She steps past him while he closes the door, and she stands still with her back at the wall. He stands opposite her in the narrow entrance hall to the suite, with his back at the other wall. They hold one another's gaze, unflinchingly, each hoping against hope that they haven't horribly misread the other.

They haven't.

The attraction is palpable, and just as her back leaves the safety of the wall to move towards him, so too does his. He has to stoop to kiss her, but her willing puts her on her tiptoes to meet him at the lips. In one rush, so much happens, so much is suddenly known. She learns that the skin on his face is soft, but his lips are firm, she learns that he is nervous and eager, she learns that he smells like limes up close, she learns that he murmurs whilst he kisses, and she learns that her arms barely meet when they are wrapped around his great ursine torso. His kisses are light and many to begin with, and as he gradually believes her consent, he risks the real deep kissing he has missed so much, and Rosie submits happily.

Later, after, it's dusk and the room is slowly turning orange. Thomas and Rosie lie naked and easy together, their legs still entwined, but their bodies separate, seeking out the cool of the sheets. The sweat is drying on their skin, and they can hear each other's short gasps returning to normal breathing again. They've done it, they've had sex, they've crossed the line. Here they lie, masculine and feminine, now known to each other in the most intimate way, in the way they can never unknow. They lie quietly like this for some time, letting the actuality of it sink in, letting it be wonderful, and right now, letting it be . . . this.

Rosie is thinking, 'So that's what it's like to do it with a much older man. Well, with this man. He takes his time, he knows where everything is, and he puts in lots of effort, and best of all, thank you God or Venus or whoever, he knows himself so well that he isn't embarrassed or shy. He lets me know what he wants and he isn't afraid to ask for it. He *talks* to me, looking me right in the eyes, and tells me what he likes. Oh my god, he told me that my body was "made for love" and that the touch of my flesh sent his senses "spinning" and that the hollows at the back of my knees are "the most erotic thing" he's ever seen. Bloody hell! Something about how comfortable he is in his own skin makes him utterly gorgeous. I love how hefty he is, and how tender, and how . . . just *how* he is.'

Thomas is thinking, 'What a woman, so irresistibly plump and inviting . . . and so completely unashamed. She actually *wants* to make love, she *wants* pleasure, she *wants* me. She's a cascade of a person, full of light, and . . . look, she lit me up. At last. Nothing was difficult or awkward, it was so . . . natural. I can say anything. I did. I said everything that was in my mind, and it was OK. More than OK. It was great. And I love the smell of her hair . . . *all* her hair. She has real English pubic hair, soft and curly and unshaved. And I love the fullness and the taste of her lips . . . *all* her lips. She's – fresh and salty. Christ, she's something else, and for this little chink of time, she's mine.'

Rosie rolls in towards him and lovingly cups her hand over his cock.

'Hey, you're shaking,' she says.

'It's my age, things shake.' He says.

'You're getting cold, come on,' she pulls the sheet around them both, and cuddles into his shoulder. Gradually, he stops shaking and warms up.

'I'm amazed by this, just so you know. . .' he reassures her, 'Amazed. Thanks for . . . turning up. I wasn't sure you would.'

She sighs, 'I wanted this as much as you. I just didn't realize until I read your letter. But I knew straight away that you'd take care, of this . . . of me . . . , of us . . . . that it would be really private. And I knew that you saw the real me, the same way I believed I saw you. It's need, isn't it? With both of us. How could I resist? And anyway, the timing is great, because you are lying next to a person who has just recently decided to live her life according to yes. Enough of "better not" and "thanks but no", I'm trying "yes please" for size.'

'That's good,' he strokes her nice-smelling hair. They can hear strains of 'Danny Boy' in the streets outside. He holds his hand up as if to grab the orange light. 'Everyone else seems to love a sunset. Postcards. Photos. Sunsets all over the world. I hate them. Don't get me wrong, I know it's pretty 'n' all that, and . . . natural . . . and . . . God even, but I don't appreciate the light seeping away from me like that, deserting me. No thanks. Keep your sunsets. I'll take noon every time. Seriously. I get why wolves howl.'

'Why?'

'They are crying, grieving the end of another day of glorious light. They are yelling at the moon, for celebrating another day gone,' he explains.

'No-one's stopping you from howling,' she teases him, 'howl all you like.'

Thomas lowers his arm and lets his finger circle Rosie's nipple, which instantly responds by bunching up and out for more. It sends a shiver of delight right through Rosie.

'There are other, more pressing things I'd rather do,' his deep voice buzzes in her ear.

'Right.' She puts her hand over his. 'Are there? Are there things you really want to do?'

'Well,' he thinks about it, 'what, you want me to tell you now?'

'Yeah, I think so. You were inside me twenty minutes ago. I'm supposing now would be as good a time as ever to do the "getting to know you" stuff? Whaddyathink?'

He laughs at her cheek, and lies back to properly think. 'OK,' he says, finally. 'Let me see. I want to wear shorts to board meetings.'

Rosie chips in immediately, 'But you're one of the founding partners of your company, your name is in the title, pass a law: "shorts can be worn". Ba-da-bing-ba-da-boom. Done. Next.'

'OK. I want to play electric guitar again, I used to be in a band . . .'

'Course you did. Name of band?'

'The Right Solutions,' he is nearly proud.

'Hilarious. Appalling. That's achievable easily.'

'I guess so. I want to go on a date with Nicole Kidman and have her beg me not to go home, I want a motorbike . . .'

'No! Cliché. Not allowed.'

'OK. I want to drink absinthe and sleep in a field under a huge moon. I want to dance a waltz.'

'Oh please promise they're not *all* sentimental.'

'No. No.' He thinks hard. 'No. Well, yes, but no. I want to paint a portrait, a good one.'

'Can you paint?'

'No, but I would love to. And I want to hold a younger, stronger man down in osaekomi-waza, it's a judo hold. I want to get it so right that he can't move at all, be in charge with skill and device, not just brute force. Would love that, and know what? I'd love to dye my . . .' He nearly says it, but his smile fades, and Rosie slumps a little as it does. He continues, 'Listen to me. I want, I want. It's all too late anyway. There's no time . . .'

Rosie kisses his big chest and looks deep into his eyes. She dares him, 'Oh, we have time. We have plenty of time. So finish that sentence, please . . .'

It seems you can find anything in downtown New York. Half an hour later, Thomas is sitting on a chair, naked except for a draped towel. Rosie is dressed and sits on the edge of the bath next to him. She flicks off a rubber glove cheekily, and asks, 'Any burning, sir?'

He looks up at her, wide-eyed, 'Believe me, if there was any burning you'd know about it, Toots.' They sit in silence and look at the towel.

'Your turn,' he says.

Rosie knows he is inviting her to reciprocate and open up about herself. She smiles fondly at him, shaking her head and fiddling with the rubber glove. 'Honestly, Thomas, I'm better off as a bit of a mystery. The actual truth is a bit boring.'

He stares at her as if to push the matter, but it doesn't work, so he softens, and tentatively asks, 'Is there someone? At home?'

'Do you mean physically or mentally?'

'Why are you British always so evasive? You know I'm asking if there's someone special in your life . . .'

'No. Yes. Not sure.'

'One of each. OK. Is that why we did this?' He kisses her hand, just to reassure her there's no judgement in his question, just a need to understand her.

Rosie isn't ready to be entirely understood just yet. 'We did this because there's a funfair in those eyes of yours.' She stands over him, and takes his lovely big face in her hands and kisses his lips fully, savouring every lavish moment of it, mingling her tongue with his in succulent shared bliss. When they break apart, she looks under the towel, and says, 'What if the missus sees this?'

It's the first time Glenn has entered the room, and Rosie is aware of how uncomfortable that is, but she's not one to pretend the difficult stuff away. Glenn is part of the truth of all this.

Thomas responds, 'Not much chance of that. We stopped the naked together stuff years ago. We used to, yes ... but the nightclothes slowly crept in ... like the hairy ears and the enlarged prostate ... mine not hers.'

'And I'm not the first, am I?' questions Rosie.

He half smiles in a sad way, then he suddenly winces.

'OK, now there is a slight, hot ... ness ...' Rosie looks under the towel and clasps her hand to her face. He continues, 'If this all ends in my death, I want you to make up something very dignified.' He suddenly looks like an excited boy up to no good. A timer bell rings on his watch.

'And rinse!' says Rosie, as Thomas drops the towel and steps into the shower.

Much later in the evening, back in the apartment kitchen, Rosie is tucking into a steaming bowl of chicken noodle soup she picked up in a Vietnamese grocery store on the way home. However much she uses these stores, she cannot get used to the bounty they offer, so different to corner shops in Cornwall. At home, she'd be lucky to get a decent block of cheddar and some Twiglets for a munchie. Here there are deli counters and hot cheesy pizzas and Chinese food and meatloaf and aisle upon aisle of soups and salads and sandwiches. For a woman with a thumping appetite, all of this choice is dizzying. Rosie thinks it a crime to pass an ice-cream fridge without giving a home to a tub or two who might . . . otherwise be rejected. So here she sits, cosy in the kitchen, scoffing her soup from the cardboard shop container. Iva has, unusually, chosen to sit with her, and is tucking into kielbasa sausage and sauerkraut which she cooks in beer. She looks at Rosie.

'What?' says Rosie.

'What?' says Iva.

'You're staring at me, Iva.'

'Free to look, isn't it? No tax on that. Just watching you with the soup, you are liking, yes? Liking so much, like you have not eaten food for three years. Hungry, hungry. You must have busy day, no?'

'It's my day off.'

'OK. So, you been doing what? Walking or shopping or what? To make you so hungry?'

'I've just been enjoying myself, Iva.'

'Enjoying yourself. Yes. I can see somebody is happy.'

'When is your day off?'

'Tuesday.'

'What will you do?'

'I go to Greenpoint. In Brooklyn. Little Poland, and I eat with my friends. I can speak there. We speak. My language. And I go to my bank. Put my money there, for my plane home three weeks in summer.'

'Oh, lovely. So you will see your daughter?'

'Yes, I will see.'

'When did you see her last?'

'The summer before.'

'Last summer? Blimey. That's a long time.'

'Yes, she live with my sister, and I will bring her to America for college.'

'Oh, that will be great. How old is she?'

'Fourteen.'

'Do you have a picture? What's her name?'

A pause. It all becomes a bit too difficult for Iva.

'No. I keep her for me. No photo, no name for you. Just for here . . .' Iva pats her heart, and gets up to wash her plate.

'Sorry, Iva, I didn't mean to pry or upset you. It must be so hard for you.'

'No. Not hard. Not difficult to keep her safe inside me. That's the job of the mother. You should try.'

'Yes. Maybe one day.'

'One day, if it doesn't go all the shape of a pear.'

'Pardon?' Rosie asks.

Iva clatters around clearing up. 'Nothing. You be careful. This family . . .' Iva makes a spiral with her index finger next to her forehead, indicating that they are crazy.

Rosie laughs, 'I'm here for the boys, that's my concern.'

'Yes, good. That is right. Goodnight.' Iva purposely turns the lights off, save one that's over the cooker, and always left on overnight.

Rosie is still finishing her soup, and sits alone and quiet in the strange night light, feeling distinctly like someone's just taken a nosey peek inside her.

Meanwhile, in their bathroom, naked Thomas is brushing his teeth and looking directly into his own eyes in the mirror. He is checking to see if any guilt is discernible. He doesn't think it is. Why? It hasn't happened that often, but it *has* happened. Could it simply be that he doesn't actually feel guilty at all? Maybe, he thinks, a person is entitled to no regret and no shame if what they have done feels so . . . right? He's not going to strangle the joy with guilt. Especially not when he doesn't even feel one single tiny tug of it.

What he *would* feel guilty about is hurting Glenn, because she hurts so much already, she's fragile somewhere inside that brittle front. So. No. He won't be visiting these questions again. Besides which, how can he feel a jot of sadness looking at THIS in the mirror? He smiles to himself, finishes cleaning his teeth and struts back into the bedroom.

Glenn is sitting on the bed, turned away, as usual, putting this and that safely into her bedside drawer.

Thomas stands boldly, nakedly, on the opposite side of the bed, hands on hips. 'I'm getting fatter,' he says, flagrantly slapping his belly.

Glenn glances behind her, 'You seem just fine to me.'

Thomas looks down at his bright green pubes, 'Happy St Patrick's Day, honey!'

'Yes dear,' she replies. 'Happy St Patrick's Day.' She begins moisturizing her hands. Thomas hums 'Fly me to the moon' as he pulls on his pyjama bottoms, tucking his secret away.

Another Breakfast

It's an ordinary weekday, and Rosie is in the twins' bedroom corralling them to get dressed, to get their school gear ready, and to get to breakfast. She is herself still dressing, throwing on a bright red cardigan over a blue polka-dot dress and scooping her unruly hair up into a huge messy high ponytail. She is right next to their iPod, and with her finger poised above the play button, she says, 'OK, gentlemen, here we go. If you aren't standing to attention by that door, completely washed, dressed and ready for school action by the end of this song, there will, repeat WILL be serious consequences which involve extreme pain. Yes, I hereby declare I am threatening you with physical violence, intent to harm, call it what you will, it will hurt. Do you understand?!'

'Yes, Rosie.'

'We understand.'

'Right,' she continues, 'here goes.'

She presses the button, and very loudly, Pharrell Williams'

'Happy' blares out. You have to be dead to resist dancing and singing along to this song, so of course they bop away as they clear up their room, pick up their books and get their school uniforms on, lip-synching all the while. On the very last beat, they jump into position near the door. Phew.

'Good, I don't have to injure you after all. By the right, quick march, follow me . . .' Rosie stomps out of the door towards breakfast. She leaves the boys' bedroom door open, their den door is also open, her door to her set of rooms is open, and as they pass Thomas's office, his door is *also* open. She glances in. He is dressed for work. As he sees her, he grins and steps out from behind his desk. He is wearing pink Hawaiian shorts. Rosie smiles and carries on marching to the breakfast room, leaving a trail of light from the open doors flooding the dark corridors behind her.

Five minutes later, Glenn's face is wearing its most distasteful expression Rosie has thus far seen. Her eyes bore their disapproval into Thomas as he turns from the sideboard where he is loading his plate up with bacon. For a tiny second he could be embarrassed, but then he knocks his knees together in a funny little dance for her and winks. He hopes this will thaw her. It doesn't.

When the derisory comment eventually comes, it is from Kemble. 'Pop, only a fag wears pink shorts.'

Rosie flinches at this. 'Wooo. Massively un-pc there!'

Teddy, who is home to visit again for a few days, agrees. 'It's not OK to say that, Dad, the little guys . . .'

Kemble perseveres. 'Oh sorry . . . Queer then?'

'Really?' Teddy questions him. He says to his grandfather, 'I personally think you look edgy, Granpop.'

'I'm hoping this is for some kind of sponsored charity event?' Glenn remarks.

Thomas grins at her, giving her every indication that she couldn't be more wrong. He's doing this because he wants to, 'Nope. Got an important board meeting.'

Kemble says, 'OK, he's full on senile. Fact.'

Rosie has remained quiet, watching the scene with interest, and trying to keep the twins distracted from the casual homophobia that is being bandied around. She gets up to help herself to coffee. Thomas holds the cup out for her and, as he gives it to her, brushes her hand. For the briefest of seconds she catches his eye. A tiny thrilling fleeting moment, which Rosie reacts to in the carnal pit of her stomach. And then just as quick, it's gone.

Iva bundles in with a huge parcel. 'The porter just deliver this. Is for you, Mr W.B.,' and she hands over the large cumbersome package.

'Ah,' says Thomas. 'Thank you Iva. I know exactly what this is. My latest eBay triumph.'

'Wow!' says Three.

'What is it, Granpop?!' says Red.

'You'll see boys, you'll see. All in good time.'

Glenn watches all this unnecessary excitement, a General losing control of her army.

Saturday

Glenn is irritated. Not only are the doors open all over the place in the apartment, and increasingly so, it would seem, allowing pesky light in, everywhere. But now there are two further abominations. The first is air. There is a distinct breeze blowing fresh air right through, which is another reason to keep the wretched doors shut. Never mind the windows, which also ought to be closed. Why are they open? Who has opened them? She knows full well of course, but she is rehearsing her outrage.

The second horror is . . . leaves. Bringing with them a third aberration, which is dirt. The leaves are on the hallway floor, and she follows them like a Hansel and Gretel trail, til they lead her to the open service door at the back of the kitchen. Clearly, the twins and that woman are ferrying plants through the apartment and up the back stairs to the roof. This is precisely what Glenn predicted. Utter chaos. Easily five or six leaves cluttering up her space. Well, mainly the boys' space.

Well, mainly the back steps where she never ventures. Nevertheless, it's utterly unconscionable. Words will be had. Firm words. Making sure everybody concerned understands who the damn boss is here.

As she retraces the trail of leaves, picking them up one by one, another annoying thing occurs. She hears the faint sound of an electric guitar. Where is it coming from? Is it Teddy? As she walks towards the direction of the sound, she realizes it's coming from Thomas's office. Oh Lord, she thinks, now I have a husband who is retreating into adolescence. Nothing in Glenn wants to go in and share in his excitement about his new acquisition. Everything in her wants to flee, there's just too much light and air and music here.

She can't leave though, because her friend Betty is due to come for coffee. Betty is Sharpe's widow, and since Glenn didn't go to the funeral, this is the first opportunity she's had to offer her condolences. It's the right and proper thing to do, so Glenn can't escape it. It's a duty, and Glenn is big on that. She tuts and walks away wondering why on earth she has to deal with so much chaos. It's so very tiresome.

Up on the roof, surrounded by masses of light and air and chaos, Red, Three and Teddy sit side by side on deck chairs. There is quite a lot of garden mess in one corner, and all three are wearing wellies. As is Rosie, who is parading up and down behind them. Their eyes are firmly shut, and they are laughing at her. She is pretending to be an old fashioned German therapist, 'Imageen ze garden. Feeeel ze garden. Vot do you see in it? Answer zis now, boy,' she pats Three on the head.

He answers hopefully, 'A swing?'

Red joins in, 'A little house?'

Now Teddy seizes his opportunity, 'I say "cocktail bar", I say "hot tub", I say "two person hammock". Call me horny.'

'Hmm,' says Rosie. 'I'd rather call you hopeful or even possibly deluded?' He laughs easily at her teasing. She is well intentioned and he knows that it's impossible to take offence at anything she says.

Red is still wracking his brain, 'Any chance of a kinda water gully log-flume?'

'Yeah,' Three pipes up, 'or like, a huge fountain?'

'I still say hot tub, y'know, for all our babes to sit in,' Teddy tries again.

'Babes, eh?' Rosie asks. Teddy doesn't open his eyes, but he grins and flicks his hair in mock confidence.

Later on, Teddy wanders in to the kitchen, and while Iva is busying herself washing up, he drifts from fridge to larder to cupboard, taking out all the ingredients to make himself a super duper Scooby-Doo snack sandwich. He gets out pastrami and tomatoes and gherkins and Swiss cheese and rye bread and butter.

As he is constructing his giant treat, Thomas ambles in. Neither speaks, they don't need to. Thomas is humming 'Fever' in the style of Peggy Lee as he weighs up what Teddy is doing. He goes foraging in the cupboards and fridge himself, to see if he fancies anything. Quite a bit of time is spent with his hands in his pockets just eyeing up possible ingredients. Eventually, he commits to lettuce, cooked bacon slices, and some Monterey Jack cheese. He brings his armful of bounty over to the worktop where Teddy is building his sandwich, and slowly but surely, Thomas starts his own stacking, stealing some of Teddy's booty and adding his own. Before too long, an unspoken sandwich war is subtly declared. Thomas is grinning, so Teddy says, 'You seem happy,' to which Thomas winks,

'Life is looking up, kiddo.'

Teddy finds himself suddenly and inexplicably jealous of his grandfather, and for some reason he knows he must make a bigger, better sandwich than Thomas. He revisits the larder and gradually starts slapping on the layers, pickles, white bread for stability, onions to chop into raw rings, and mustard. Thomas retaliates with crabsticks and mayo, Teddy adds a slice of meatloaf, Thomas smears peanut butter onto the underside of his last edge of bread to form the top of his sandwich. Teddy copies, then goes to the fridge and gets the ice-cream. He defiantly scoops two dollops on top of the meat-loaf, adds the peanut-buttered outer slice, then gets a Morello cherry and skewers it into the very top with a toothpick. At which point Thomas respectfully shakes his grandson's hand whilst simultaneously watching his own entire stack collapse and fall. Teddy lifts his up triumphantly, and takes a huge bite.

'Awesome,' concedes Thomas.

'Make way for youth, ol' timer. Mind you, I was taught by a Grand Master.'

The Grand Master is picking at his fallen sandwich. True to form, after all the back-slapping, they both exit the kitchen and leave the mess for Iva to clear up.

Glenn sits in her impressive drawing room with Betty. This room is Glenn's favourite in the whole apartment, mainly because it is hardly ever used, so it remains in pristine condition at all times. Fifteen years ago Glenn used the services of an interior designer, the same woman who had done the refurb at The Colony Club. What Glenn really wanted was the club inside her own apartment and so, here it is, on a slightly smaller scale. The colour palette is peach and cream. There is one large peach-coloured velvet sofa and several armchairs and low Georgian chairs upholstered in paisley and tartans of peach and cream. Another Persian carpet adorns the floor and a huge glass coffee table impressively displays all the right art and travel books. As in the library, acres of expensive fabric drape and adorn the windows in huge swathes, reducing the rare and lovely light. There is a chandelier of clear glass and plenty of large side-lights on tables with cream shades. Over the never-used fireplace there is a massive ornate French mirror and plenty of tasteful, palatable art on the walls, mostly of landscapes and vases of flowers. Glenn rejected the designer's attempt to 'jazz up' the colour scheme with the odd crazy maroon cushion or even the one astonishing attempt to introduce leopard skin. What the designer didn't know about Glenn is that although, yes indeed, she is seventy-eight now, in all things domestic she prefers to be a hundred and twenty, thank you.

So here she sits with Betty, whom she has known for fifty years or more. From the moment Betty arrived, it was clear that she was in no state of mind for a round of cards, which is what Glenn had hoped would happen. It's easier to talk about difficult stuff when there's a distraction. Instead, Betty wants comfort and warmth from her old friend. She wants to tell Glenn over and over again about what happened during Sharpe's illness and subsequent demise. She wants to alleviate the unbearable grief she feels by doling out some of the heaviness. She wants to feel lighter. This is what she has been doing for weeks with her nearest and dearest, and in small ways, it is working. Each time she shares her story about the death of her beloved man, her life partner, the other half of her soul, she hears herself and accepts more, that he is truly gone. But simultaneously she feels connected to him in those moments too, which she relishes, so for lots of reasons, it's important that Betty goes through this pain with those she trusts. Glenn is one of those people. Sadly for Betty, something she has never fully realized about Glenn is that really, Glenn herself, is already dead.

Betty is weeping quietly into a handkerchief as she sits next to Glenn on the sofa.

'My daughter gave me a copy of C. S Lewis' essay, 'A Grief Observed', have you ever come across it? It's remarkable Glennie, it begins with the words, 'No-one ever told me that grief felt so like fear . . .' and that's the truth, I feel afraid . . . of what?'

If only Glenn could answer, but Glenn realizes she has no reference point from which to empathize. She knows that there are customary hoops she ought to be jumping through right now, she should be hugging Betty or holding her hand or saying 'There, there' and 'it will be alright' or 'he's at peace now' or anything consolatory like that. She knows the script, she knows the stage directions, but she is sitting next to Betty, paralysed with the creeping realization that she doesn't genuinely feel anything.

This is a common occurrence for Glenn, but it seems particularly stark right now, here, in her own drawing room where just the two of them are. Maybe if someone else was leading the charge of the solace brigade, she would be able to fall in behind, and sound authentic, but this one to one is unbearably awkward. If Glenn is honest with herself, and she is, what she genuinely thinks at this moment is that Betty is full of self-pity. Glenn knows enough about manners to realize that this would be the wrong thing to name, it would be insensitive and would only lead to trouble, but that's her truth. For Glenn, self-pity isn't an option. Not only would it be pathetic and weak in her opinion, but in order to pity yourself, you must surely have a self. That's a problem for her. The only self Glenn has concerned her time with for sixty-odd years, is the one who must appear to be tippety top in every way. Little vexations like Kemble's divorce are a possible threat to the status quo, but Glenn is adept enough to ride those storms whilst still maintaining a fixed veneer of calm and restraint.

This Betty situation though, is a challenge. A woman physically leaking from the nose, shaking and sobbing, is the last thing Glenn wants. How very unseemly she finds all this emotion. She decides to recite some of the requisite script.

'There, there dear,' she says as she pats Betty's hand.

'I miss him, Glennie. I just miss him so much.'

How sentimental, Glenn thinks, and wonders how long this is likely to last before she can justifiably put Betty in a town car home?

Noguchi

Rosie, Red, Three and Teddy stride up the steps onto the plaza outside the Chase Manhattan Bank. There's not much to interest eight-year-olds in the Financial District, but Rosie has told them it's important to see the garden here to help them with ideas for theirs. She bids them to stop still for a moment and asks them what they see.

'Umm, high rise buildings,' says Red.

'Yeh, some old, some new, lots of glass. Ooo, and a huge totem pole! Wow. Is that what we came for?' says Three.

'No,' she answers, 'but I agree, it's a thought. So this is a flat area, isn't it? It's called a plaza, and there are lots of places to sit, maybe people eat their lunch out here? Can they sit in the sunlight?'

Red looks about, 'Not much. The buildings are in the way.'

'Right. So at different times of day, the sun will come into this plaza in different places, it's mainly over there now because it's afternoon. Would you call this a garden?' She wants them to think.

'No,' they all agree, and even Teddy gets drawn in to the discussion, 'I guess we think of a garden with grass and trees 'n' stuff, or vegetables, this is all concrete. Central Park is better for gardens. It's one giant garden.'

'Yes,' Rosie agrees, 'but gardens can be many things . . .'

Three interrupts, 'Some gardens are, like, just flowers. Tons of flowers like, everywhere. That would be so cool.'

Red can't help his enthusiasm, 'Yeh, with like giant bug-eating plants.'

'Triffids,' says Teddy.

'Oh I love that book,' Rosie agrees. 'All of that is true, but I just want you to see something here. Look ahead, right? All you see is flat plaza and a few trees in raised beds, and huge paving slabs on the floor. But follow me . . .'

She walks, and they fall in behind her, across the vast plaza towards a circular rail, where some other people are leaning and looking. As they draw closer they see that beneath the rail is a sunken circle, about thirty feet in diameter one floor down. It contains an undulating mosaic-style stone floor with occasional holes in it and about eight or nine rocks of various sizes scattered about untidily. Some of the holes have water spouting upwards, which eddies around on the stone, then filters away, playfully. The boys have never seen anything quite like it before and stare.

'Look at the sunlight falling on just one stone over there,' Rosie says, 'and I bet it would be on that one or that one or that one, depending on what time we were looking. This is a garden designed by a very cool guy called Isamu Noguchi. He was a bit Japanese and a bit American, and if he used stones in his gardens, he brought them all the way from Japan. Lots of people thought there was something significant about the stones, but actually, he just wanted someone to pay for his holidays to Japan, which was very cheeky. He loved going there, because it reminded him of when he was a little boy and lived there. And it reminded him of his dad, who was a bit too busy most of the time to remember he had a son. Which was the dad's loss. Because, what a son to have! Someone who can make such an interesting place, that lots of people come to, to enjoy. What do you think guys? Like it or not?'

'This is so not what I thought was going to be here,' Red tells her, 'so a garden *could* just be stone, you mean?'

'Well, it can be anything you want it to be, but the thing to remember is that it doesn't have to be like any you've ever seen, or like anyone else's, it just has to be what you like, that's all.'

'I like it. I really like it. It's sort of, a boys' garden. For boys,' says Three.

Rosie laughs, 'Is it? Why?'

'Coz you can climb on stuff, and there's water spouts and everything.'

Rosie moves towards the entrance to the building. 'Let's go have a look at it from inside,' she pushes open the huge glass doors. The atrium is towering and bright. Rosie beckons the boys to join her on the escalators heading down to the floor below, which brings them directly into the actual bank, with all its bustling business going on as usual. In the centre of the bank is a wall of circular glass that looks out onto the secret garden from ground level, where it's even better, and much easier to see up close. Red and Three push their faces onto the glass and then run around the circle, looking at the remarkable structure from all sides. Rosie hands each of the twins a pad and a pencil, 'OK, I want sketches and ideas for how we might do something like this on the roof. Go.' The twins find a table to sit at and draw, yabbering away happily to each other.

Rosie sits down with Teddy near the glass, and looks at the garden. They are in the very last sliver of afternoon sunlight that is seeping in through the plaza, through the garden and through the glass onto their legs. Even through their trousers, they can feel the early spring warmth, and it's lovely. They sit side by side quietly.

'This is pretty cool. I didn't even know this was here, and I've lived in the city all my life,' he tells her.

'Yes. It's something. It's sort of weird to be . . . in a bank . . . looking out at this. Surprising. I like that,' she says.

As they sit, a young dark-haired pretty woman walks by, and Rosie watches closely as Teddy can't take his eyes off her, but pretends to be disinterested, 'Hmm, gardening trip is looking up. Babelicious.'

'He he he,' Rosie chortles.

'Maybe she could offer some horticultural advice?'

'Well, go on then.'

'What?! I'm not seriously going to speak to her, look at her, she's a goddess, I was just kidding.'

'For a start, she's a mortal. A gorgeous one, I grant you that, but she is human y'know. And even if she was a goddess, you'd still be entitled to speak to her, you gurt ninny.'

'She wouldn't talk to me. Totally out of my league.'

'Nah.'

'Isn't she? D'you think she would?'

'Yeh.'

'Really? No. Anyway, she's busy,' and he keeps quiet, all the time with one eye on the dusky beauty as she goes about her work.

Rosie twiddles her feet, until Teddy wants to speak, 'Do you think Dad has a chance?'

'Of what?'

'Of getting custody of my brothers. You've noticed Mom and Dad are fighting about it?'

'Can't really miss it.'

'But he knows that's not what they want. They want to be with Mom. See him, of course, see him plenty, but stay with Mom. She's . . . more . . . like a parent than him. And they don't

131

have to feel like they are disappointments all the time with her. Because you're not, you're her son with her, and she doesn't really mind if you get it wrong occasionally. Her family are chilled. The French . . . just are. Y'know it's OK, and they want *you* to be OK.'

Rosie is instantly aware of just how heavily Teddy carries the weight of all the secret squabbling, and of how protective he is over his little brothers. In the absence of a step-up dad presently, Teddy has stepped up himself, to try and fill that space for them, and in the meantime, everyone involved seems to have forgotten that he's only eighteen, and is of course wondering where *he* fits in all the fighting. But he's proud, and being eighteen and proud means that it's difficult to find a way to say that you want to matter as well.

Rosie's heart hurts for him. 'Why don't you talk to your grandfather, Teddy? I'm pretty sure he's on your team.'

'You know that for a fact?'

'No. Just guessing.'

'Listen, he's a great guy an' all that, but he has to be on team Granma, or he won't have any balls left. Seriously. And she hates Mom, so . . . y'know, I don't think he's the guy to talk to.'

'OK, but . . . it's a thought . . . keep it in yer back pocket just in case,' Rosie advises him. 'Why don't you say hello to that lovely girl . . . ? Bust some loverman moves on her, guy.'

'Yeh, sure. Not.' He tentatively looks over to the girl, who is oblivious to him and, as so often is the case for the virginal

Teddy Wilder-Bingham, even though he is six foot two he feels terribly terribly small.

The twins return to where Rosie and Teddy are sitting. They have done a few drawings, but mainly they have spent their time filling in the paper cheques and paying-in slips from the bank consoles. They have awarded each other millions of dollars and are poised to withdraw their booty soon as, so Teddy and Rosie take this as an ideal opportunity to adjourn to a café for hot chocolate and to explain how banking works. Rosie does the hot chocolate part. Teddy takes care of the pecuniary matters, during which the twins nearly nod off. Before she loses their attention entirely, Rosie has another adventure up her sleeve . . .

Trying

On a side street in Brooklyn, Kemble is sitting on a bench looking up at the window of a red brick house opposite. This is where he should be, with his family, like it was a year ago. All of them together under one roof.

Natalie has seen him from her bedroom window which used to be their bedroom window. She can't decide what is best to do. If she lets him in, it will encourage him to come back, and they've gone through such a lot to reach this point she doesn't want to retrace any of those painful steps, and lose ground.

Natalie is only now beginning to define and understand herself as single. Slowly. She hasn't been alone like this ever in her life. An attractive girl, half French, clever and sassy, she has had a lot of attention – firstly from boys, and then men – her entire life. She took it totally for granted that she would always be attended to, looked after, desired. Not for a second did Natalie imagine that she would eventually be parenting her three gorgeous boys on her own, with a failed marriage staring her in her pretty face. Neither had she considered for a second that her face might not remain quite as pretty, and how this would erode her confidence as she grew into her forties.

Only now that she is a person in her own right, and not one half of a couple, does she realize that she has defined herself partly – or mostly, if she's honest – by how she looks. It's only in these last few months that she has let some of her anguish about her fading beauty and her chaotic relationship go. No way is she going to open the door and let all that trouble back in. She has just started to build back up the foundation stones of the self-esteem she once had, and this time, she is building on the solid ground of her independent self-knowledge and truth, not on the shifting sands of the reflected self-image that she had before. She must be strong now and stand firm. She must heed her instinct. No longer will she allow her prior, hidden sense of unworthiness, to halt her progress forward with her life.

BUT.

Natalie *did* build a life with Kemble. She did once share his fears and his worries and, most of all, that package of inadequacy which emerged later in their marriage as, frankly, a surprise. They did make those three beautiful boys.

She hates to ignore him. She worries about him. So, after a couple of hours, as the light starts to fade, she opens their front door and crosses the road to where he sits, slightly dishevelled in his expensive, slept-in coat. She remains standing, 'You should be at work.'

He says, 'You should be with me.'

'Go home, Kemble'

'I am home. This is my home.'

'Go home.'

'Come with me?'

Kemble is pleading with his eyes. Natalie is very sad to be having this moment with him. Like this. Here. She shakes her head slowly. No.

'Go home, Kemble.'

Now Kemble shakes his head. No. 'I'll try harder . . . ?'

'There's no more trying, K, it's finished. You know it. I don't . . . love you any more.'

Suddenly, there's glass in his blood and deep down he knows. He looks at her and nods. She sits down next to him, two soldiers, exhausted from the battle.

Kemble surrenders. 'I'll deal with the kid stuff. I promise. I know what's best for them. And it's not me.'

They sit in silence for a minute, allowing that giant truth its moment in the light.

Natalie says, 'That's not what your mom wants.'

'I'll tell her. I promise. It's OK.'

Natalie looks at Kemble, searching his face, to see if this is true. Can she believe him? Two big promises.

'Thank you, Kemble,' she says, softly. 'I hope you do tell her. Tell her everything.'

'Fuck my mother,' he mumbles into his hands as he rests his

face there. The two of them sit in silence, looking back over the road, at what should have been.

Under the same fading light, elsewhere in New York, Rosie has brought the three Wilder-Binghams to a place none of them will ever forget. They needed to rush here because the light is the thing, the whole thing. Luckily, they are the only four souls in here. They are all lying on the floor of the James Turrell light room, his *Skyspace*, which is a white room with a round hole where the roof should be, so that the sky is framed like a roof picture. The four horizontal folk are lying in a starfish shape on the floor with their heads touching, looking up directly at the sky, watching the clouds skid over and noticing the change in the light, and how it transforms the room. For some reason, they whisper.

Red says, 'The sky is just the sky, isn't it? Like, it's the same sky for everyone, isn't it?'

Teddy says, 'Yes, basically. I mean for some people, say in Japan, it will be night time, so they will be looking at the same sky, but dark.' As he speaks, he glances over at Rosie just as the light crosses her face and he notes how pleasurable it is to watch that.

Three says, 'So, wait a minute, is Will Smith looking at this same sky?'

Teddy, 'Yep.'

Red, 'And Jay Z, and President Obama . . . and Hermoine?'

Rosie, 'Who's Hermoine?'

Three, 'From Harry Potter. He loves her.'

Red, 'No I don't, douchebag!'

Rosie, 'Shush, please. But yes is the answer. All of those folk will be seeing the same sky. And look at the colour in this room now, it's so different to when we first came in, and look where the light is on the wall. How long do you think we've been lying here?'

Red, 'Ten minutes.'

Three, 'No! Two minutes.'

Teddy, 'Thirty minutes.'

Rosie, 'I have no idea. How great is that?! We have been lovely and still, and time has just ticked by . . . can you feel your heartbeat? Mine has slowed down, I think.'

Red, 'I can't feel mine.'

Three, 'You're dead dude.'

Red, 'I'm like totally dead.'

Rosie, 'You're not dead, you're just peaceful and resting. It's really OK to slow down sometimes. That's when you can hear the other noises in your head.'

Three, 'Like mad murderers do?'

Red, 'Kill him! Kill him!'

The twins convulse themselves with laughing.

Rosie, 'No, not weird voices, more like quiet . . . thinkings . . .

that don't get thought if you're too busy rushing about and being noisy all the time.'

Red, 'Yeah.' He thinks he gets it. He doesn't. 'Like what?'

Rosie, 'Like . . . well for me, it's stuff to do with how I am feeling. So, say, today I am feeling very very happy, so my little thinkings are making words pop up. Words like – smile, jokes, bright, cake.'

Teddy suddenly snores very deeply, so much that it wakes him up, 'Sorry, what were you saying? I was so chilled man . . . just dropped right off there.'

Three, 'Rosie has happy words like smile and jokes in her quiet head she's saying. I have candy and . . . ice-cream . . . jumping . . .'

Red, 'PlayStation, Mom, gummy bears . . .'

Teddy, 'Girls . . . music . . . girls . . .'

Rosie, 'Music, yes! Clapping. Clap your hands . . .'

They all join in, still whispering, but getting louder, '. . . If you feel like a room without a roof!'

They look up. Red says, 'Hey! Yeah!' and they carry on with their whispered Happy song as they get up and do funny little dance steps all the way out of the room and the evening light through the roof casts a soft twilight in their wake.

'Clap your hands, if you feel like happiness is the truth . . .'

Tents

On the roof of the Wilder-Bingham apartment block, under the stars, there are three pop-up tents in a row, right next to the detritus of the developing garden. A string of fairy lights illuminates the area and there is light and warmth coming from the lit gas of the camping stove. A supper of sausages and bread has already been stuffed, but Teddy is still cooking the last two sausages in a frying pan. There are stripey deck chairs and a small table on top of which is all the equipment Teddy has used to make cocktails. The twins have had Shirley Temples, their favourite. Natalie is the one that normally makes them, and she knows the proper ingredients, ginger ale, grenadine and a cherry. Teddy wasn't too sure so he tried to replicate it. He got the cherry part right, and he even added little Chinese umbrellas, but he improvised with seven-up and cranberry juice. It wasn't 'the bomb' according to the twins, but it was still pretty good, and they gulped it down.

With sausage and Shirley-full bellies, the twins have climbed into their joint tent and settled into their sleeping bags on a blow-up mattress. They wear their coats and hats and gloves over their pyjamas and hoodies, and with a camping heater inside their tent, they've cosied up with Rosie in the middle who read *The Velveteen Rabbit* to them. They love that story, all about being real, they request it time and time again, understanding it a tiny bit more each time.

That was half an hour ago, and now Rosie is backing out gracelessly on all fours with her lovely big bum leading the way, whilst the twins audibly snuffle and snore and occasionally garble muted nonsense from their deepest, tired-outest sleep. Rosie stands up, pulls her coat around her, tugs her hat further down on her head and sits down on the deck chair nearest the big outdoor heater. She grabs the glass she left when she went into the tent, and she drains the last of the potent mojito Teddy has made.

"Nother one?' he offers.

'Yep. Why not?' she replies.

'Sausage?'

'No ta. Full.'

Teddy makes the mojito with pride. He has all the correct ingredients for this since at school he is renowned for being the best covert mojito-master in Roosevelt dorm. The full equipment lives under his bed and no birthday slips by amongst his pals without a celebratory 'Mojiteddy', in which he generously dollops three times the amount of rum that he should. He delights in using real Jamaican white rum, John Crow Batty Rum, 160 proof and stolen from his grandfather's drinks cupboard. This is not a drink for sissies, and Rosie is no sissy. But sadly she *is* a lightweight when it comes to alcohol. She is already delightfully merry when she drains her glass. This next one will slowly do for her. Teddy pours one for himself too, they clink glasses and raise a cheer to 'sunlight' in honour of their day, and then they clink again for 'moonlight', in honour of this lovely night and their camping adventure. They sit comfortably and quietly in each other's company, gradually getting delightfully sozzled. The sound of traffic below drifts up.

Rosie cups her ear to hear it better, then says, 'Bub-bubba-bub-bub . . .'

From down on the street, a taxi hooter completes the sequence – Bub Bub.

Then Teddy gives it a go, 'Bub-bubba-bub-bub . . .' they listen, they listen. No response. Rosie does a quiet cheer and licks her finger to draw a point in the air.

'One-nil. Lllllllllooooooooooser!'

There is a distant mumble from the twins' tent. Rosie darts over and peeks in to find them both still fast asleep, though Red is fighting an enemy in his dreams. She lays her hand on his sleeping bag, where his shin is, and slowly he drops back off.

As she returns to the deck chair. Teddy decides to give the traffic game one more try, 'Bub-bubba-bub-bub . . .'

A taxi hooter finishes the jingle. Teddy does a punch of victory, 'Yes! One all. Slam dunkety dunk!' They laugh. A bit too much.

Rosie takes another slurp. 'I'm guessing, then, from the banking-babe incident, that you don't currently have a girlfriend?'

Teddy, 'Correct, Miss Marple, I don't. I'm too young and good-looking to be tied down, baby.'

'Right,' says Rosie.

A long pause. Teddy has another swig. He looks at Rosie and suddenly he is a less confident boy. 'I haven't ever had one . . .'

'OK,' Rosie nods. 'It's not a big revelation, Teds. Doesn't matter. In the slightest.'

Teddy looks at his feet, and blows out a big sad sigh, 'Yeah. But. Y'know. It is too much to ask? That one girl might check me out, just one? I'm not saying it has to be a model or a hot dancer or whatever. I'd be grateful for a head and legs, to be frank. Well OK, not necessarily a head . . .'

Rosie chuckles.

'I know I'm not exactly a catch,' he continues, 'nothing on me behaves right. I know that. Skin doesn't, hair doesn't, no chest, skinny arms, torso's not cut, no kick ass . . . ass. I'm not built, I'm not a beast. Women want a beast.'

'Bollocks,' chides Rosie, 'that's so not true. A hunker-chunker might be quite nice to look at occasionally, but trust me, hon, no woman worth her salt wants to be with that kind of vain twot. Too high maintenance, truly. And doesn't make you laugh, which is the sexiest thing of all. Believe me on this. Some of my most favourite, unforgettable boys have been decidedly odd-looking – which you are *not*, by the way – but all I'm saying is that any girl worth having won't be looking for all that stuff you're wishing you had, so it's a waste of time worrying about it. What you need to do, Teds, is inhabit what you've got, and honestly, what you've got is pretty bloody good from where I'm sitting. And I am of the female persuasion. So I know. Wear this body here, that you've got . . .' she pats him in a way she wouldn't if she weren't so disinhibited by drink, 'like a nice comfortable jacket, that fits you just right. Which it does.'

'But, look, basically, I'm not attractive. Am I?'

'Teds. Hon. Are you barking bonkers mad or what?! You are properly lovely. AND you are charming.'

'Oh great' he replies sarcastically, 'I'm a thatched cottage.'

'Listen, Ted, seriously darlin',' Rosie doesn't quite slur her words, but she's only one slurp away from it, 'you will have no trouble getting a girl. I promise you. You just need to . . . relax.'

'If it could happen before I go grey, it would be good. I'm the last guy . . . y'know . . . amongst my friends . . . the last sucker . . . not to . . .'

'Oh God. And you're feeling so rubbish about it I can't bear it. It's not your fault sweetheart, really it isn't. These . . . stupid . . .

144

girls. They don't know what they're missing, you are such a diamond. C'mere, give us a hug, it'll be OK . . .'

Rosie gets up and grabs him in a heartfelt, boisterous hug, which Teddy is very happy to have.

She eventually lets go and sits back down again. 'Honestly, when I was your age, I thought I wanted a dirty nasty brute who didn't wash and treated me like I was a shit sandwich. Maybe you should try that!' and to illustrate, Rosie does her best mean face for Teddy to copy. He does his best mean face back, which isn't very mean at all.

He wonders out loud, 'Why the hell do girls go for nasty in the first place?'

'Because girls really like a mission. We want to be the one responsible for turning the brute into a slush bucket. I know, it's pants.'

Teddy tries the mean face again and this time beats his chest like King Kong, and then quickly turns the volume down to avoid waking the twins.

Rosie finds it hilarious, 'OK, so it's a resounding no to Teddy the giant hairy brute. How about jocular Teddy the joker? You are properly funny, Teds, truly. You are. Try laughing them into bed. Y'know, "Knock knock – who's there? Me in my under-pants, willy at the ready", that kinda thing, only better. Well . . . funny.'

Teddy thinks about this, 'The thing is, when I'm next to a girl, I don't feel funny. I act funny. Not so good, total turn off.'

'I tell you, the other good strategy is to be massively powerful. Look at some of those kings and presidents and prime ministers. You can be badly battered with the ugly stick, and still negotiate a girl into bed IF you run a country.'

Teddy puffs. 'I'm eighteen, Rosie.'

'OK, OK, yeah.' She takes another little sip of the sinful cocktail. Then, 'OK, right, we must go for the deep and interesting type. Which is what you actually *are*, Edward Wilder-Bingham.' She leans over and grabs his chin, to make him look directly at her. 'Give me your deepest look, let's see.'

Teddy tries to appear interesting and sensitive.

She doesn't buy it, 'Hmm, that's more like constipation.'

He tries again, but it's still no good. 'Terrorist,' she confirms.

He splutters and surrenders, 'I think I'm just going to do celibate, for the rest of my life.' He takes a deep resigned breath and leans back in his chair with his hands behind his head, checking out the stars. His mind wanders, 'Do you have a boyfriend?' She doesn't answer. He looks at her long enough to get one. She nods. He pursues it, 'Is he a brute? Or funny? Or powerful? Or deep?'

Rosie avoids the questions and tries the traffic game again, 'Bub-bubba-bub-bub . . .' a hooter completes the jingle. 'Get in!' she shouts as a whisper.

Teddy is intent on looking directly at her in order to have his answer. She can't escape it.

146

'We're not really together anymore, Teds. It was a long time, he's my slippers.'

'So where is he?' asks Teddy, 'Under the bed?'

She points at the moon, which confuses him.

'Is he an astronaut? Alien? Dead?'

'No. He's just . . . looking at this same sky, but from England. From Cornwall.'

The mixture of alcohol and the far away from home-ness kicks in. She doesn't allow herself to have these difficult thoughts currently. She's on the run, she can't afford to go home in her head, but the delicious and potent alcohol has blurred her line of resolve, and she feels a lurch in her heart. The heaviness in her heart moves to her throat, and she knows she will cry if she doesn't distract herself.

Luckily, Teddy is thinking aloud. 'Y'know, I'm starting to really dislike Dad for . . . well, for everything. This divorce is his fault. I know that. Mom won't really say exactly what's happened, but if it was her fault, I just know she would own it and say, so it must be him. Neither of them is being real about it. They give the little guys the ol' "mommy and daddy can't live together any more, but we're still good friends" shit, but hello, I'm eighteen. I don't buy it. What about treating me like an adult and telling me the truth? I'm gonna re-surface after it's all over and I'll have missed out on a huge chunk of my life, totally pow, gone. My buddies will be married with mortgages and I won't have touched a froo.' Rosie looks quizzical, so he expands. 'A froo-froo. Girl's . . . front . . . part.'

'Right, got it,' she says, 'something you should know, Teddy, is that . . . you're never a fixed thing. I've been a woman I didn't want to be, in my time.'

'What changed?' he asks.

Rosie shrugs, she doesn't really want to answer. She takes another big slug of her Mojiteddy, and stands up. She is shifting gear.

'OK, sweetcheeks. Seeing as it's you, I'm going to show you the Rosie Kitto "it never fails" seduction technique. You get a girl alone with you in a room, you do this, and . . . I promise you it will get results, or your money back.'

'Are you a lesbian?' he suddenly blurts out.

Rosie is confused.

'It's just,' he continues, 'you seem very sure, about seducing a girl.'

Rosie laughs, 'I'm an insider, mate, I've got the lowdown.' She tells him to sit tight and disappears through the door to the roof. Teddy drains his drink in one go and slumps back in his chair, happy to let the liquor stampede through his blood, trampling on all reason and inhibition in its path.

Rosie is heading for her rooms when she spots Thomas in the corridor near her door.

'Hello there,' he says in hushed tones, searching her face to see how the emotional land lies. 'I just knocked on your door. No answer. You're out.'

'I'm up on the roof with the boys. We're camping. Want to join us?'

'It's OK, you guys have fun. I'm ready to turn in. I just wanted to say,' he whispers, '. . . can I see you again?'

'Yes please,' she smiles at him.

He nods his head and backs off, blowing her a small silly kiss as he does.

When Rosie clambers back through the roof door she is equipped with her iPod and two sets of headphones. She is wearing one pair, the other one is dangling from the machine. Rosie drags her deck chair directly opposite Teddy's and places the other set on his head. She takes a dangerously big gulp of the cocktail, and now the real giddy begins . . .

'The key to seducing a girl is learning to wait and listen. What is it?'

He goes to repeat it, and she instantly cuts him off, 'Don't speak! Wait. And listen. Right. First, you have to get both of you into the zone. Right in there with each other, to the exclusion of all others. Music is definitely the way to do that. So listen to this and think about all the gorgeous, loving, sexy things that are going to happen the second it's over. Because she needs to know *that's* what you intend. You intend to take some control and you ARE going to make love to her. It should only take one song for her to realize you're serious, get used to the idea, then agree. The song has to be the right one. She's never going to forget it, and neither are you. This is the one that would do it for me . . .'

With that, she clicks the button and through the headphones, loudly, they both hear the slow strains of the opening bars of 'Sexual Healing' by Marvin Gaye. The drums and the whispered 'Get up, get up, wake up wake up' are the unmistakable rhythm of a heartbeat, and slowly but surely they both sway in time to the beat, moving their hips in their chairs.

Rosie smiles 'isn't this amazing?' and gives thumbs up to him.

Teddy smiles 'wow, phenomenal,' back with corresponding thumbs up.

Rosie closes her eyes to disappear into it. Teddy doesn't close his eyes, he wants to watch her in this acutely intimate moment as she abandons herself to the music. He doesn't know females like her. She is unashamed and sensual and real.

And drunk.

She is the level of drunk where the edges between music and meaning are blurred, where you can believe you ARE the music and everything it speaks of. In this case, the conversation is thrummingly evident. This intercourse is about intercourse. No doubt. The music and the insistence of Marvin Gaye begin to work their effect.

'I'm hot just like an oven,

I need some lovin'. . .'

Rosie throws her head back and smiles. How often did this song work its magic for Marvin Gaye himself? Did it succeed a hundred times? Did Marvin make a thousand conquests? A million? Teddy sees her throat in the moonlight, and he is baffled by why it seems as if he's stolen a glance at something supremely private. He sees her throat every time he sees her. It's not a secret, she doesn't cover it up. Yet here and now, in this light, and urged on by the powerful coital message of this throbbing song in his ears, her neck, flung back like this, is irresistible. Gorgeous and inviting. Christ, she is really . . . sexy . . .

'And baby, I can't hold it much longer,

It's getting stronger and stronger.'

She opens her eyes and looks at him. He suddenly fears she might see into him, and he looks away, but only for an instant. He looks back. Her gaze is unwavering, honest, inviting.

'And when I get that feeling,

I want sexual healing . . .'

The music is winding its way into their souls, and grinding its way into their groins. Teddy lets his eyes wander from her face, down past that lovely throat he is so desiring to nuzzle, to her cleavage, which is visible at the top of the buttons on the front of her dress. Is he mistaken? Has she arched her back a little bit so that her coat falls open? Is she allowing him to see? He looks back at her eyes to see if she is letting this happen, and he knows straight away that yes, she most certainly is. Teddy has never had permission like this before, and it's thrilling, his breathing starts to change to shallow and often. His breath synchronizes with the beat of the song.

'Let's make love tonight

"Cause you do it right.'

He feels his teeth tighten and he's aware of the twitch of life kindling awake in his lap.

Rosie can see that his face has changed, he has the unmistakable look of a focused, aroused man. Even his nostrils are flaring slightly. His chest is moving fast, his eyes locked onto hers.

'I think I'm capsizing'

The waves are risin' and risin'.

Rosie observes small beads of sweat on Teddy's brow, and as one rolls down his temple, she follows it over his cheekbone, and down to his jaw just below his ear, on the edge of his stubble, where she notices his skin is particularly smooth. He is jigging his legs excitedly, which is rocking his whole body. He moves his hand from his knee, up under his sweatshirt, under his t-shirt, and he begins to rub his belly. Rosie sees this and looks at his mouth, his lips, his lovely lips. She automatically lifts her fingers to lightly touch her own lips, unconsciously hinting what she wants to be doing to him.

'You're my medicine,

Open up and let me in . . .'

Teddy wants her. He wants her urgently, so much so that he's forgotten to be shy or awkward or scared. He just knows.

Then, zip, the music finishes and Rosie is jolted out of it. She stands up, takes off her headphones and turns off the iPod, suddenly all school-marmish, 'Right, so you get the idea. Well done. You pass.'

Teddy stands up too and takes his headphones off like her. Rosie turns to go, but Teddy steps closer, to stop her. He takes her shoulders and leans down to kiss her. In the fug of her inebriation, Rosie leans back to avoid the moment which she knows is strange and forbidden.

Teddy softly says, 'Please?'

Rosie honestly doesn't know what to do. They seem to have travelled to a different, new place together in the last three minutes. This is unfamiliar, uncharted territory. She searches his face to find him searching hers. For him, the moment is now, just as she said it would be at the end of that song.

He repeats himself, 'Please. I'm so useless . . . please.'

She makes the decision, and pulls him in towards her.

When Rosie wakes up in the fuggy tent, it's still dark, but only just. There are threads of pink morning light piercing the gloom outside. She is inside the sleeping bag, with a naked Teddy wrapped around her. As she gradually surfaces, flashes of the night come tumbling back to her . . .

Teddy's warm hands seeking out her breasts. The pulling off of clothes, the catching of sleeves on wrists. His kisses up her spine. Her hands in his hair, his ears in her mouth, her face on his stomach, his fingers in her fingers, his gentle bites, his cold toes, his warm penis, his moist mouth. Her guidance to where she wanted him most. His coming in. The shudder of him as he entered there for the first ever time. The panting on each stroke, the suckings, the nippings, the grunt, the writhe. The delightful weakness and the sticky soaked bed. Her hands on his face in the dark, discovering how wet, kissing his tears, touching his smile, hearing his gratitude in her ear, over and over, 'Thank you. Thank you. I love you.'

And all the thousands of kisses, so freely, lovingly given. And then the gluey deep sleep.

And now.

The morning.

The temples pounding. The dry acrid mouth. The smell of armpits and breath and sex. Christ. It really happened. Look at him lying there all . . . ruffled . . . and stunningly lovely. So flawless, so young. Rosie inches herself out of his sleepy grasp, pulls on her knickers and dress, unzips the tent quietly, and clambers out. It's a fresh morning, with more light tipping up every passing minute. She walks to the edge of the roof, pulling on her wellies, and looks out over the emerging, greening park towards John Lennon, and she hums, 'Beautiful Boy.' She flings her arms wide to ride the delightful breeze for a fleeting moment before she knows she's surely going to feel horrified in retrospect.

Rosie hears the zip of the other tent and a croaky call. 'Rosie!' It's Three, just awake and sleepily bewildered. She runs over, gives him a hug and whispers, 'Wake your brother up, c'mon, let's go and get breakfast. Keep the noise down, Teddy's still asleep.'

Morning After

Doors are rebelliously wide open all over the apartment. There are four pairs of varying sized wellies standing messily in the hallway, radiating dirt. Gardening clothes and coats are on the hooks. Seeing this welcome sight and smelling the earthy smell is Thomas in his office, visible to all. He is sat with his electric guitar on his lap, attempting to master the opening riff of Chuck Berry's 'Johnny B. Goode'. The window behind him is open and he is enjoying the breeze on his neck. It's that same breeze that is swirling past him, on out into the hall, around the soily boots and bobbing back in to his office, flicking his nostrils on its way back out of the window, leaving him with the faintest whiff of garden life, a rare treat in this stale city flat. That, the sunlight and his guitar are cheering him up more than he thought possible. Such simple pleasures. Plus, of course, his snatched rememberings of Rosie-related lust. They certainly contribute to his contentment. Closing his eyes and daydreaming about her has become his favourite pastime. He has to be careful not to smile too much, but the fact is, he's nearly bursting with it, and better still, she's agreed to more. So he has the *double* delights of memory and anticipation. He feels desired, and loved, and mighty. It's just a shame that he's not as accomplished at 'Johnny B. Goode' as he is in his guitar-hero fantasy. Still, he's giving it a go. And he's loving every minute.

There is the distant sound of laughter coming from Red and Three's room where Rosie and the boys are trying to paint sketches of their garden designs, but seem to be mainly painting each other. Their giggling travels on the breeze up the corridor. Teddy has had a shower, dressed and is now checking himself out in the mirror. Does he look any different? Because he feels MASSIVELY different. The person he sees in the full-length mirror is entirely grown up, someone to be reckoned with, dare he think it, an adult? He is amazed at the difference a simple, natural human act can make. Everything before last night was chapter one, Teddy the boy. Everything after today is chapter two and beyond, Teddy the man. Are his eyes deceiving him, or is he just that tiny bit taller even?

Armed with his new height, Teddy sets off to the kitchen to pillage the fridge. He is ravenous. Of course he is. Men are. En route and with no acknowledgment whatsoever, he passes a formal photo on the wall, of his own high school prize day, where he was presented with an award for 'Most Motivated

Student' last year. Here he stands, between Kemble and Natalie, and all of them are grinning, but none of them are really smiling. Teddy hates this photo and couldn't believe that his grandmother wanted to frame it. Little does Teddy know that the same sophistry is evident in almost every photo Glenn has chosen to have adorning their walls. Her corridors of pretend.

He finds Kemble sitting at the kitchen table munching on raisin toast. Iva is flitting around wiping surfaces, but she knows enough to stay out of the fractious father and son energy field.

Ordinarily, Teddy might have chosen to stay quiet and avoid any confrontation, but today he's different, today he is bolstered by a couple of degrees of new-found confidence.

He helps himself to a tumbler, and opens up the conversation, 'I had a call from Mom.'

Kemble looks up at his son, and sees nothing but contempt in his eyes.

There is a pause.

Teddy tries again, 'I said Mom called.'

'Yep. I heard.'

Teddy stands his ground. In every way. He literally stands opposite Kemble, who raises himself up so they are face to face. Father and son, who look so alike. If ever there was a chip off the ol' block physically, here is the perfect example. Kemble is looking at himself thirty-four years ago. There's his nose, his skin, his mouth. But there's more, because there, also, is Teddy's resolve, his courage, his hurt, and those are the very things Kemble never showed his own parents at Teddy's age. Especially not his mother. Here is Kemble, looking at the very truth in his son's eyes. His parents never saw or heard that from him, and there was so much truth to tell. So much. That profound sliver of opportunity passed him by, and the weight of his cowardice back then has hung heavy on him ever since. He has nothing but admiration for this fine young man that he and Natalie have made, in this seminal moment. But much as he supremely despises the weakness in himself, he has a profound unease around strength in others. Even if that 'other' is his own son. Kemble is too tired of himself to find the energy to support Teddy. Being real is exhausting, he thinks.

Ironically, Teddy is galvanized by the lack of steel he sees in his father, and calmly but firmly he says, 'It's the lawyers tomorrow, I hope you're going to tell them we're better off living with her.'

Kemble tries to stare his son down, he glowers at him. This would usually work, but that's simply not happening today for some reason. Teddy stares right on back. Man to man.

For the first time ever.

Teddy chances it even further. 'I said we're better off with her.'

Even Iva, with her back to them at the sink, has stopped still in her tracks to let this cockerel fight play out. Kemble so desperately wants to tell his son that yes, he knows, he's right. Instead he slowly gets up and walks past him out of the kitchen.

Teddy sits down in Kemble's seat, shaking with shock. Everything and nothing has just happened, all inside a couple of sentences. If he lived in Southern Sudan, Teddy would be bearing three parallel bloody lines across his forehead right now, lacerated with a red hot knife by the local sorcerer to indicate his rite of passage into manhood.

Teddy lives in Manhattan. He gets a glass of apple juice poured by Iva, and a pat on his back. Good lad. Good man.

Dig Dig Dig

Rosie and the twins spend the whole morning getting stuck in to the garden.

Three has chalked out an area where he is carefully placing a circle of large pebbles he has collected from beach holidays with his grandparents and kept in his room in a box. Now he can see how to use them out in the open, Noguchi-style.

He has brought a bowl up from the kitchen, filled it with water and placed it in the centre of the stone circle. He stands back to look and quickly changes his mind about the positioning. He returns to the bowl and decides to move it a foot to the right, so that it's not dead centre. He stands back again, and is much more satisfied.

Rosie observes this from a distance and notes how precise and sophisticated a process this is. Three is really exploring his own aesthetics, learning what he prefers and making decisions and what's more, he has a really good eye. Somewhere in his deeper self, Three knows it too. He knows that he knows something about this, whatever it is. He actually knows about shape and form and composition. He knows what pleases him. He knows for instance, that he would prefer these pebbles to be big rocks, taller than him, and that he'd like to bash them into the shapes he has in his head. Rounded and swirly shapes that wind back into the circle and make you think of spirals and shells and stairs and stars . . .

Red, on the other hand, is enjoying the earth under his fingernails as they plant out the containers with compost. He is hungry for all the information Rosie is reading out from the books she bought. They are both learning about not using soil because it's too heavy and it dries out quickly, and could be full of weed seeds. They are learning about the ratio of the size of the plant to the size of the pot, about how to make sure the plant isn't in line with the top rim of the container, so that there's room to pour the water in without the whole thing overflowing.

They plant some tall bamboo, some geraniums for a bit of colour and some pink ice-plant to attract butterflies and bees when the time is right, later in the summer. Then, they plant lavender and rosemary and mint and sage, all together in one short fat wide container. They even plant a cactus they bought, and they use plenty of new swear words to curse it for having such spikey spines. Red leans his old Sheriff Woody doll up against the cactus and he revels in the funny, awkward positions the Sheriff finds himself in. Cactus up arse for instance, is particularly hilarious. They lug the heavy containers around, placing them so that they make a cosy sitting area around the chairs.

Rosie has started a chanting game where she randomly starts off the 'Dig Dig Dig' song that the seven Dwarves sing, the rule being that they have to sing it one word each in a roundelay, getting faster and faster until someone fails. That someone must then perform a dance for the entertainment of the others. Rosie is the worst at the game, so has already given her Kate Bush, her M C Hammer and her pitiful Michael Jackson Moonwalk. Three has given a surprisingly accomplished Beyoncé. Red hasn't been caught out yet . . .

After all their hard work they trudge back down to the kitchen for some grub. Rosie washes the dirt off all their hands under the running tap, while Iva dries them roughly with the kitchen towel. All the jollity stops abruptly when Glenn sweeps imperiously into the kitchen, 'Thomas, Kemble, please finish what you're doing and come see me in the library immediately,' and she marches out.

The twins rarely hear their formal full names like that, and the fear of God is now suddenly in them.

Rosie can't imagine what could be so awful that they have to be frightened like this, but she wants to keep it all light, 'OK guys, let's have a quick bite to eat. It may be your last ever meal, by the looks of it, so name yer poison . . . ice cream anyone?'

Whilst the twins are captive in the library with their scary grandmother, Rosie returns to her rooms and sits down on her bed to mull over some of the beautiful gardening books. She needs to stay one step ahead of the boys to appear to know what she's doing. She turns to the pages which hold the plant names, so that she can compare them with the remaining seed packets she has left to plant.

There is a soft knock at the door. It's Teddy.

'OK to come in for a sec?'

'Yeah, sure,' she replies as she gets up from the bed and purposely relocates to the sofa. 'Leave the door open, Teds.'

He enters sheepishly, moves further into the room a few paces at a time. 'Hey.'

'Hey.'

It's an uneasy pause that follows. Teddy is blushing, much to his mortification. He inspects his jumper closely and then grins at Rosie, 'Bub-bubba-bub-bub . . .'

No hooter. Rosie laughs politely to make it easier for him. Teddy so wishes he could shut the door. He wants to gather her up . . . now now now. He reaches out his arm and tags his finger around her little finger.

Rosie smiles, but wriggles her finger free, and summoning her best courage, hopes she will find the right words. 'Teds, look, I'm the first woman . . . the only woman . . .' she speaks in hushed tones, 'that you've seen in the buff after ten o'clock, just keep that in mind . . .'

'No Rosie, you don't get it, I love you.'

'No, you don't!' she shuts the door. 'You're grateful, hon, it's completely different. Seriously.'

'But, no kidding, I feel, like, so . . . all over different today. I can say stuff I couldn't before. It's you, you've given me something . . . strength.'

'I haven't, darlin'. You already had that strength. You were due to find it any day now.'

'No.'

'Yes. Listen. I'm not saying it was wrong, or horrible, Teds, it wasn't, it was bloody lovely, you're such a dreamboat. And it wasn't a mistake. But I AM saying that it won't happen again, OK?'

Teddy slowly nods like he understands, but then he looks her in the eye, and Rosie realizes he is trying to start the seduction technique again. He even licks his lips, 'No, Teds, it's no good doing "the thing" again, it won't work . . . really.' She is amused though, and he sees this, so he starts to move towards her.

'Come on, come on, come on . . .' he sings quietly.

'No.' she says firmly.

'We could still practise . . . ?' he suggests cheekily, 'after all, I want to get it right.'

'You *do* get it right, Teddy, you really do. You've done the practice, it's time for the real thing – with a girl your own age.' He stares at her. She touches his cheek.

This really is it.

'C'mon now, get lost, we don't want your type round these parts and I need to go and rescue your brothers from the guillotine . . .'

As Rosie approaches the library, she can hear the muffled end of the telling-off happening inside. Glenn is admonishing the twins in her best Judge Judy tones,

'So, to be clear, and listen well both of you, I shan't be repeating this . . . if I ever hear another whisper from anyone that questions the moral fibre of *any* member of this family, there will be serious consequences. I kid you not. Look at this face, and remember the anger . . .'

Rosie knocks on the door and goes straight in, 'Hello, just wondering how long you might be?'

'Ah, Miss Kitto,' Glenn keeps it formal. 'You might as well know that it has come to my attention via a source at the school that one of these boys . . .'

'Your grandsons,' Rosie interjects,

Glenn stalls, annoyed, but then continues as if stung by a bee, '. . . my grandsons, yes, precisely, members of the Wilder-Bingham family . . . has been involved in a theft. Understandably this has sent shock waves through the school and now, through this house . . .'

'Apartment . . .' Rosie corrects, as she once was corrected.

'Through this house.' Glenn stands firm, and continues, 'Neither of these two boys . . .'

'Your grandsons . . .'

'. . . These two boys has had the honour to step up and admit to it, they are rather pathetically covering for each other, so I'm afraid the punishment will have to fit the crime.'

'I see,' says Rosie, turning to Red and Three, both of whom appear shell-shocked and have trembling lips where they are fighting back tears. 'Might I ask what has actually been stolen?'

'It doesn't matter what, it's a disgrace, and consequences will follow, especially since neither one has the spine to own up. So, no more garden today. They must sit and think about what they have done. No TV, no games, and there will be no treats for a week.'

'Understood. Yes. This is very serious, I can see that. I can only assume the crime is major? What did you steal, boys? Gold bullion or perhaps precious jewellery or a car?'

Glenn flashes a furious face at her.

Red snuffles and mumbles, 'It's a pen, and it's a mistake.'

Glenn is ruffled by the clear effort on Rosie's behalf to diminish the crime, 'It is not simply a pen. It is a theft. It is a felony. Now, you are free to go and I look forward to hearing the truth at some point, when the two of you have mustered the courage to tell me. I will be informing your grandfather of this. Thank you.'

Rosie and the boys silently file out of the library, tails firmly between legs.

Within half an hour, Rosie and the twins emerge from the Canal Street subway and walk uptown on Centre Street. She has a plan. This is purposeful walking. Rosie strides along with a twin holding each hand. The mood is sombre, the boys are still bruised from the ear-bashing they've had from their grandmother.

They go up the steps of a large imposing civic building. Once inside they remove their coats and hats, their bags go through an x-ray machine and they are patted down by a guard in a bulletproof jacket as if they are at an airport. The central foyer of the building is high-ceilinged, with massive municipal lights hanging down in front of long windows which don't ever appear to have been washed. The grime is sticky on the windows, the ledges, the chains the lights dangle from, and on the very air itself. This grand sad echoey hall is gloomy and forbidding.

Rosie collects the wide-eyed twins to her. 'Right, gather in, m'lads, and listen up. You are standing in the heart of New York City's criminal courts. This is where something called 'arraignments' happen. After a person is arrested for, say, stealing . . . this is where they are brought. The judge listens to what the crime is, and tells them if and when they will go on to a bigger court to decide if they have to go to jail. While they are waiting to find out, the judge can give a person something called bail, which means that the family will have to pay proper money to promise that person will definitely turn up, and if they don't the money is lost, gone for ever. We are going to go and sit in a courtroom down there, and believe me, the judge won't look kindly on any pesky kid disturbing their court, so keep it schtum, look and listen, OK? Follow me . . .' and she sets off towards Arraignment Court No. 1, with the silent twins in tow.

They rush to keep up with her, striding up a long passage with mustard walls and wooden benches along each side. The benches are full of people waiting to go in to court. It's like a tunnel of damnation, one Bosch would have been inspired to paint. Here and there are whole families, supporting their mum or dad or brother or sister. Many of the clusters of people have a policeman or woman accompanying them, or a lawyer in a worn, ill-fitting suit on the phone desperately calling someone, trying to fix this mess at the eleventh hour. Some people are alone, some are handcuffed, all appear haunted and tired. One man sits with his hands cuffed behind him, whilst he hangs his head, guarded by a solitary policeman who is chewing and checking his texts.

Somehow, here, this is normal. People on the edge of their lives, at the limit of their pain and at the finish of their hope are assembled here to face their consequences. It saddens

Rosie to the pit of her stomach that such a high proportion of these lost souls are black. How has this happened? What is going on in New York City that this can be so? Why should the baffled, the corrupt, the fallen, the raging and the vilified be predominantly one particular colour? The imbalance is stark and shocking, and she wonders if she has misjudged this decision. Perhaps Tom-peeping at the wreck of social order that's here is a graceless and rude thing to do.

Or maybe not. Maybe Red or Three will one day be part of a new generation who forge a different system that goes some way to changing this, if it offends or touches them enough. Maybe they can learn not to stand apart and judge, but instead to get involved and change. Maybe some of the young people here, at the centre of it all, learning how it works the hard way, will be the ones to stop the rot and make a difference. With each step, Rosie clings to these hopes for ballast, until at last they come to the huge wooden doors of Court No. 1, where a guard instructs them to turn off their phones and to keep quiet. In they go.

Rosie and the boys slide into seats three rows back from the front. Only one other family are sitting nearby. Rosie assumes these are the relatives of the next defendant, since they are in a scrum, speaking in hushed and hurried tones with an interesting-looking man who is clearly their attorney. He is a short chunky dapper chap in a subtly striped suit with a purple shirt and matching tie. He has long neat grey dreadlocks hanging down his back to his waist and wears two sets of spectacles, one on his head and one on his intelligent face. He apparently has a hell of a *lot* of things to see. He has his hand on the arm of the weeping mother and seems to be reassuring her.

As they settle into their seats, the junior Wilder-Binghams and Rosie look about and take in everything in this unfamiliar daunting new environment. There is a barrier separating the observers in the gallery from the real court action which takes place in the front half of the lofty wood-panelled room, which clearly hasn't changed since it was built in the forties. The judge, a surprisingly attractive polished woman who looks to be in her early fifties, with a sharp flicky auburn bob and good tortoiseshell designer glasses, sits at the highest point in the room, behind a large wooden desk on a podium. Either side of her are two tall, drooped flags; one is the stars and stripes, the other is the flag of the State of New York, blue with fancy gold edging. Above her head, on the wall behind her is a large crest with an angry standing eagle and the words, 'In God We Trust' emblazoned across it.

Everything about this room tells you not to mess with anyone in it. Rosie looks at the boys who are sitting bolt upright with their hands in their laps, eyes as wide as saucepan lids, taking it all in like sonic radar.

Above them hang two giant upturned-dish-like opaque glass chandeliers. In the lowest part of the hanging dish, but still very high up, Rosie notices lots of elastic bands. How did they get there? Rosie looks around the room at all the official people; policemen and guards in blue shirts and badges, clerks in drab suits, sitting at computers, various random self-important people in grey flicking through box-files, assistants and their assistants. Who, out of all these, chooses to wait until the room is empty to have an elastic-band-pinging competition? Perhaps that's the kind of levity which makes working here more bearable?

A tall bullet-headed man with a deep voice announces that 'Court is back in session.' There is a bit of fussing around the door at the rear of the court and eventually, two court marshals escort a young black man in. He is in his own baggy clothes and attempts to swagger with attitude. He is small in comparison to the large guards either side of him. Mr Purple Shirt goes to be at his side in front of the judge, who immediately instructs him firmly to 'Take your hands out of your pockets please, Mr West.' Mr West does as he is told, and in an instant, all swagger is vanquished. Mr West, who would love everyone to believe he is a powerful and scary gangsta man, is in fact a naughty boy who can't fake it in front of the judge before him, and even worse, his momma behind.

The prosecutor reads out the accusation. It would appear that his warrant relates to a firearm found in his possession, which he has stolen.

His mother's soft gasps can be heard as she cries, 'No, Keiron, not a gun. Not you. With a gun, Keiron? You coulda hurt y'self, son.' The rest of the family try to mollify the distraught Mom, who can see nothing but the fact that her baby boy has put himself in harm's way.

The attorney attempts to mitigate the accusation, with snatches of background information about the boy, which he hopes will help his defence. 'He works at a coffee shop … eighteen years old … no previous criminal record … in with the wrong crowd … his father just passed away last month …' As he references each point about Keiron West, the boy hangs his head further, unable to look anyone in the eye.

The judge is matter of fact, 'I am going to adjourn, the court date is pending, and the bail is set at three thousand dollars. Thank you.'

Keiron West looks back over his shoulder at his mother as he is led off by the marshals, and with tear-filled eyes he mouths 'I'm sorry.' To which his mother mouths 'I love you,' which she so clearly does.

Rosie, Red and Three have watched the whole interaction between them. In such a public place, they have been privy to an intensely private moment. Three has tears on his face, and his brother comforts him, 'It's OK dude, he's gonna be OK', to which Three replies, 'It's not him, it's the mom I feel sorry for. She's so … disappointed.'

All of them shuffle out of the seats and out of the courtroom, and home.

Job done.

Roof Food

Glenn sits alone in her usual place at the table in the dining room for supper. The places are set but the people are not here, and she appears to be the queen of no kingdom. She is on the verge of letting her feelings be known, when she hears the sound of sneakers running up the corridor outside. She sits still and listens out. A door opens. And shuts. More footsteps pass the dining room. Glenn is growing increasingly uneasy.

Suddenly Thomas pokes his head around the door, 'Barbecue on the roof. My surprise.'

Glenn smiles a weak smile. 'Oh, Tommy, I'm just not that hungry.'

'Please try, Glenn. C'mon, it'll be fun . . . ?' Thomas winks at her and leaves.

She stares at her table setting. She hears laughter in the distance . . . exactly what she didn't need while she's hunkered down into a nicely familiar irritable mood. She doesn't want to have to adjust herself in any way. Especially not if it involves 'fun'. She pauses, takes a deep breath, slowly stands up, and smoothes herself down.

When Glenn opens the door to the roof, she sees the garden for the first time. It's half finished, but it's already pretty impressive. Rosie has slung up more fairy lights, and strings of multi-coloured bulbs around the seating area, and in the dwindling light, it's very cheerful.

There is a barbecue well underway and Thomas is in charge, with Iva flitting around as his sous chef, ably assisted by waiters Red and Three. Thomas's long fingers are covered with gooey red barbecue sauce from all the meat he's presiding over. Teddy bites into some succulent ribs and drips sauce down his chin and on to his t-shirt. Rosie attempts to wipe it off with a paper napkin and only succeeds in making even more mess. She herself has a red blob of ketchup on her cheek which he in turn tries to remove, with both of them sniggering.

Glenn clocks that all these people are comfortable in each other's company and she wonders how they can have gotten to know each other so well in such a short time. She isn't this relaxed with folk she has known for fifty years.

Red and Three are having a corn-on-the-cob nibbling competition, and have the butteryest faces in Butterville, USA. They are laughing loudly, until they catch sight of Glenn watching them. They still sting from the earlier telling-off, so they quieten down. Rosie notices the awkwardness for both the boys and for Glenn, whose first time it is on the roof after all, seeing the new garden. She quickly spears a frankfurter with the barbeque fork, places it in the bun, and offers it to Glenn. 'Sausage for you, Mrs W. B.?'

Glenn stares at the greasy meat being proffered, and at Rosie. They are both equally repulsive to her, so she shakes her head and she glides off to where Kemble is sitting, scoffing some ribs. Glenn first wipes the surface of the garden chair with her handkerchief, then sits herself down.

Kemble stops eating with his fingers and immediately starts to use his knife and fork.

Glenn surveys the scene, and somewhere deep inside her grudging self there is the whisper of a wish that she would love to take part, but she can't possibly do that, because she lives inside the invisible fence of her deep-rooted anxiety. She has come to respect its boundaries and dutifully remains within, held tight by its familiar restraint. She won't be shifting anytime soon, thank you, and she certainly won't be giving over any time to contemplating when exactly the moment was that her life became terrifying.

Red and Three approach her.

'Granma,' Three says, 'I want you to have this.' He reaches into his pocket, and brings out a complicated-looking piece of plastic. He hands it to her gingerly.

She takes it reluctantly, 'What is this?'

'It's the pen,' he explains, 'it's a Transformer pen. No-one stole it, it was given as a gift by Sammy Klein. He got a Transformer watch back for it, but he's forgotten to tell that bit. So here's his pen, you can give it to Principal Taylor. We don't want it anymore anyway.'

'I see. Thank you, Thomas, I respect your honesty for owning up and taking the correct responsibility.' And with this, she shakes his hand formally, as if she has just done business with a mini insurance man.

As the boys retreat, Red pats Three on the back and whispers to him, 'Thanks bro, I owe you, OK?'

'No prob,' replies the heroic little chap, and they return to the infinitely preferable Rosie, and the barbecue, and their grandfather, and the lovely fragrant sweet fried onions.

Thomas senior has delegated meat duty to Teddy, and he directs the rookie from the sidelines as he sits in his apron and plucks away at his guitar, still no better at 'Johnny B Goode' but loving the sound of the strings in the open air. Rosie claps along with Thomas's faltering attempts, which only serves to put him under further pressure and so he plays even worse, which renders him helpless with laughter. As it does her.

Glenn sees this shared delight, and although she can't possibly know the truthful depth of it, it bothers her. Her face sets in its old, cold mask. Kemble clocks his mother's attitude and to court her approval, snorts his derision at the happy scene. For a brief moment, the tribes are clearly marked, which gives

Glenn and Kemble a fleeting sense of shared loyalty in their grumpy clan. Then Teddy starts to strut his stuff across the roof to Thomas's chords, throwing down some of his best Mick Jagger moves.

Kemble watches his son and despite himself, he laughs. One wilting look from Glenn wipes that smile off his face in the next heartbeat. Glenn will not abide any betrayal, and boy, does Kemble know it.

'Granpop,' pipes up Red, happy and relieved now that the pen debacle is over, 'we do this thing with Rosie where we listen to noises or thinkings in our heads which make words pop up. Wanna try?'

'OK,' says Thomas, 'but you go first, so's I can see how to do it.'

Red – 'Umm, OK, umm, . . .'

Three jumps in – 'Stones, sky, heart . . .'

Red – 'Yeah, yeah, hot-dogs, happy,' then he whispers, 'Hermione.'

Teddy – 'Girls, music, girls . . .'

Rosie – 'Love love love. Sorry, bit gooey, but that's what I see and feel up here.'

Thomas – 'Yes, and apparently, all you need is love.'

Rosie – 'Well, yes, that and cake. And cotton bedlinen. And a head massage. So all you really need is love, cake, cotton and a head massage.'

Thomas – 'Right.'

Rosie – 'And a pony. Just one tiny pony, then that's it . . .'

Three – 'Stop being so greedy, Rosie! C'mon Grandad, what are yours, really?'

Thomas – 'Shadows. Light. Future. Grandsons.'

Teddy – 'Go Granpop! Awesome.'

Kemble has heard all this, and he notes that Thomas skips a generation, straight to 'grandson', when he is summoning his key words. No surprise. What would his own words about himself be, he wonders? Perhaps 'Idiot. Moron. Failure. Wuss.' Yeah, that's about right.

Glenn sips her glass of water and looks out over Manhattan to distract herself from thinking of any pertinent words what-soever. Hopefully, this irritating jollity will be over soon.

Later on, when everyone has gone in, Iva takes a moment whilst she is cleaning up to sit down. She pulls a packet of cigarettes out of her apron pocket, along with a lighter. She puts fire to the tobacco and sits back to suck in a long long drag of the deadly delicious smoke, pauses to let the vapour fill up her lungs, then she slowly releases her smokey breath into the night sky. She finishes off the half-left bottle of beer on the table next to her, which Teddy has forgotten. She sits and she thinks, 'This family is different recently. It's better in some ways, but Mrs W.B. is on edge, more than usual.'

This woman Rosie . . . yes, Iva likes her . . . but there's something . . . what was it she said to Iva in the kitchen that night? Oh yes.

'I'm here for the boys . . .'

Hmmmm.

ACT III

Nookie

They are back in room 610. Their room. Thomas and Rosie have found a kind of heaven in the huge bath together. His head is by her feet and vice versa, except he is much longer, so his feet and head are much further out. Rosie is virtually submerged beneath the mountain of bubbles, which are swirling around while she attempts to squeeze a tune out of her clasped hands which fart bubbles upwards. Phhht, phht, phht, phht phht phht,

'Come on, it's so obvious . . .' she challenges him.

'Do I definitely know it?'

'YES. YOU. DO! Unless you're dead. Which you're not . . . yet. Honestly, everyone knows it.'

'Do it again, then.'

She starts at the beginning again, spurting the water, phhht phht phht . . .

'Nope. Got no idea,' he puts his hands in the air.

'Give in?'

'Yep. Surrender.'

'You are going to kick yourself and find it hard to hold your head up ever again you'll feel such a fool.'

'OK, OK, enough with the torture, what was it?'

'"God Save the Queen". HA!'

'Ah, well, no, that ain't fair, lady, because it's not "God Save the Queen" to me. For any American, that tune is "My Country 'Tis of Thee . . ."'

'What?!'

'Yep,' he sings it to the same tune, "My country 'tis of thee, sweet land of liberty, of thee I sing." See?'

'Oh, that's such a cheat. How come you stole our national anthem? And anyway, you should still have recognized the tune . . .'

'I guess I just don't speak bubble . . . come here . . .' he reaches out to pull her over to him and as she moves towards him, she rises out of the water, covered in foam.

'Look at you,' he says, 'my frothy Venus.'

She scrapes some of the bubbles from her hips and her belly, and shapes them into a beard on his face, then sits back on her haunches to look at him with his white whiskers,

'Rip Van Winkle. He he he.'

'Hey! Mind you, I do feel like I've been asleep for years,' he reaches for her hands, 'and you've woken me up. You're a marvel, Rosie. Truly.'

Rosie kneels astride his lap and clasps his big head in her

hands, pulling his face upwards. She takes her time to really look at him. She is positioned slightly above him, and she likes the fact that she is in control of how, and how long, she can be there. It's so clear that Rosie isn't the kind of woman who needs to assert her power in any kind of overt way ordinarily, but like all women comfortable in their skin, occasionally she enjoys flexing her confidence. How else do you know where the edges of it are? In this oily bath, perched on top of Thomas, Rosie decides to take charge. Thomas senses the shift, and is very happy to comply. He is warm and wet and willing. He can see that her face changes from a tender gaze to something more serious. Her eyes focus on him in an entirely different, carnal way. She starts to press herself down on him and she rocks gently back and forth, never once taking her eyes off his. The honesty and the audacity of her is utterly thrilling, and his jaw sets as he feels the first twitches of arousal. Rosie is tuned in to him, and she perfectly knows how to grind against him for best effect. The slosh of the water making way for their rhythms adds to the sensory whirl, and Rosie starts to make low moans as she feels her own desire well up. She breathes deep and hard, synchronizing with the strokes of her movements. Thomas can tell that although Rosie is looking directly at him, the place she is ascending to is singular. This is the mystery of sex, a curious and complicated dance, where in order to be truly together, it's vital to be selfish. Thomas knows this is her moment to take, to take herself far inside her head, where her real sex lives. Rubbing and kissing and licking and murmurs have their glorious part to play of course, but the real juice comes from the pit of her, her inmost place, her animal mind. That's where prehistory takes over, and dictates it all.

Thomas slips his hand under the water, underneath her, and deftly finds the nub of her. His other hand steadies his erect penis ready for her to slide down onto. When she does, she tips her head back as if to make her whole body into an even longer channel for him. She closes her eyes and sees colours on the inside of her lids, flashing reds and purples as she gives in to instinct.

Thomas rolls with her heaves and twists, fast and slow, as he watches her fleshy body ripple and writhe above him. She's a human thunderstorm, she's a tornado, unstoppable. His temples are pounding as she gathers him up in her vortex and for a short wonderful while, they flow together, rotating on the same axis, towards a splendid inevitability. He loves how the water holds them, how she is orchestrating it. She arches her body, trembling. The exquisite judder sucks the cum out of helpless him, and for one short shot moment, they are both suspended as they hold their breath and pulsate into the stillness . . . It's lovely. It's lovely. It's bloody lovely . . .

THEN.

'You OK?'

'Sure,' he pants, 'you did all the work, toots. I just tried to keep up with the carnival. Old man dancing.'

She sits back on his lap and looks at him, then leans in to kiss his lovely mouth. He hugs her close and they stay like this for a while, listening to each other's heartbeats gradually slowing to normal.

'Thank you my love,' he whispers, 'for letting me in to this happiness. It's rare.'

They hold each other very tight, lest one of them might fall back into cold reality. They really don't want that. Just yet.

The Law

Inside an expensive midtown divorce lawyer's office, on opposite sides of a modernist concrete-topped table sitting on sleek Philippe Starck chairs, there are six sombre people. Glenn, Kemble and their lawyer, Natalie and her lawyer whose thrusting young firm this is, and a secretary taking notes. Other than the people, the table and the chairs, the room is devoid of anything except a startlingly good view of Lower Manhattan from the wall of twentieth-floor windows. The room contains nothing. Including mercy or heart.

Natalie is staring over at Kemble. His promises to do the right thing hang heavily in the air. She worries that he is not returning her gaze. Glenn, however, has no such reticence, and locks her eyes on Natalie, utterly unflinching.

She nods for their lawyer to kick off. 'My client feels that since your client has hardly seen the children in the last couple of months, she has little right to request full custody, care and control,' he says, peering over his thick-rimmed black spectacles.

Natalie's jaw drops open, she is astonished. She darts a fierce look at Kemble, who still averts his gaze. 'Kemble?'

Kemble raises his eyes to Natalie, trying to be strong. This is his moment, but he seems unable to speak.

She prompts him, 'What do *you* want, Kemble?'

Kemble is staring at her, paralysed. For a tiny second it looks as if he might keep his promise to her . . . then he makes the fatal mistake of glancing at his mother.

Glenn takes up the gauntlet, 'In the end, Natalie, you must surely agree that you have not been the wife Kemble was led to believe he was marrying . . .'

Natalie is horrified, '"Led to believe?!" What do you mean? I have never once misled Kemble into believing I am anything other than the person I've always been. Unlike him . . . Kemble, please . . . *speak!*'

'For instance,' Glenn ploughs on, 'Kemble was under the impression that you would wind down your work commitments once you became a mother so that you could be at home with your sons. This hasn't happened, and is a clear breach of the understanding between you. One of many. All of which are detailed in these documents . . .'

'*Kemble!?*' Natalie persists.

'You have misrepresented yourself, Natalie, and sadly it has come to this. The boys cannot be expected to remain living with a mother whose relationship with the truth is tenuous at best, and whose relationship with her own mental health and even her relationship with alcohol on occasion, might be brought into question should she choose to refute the claims. Don't let this get ugly, Natalie. Trust me. Don't.'

Everyone in the modernly sparse room is simultaneously aghast at the level of Glenn's caustic smackdown, even her own lawyer, and especially her son, who has overtly slumped his head down on his folded arms on the table, so hideous is all this. He is hyperventilating.

Natalie, however, can hardly breathe at all. There is so much she could, and wants to say, but unlike Kemble she is a person of her word, and she promised him way back when that she would keep his counsel. Even now, when her happiness is at stake, Natalie remains true to that word, hoping against hope that this pathetically diminished and damaged man she once loved can finally find an iota of courage in his back pocket. She pleads with him one last time, 'Kemble. Please say What. You. Want.'

Kemble slowly lifts up his head, and looks at Natalie. What he sees there hurts his eyes, his head, his heart. He turns to his mother. Will he, can he, stand up to her?

Glenn quickly answers that thought. 'Kemble. Tell Natalie What. You. Want.'

All eyes are on Kemble. He carries on staring.

He will not, for some godforsaken reason, speak. It's as though he will stare forever. They all wait.

Then Natalie gives up on him, and she turns to face Glenn full on. 'I want my children.'

Glenn answers, 'Kemble wants his children too.'

Kemble looks down at his papers, defeated, small and insignificant. There is very little left of him.

Beneath

It's Friday night, and for the first time since she arrived in this household, Rosie is alone in the apartment. The Wilder-Binghams are all away for the weekend, visiting Glenn's last and very elderly aunt in her swanky care facility in Boston. Aunt Jess was her mother's youngest sibling and is still pegging on at age ninety-three, with no teeth and a hairy chin. The boys, old and young, dread these visits, but know that they are mandatory. Glenn goes six times a year and always tries to take as many family members as possible to liven the visits up. Otherwise it's just Glenn and Jess sitting opposite each other, whilst Glenn dredges around in her childhood for any mutual memories that just might stir Jess, and form a mnemonic bridge for her to cross into the now. Jess sits and looks at the person opposite through hazy cataract eyes, wondering who on earth she could be, this woman sharing her raft in the middle of the sea . . . the sea . . . the sea . . .

Iva is staying the weekend with her Polish friends in Greenpoint so Rosie has complete peace, which is something she has been longing for, some time to properly think. The entire apartment is there for her to mooch about in, but Rosie chooses to retreat to her private lair. She remains in her rooms, turns the TV to CNN to have the wallpaper of the world for company, takes a gulp of lovely red wine and runs a bath.

As she dips into the warm water, she exhales and allows the heat to soothe her muscles and her mind. She lies down with her head back on the cold ceramic lip of the bath, closes her eyes and memories of the bath she had with Thomas come flooding in, and put a broad smile on her face and a tingle in her fanny.

Rosie is extremely skilled at compartmentalizing, she has always done it, and actually, it has served her well. If difficult or sad things are happening to Rosie, she can put them on a mental back burner while she gets on with her life. She's proud of that ability, She won't allow anything to hold her back. She can't.

So why is she crying?

A steady stream of tears drip down sideways, past her ears and plop gently into the water. It's strange to cry whilst horizontal, something akin to drowning happens at the back of the throat. Pretty soon Rosie sits up, but still the tears keep coming. At first her weeping is soundless, and Rosie thinks it will be over shortly, that it's surely controllable. Then, suddenly, her face creases into a grimace and from somewhere visceral there comes a bellowing, big sob. She tilts her head back to release it, and she cradles herself around her breasts to find some small comfort. Where is this coming from, and why does it hurt so much? She feels as though her heart is physically tearing apart, and her only release is to wail. Never before has she heard such a pitiful sound, least of all coming from herself. She is helpless to resist it, the bawling has her in its sorry grip, and a tsunami of tears engulfs her. They keep coming, and coming, until she is convulsing with it. How has she contained such sadness? Her whole body churns, retching the misery out. What is it? What is it? Get it out. Get it all out.

She wants her mum. It hurts. It hurts.

Just when she can't manage any more misery, mercifully, the howling starts to subside, and she can gasp some deeper breaths. She lets the air flow in, out, in, out of her, until she begins to believe that finally, the roaring storm of sadness has passed.

She is wracked by it. She looks up towards the light in the centre of the bathroom, as if the answers might be there, where more illumination is. Why does light help you to think? But it seems it does, because that's when Rosie knows that all these tears are in fact, grief. Here, at last, is her mourning for the relentlessly unarrived child. Rosie realizes she is crying not only for the child she will never have, but also for the child she was whilst her mother and father were alive. And for the children in her care, whose happiness in this world is fragile.

She is no-one's mother.

She is no-one's daughter.

Rosie is mourning for her whole world.

These low moans are her belated lament. Only now, alone, does Rosie know the size of the ache. It's huge. Overwhelmingly huge. At least now, with some of it cried out, she can feel a tiny bit lighter, and at least she has surrendered to it at last. She has admitted her gnawing infertility and all the subsequent levels of complicated pain she has known because of it. She's started to be honest.

She hauls her abjectly sorry self out of the bath and peers at her reflection in the mirror. 'What a puffy mess,' she thinks, 'what poor child would want this wretched potato-faced twot for a mother anyway?!' But, just as she used to witness other crabby Cornish women in her family do in moments of crisis, Rosie summons her courage, has a big sniff and tells herself to 'get on, maid'. She reaches for her green Chinese silk second-hand shop dressing gown, and she brushes her hair. The pull and pull again of the brush through the tangles is reminiscent of childhood Sunday-night bathtimes, and is soothing. She massages some moisturizing cream into her face and she dips a big puffer into some rose-scented talc and pats it all over her body. Here is the familiar smell of her darlin' mum, and her gran and her aunts to give her solace. Then she ties the dressing gown loosely at the waist, rubs her sore eyes, and pads out into the corridor, heading towards the kitchen and a restorative cuppatea, all one word.

When she turns on the light in the cavernous kitchen, Rosie stops in her tracks. Kemble is sitting at the counter, hunched over his laptop, nursing a whisky. His fifth, as it happens.

'Oh God, sorry, didn't realize anyone was here.' She feels instantly uneasy and heads for the kettle.

'Yeah, you don't sob that loud if you think anyone can hear . . .' he says, insensitively.

Clearly, Rosie imagines, he speaks from experience.

There's a quiet pause where perhaps Rosie might have apologized for the racket she made. She doesn't see the need to, so she doesn't. Rosie is brave enough to live inside her truth, even if it means her manners appear questionable sometimes. She just can't be sorry for being human, for feeling something big. And anyway, she didn't know that he was there. She thought she was private. No apology required.

Kemble stares at her through his fug of alcohol. 'Want a drink with a kick?' He proffers the bottle of Jack Daniels.

Rosie doesn't answer.

He persists. 'I asked you a question.'

Rosie is forced to reply, against her wishes. 'No ta, I'm sticking with the cha.'

'Well, aren't you the ray of sunshine?'

How rude. Rosie doesn't care to speak to him. Especially not in this sozzled state. Kemble gives up and pulls a sarcastic mimicking face behind Rosie's back which she perfectly well sees in the darkened window's reflection. Childish. How very different he is to his father. So much less sophisticated. So much less . . . everything. Kemble turns back to his screen.

There is an awkward silence between them, save the tinkling of the spoon in the cup whilst Rosie makes her tea. She has lots of sugar, she loves it, it's comforting and delicious. It's even a tad medicinal, she seems to remember some obscure advice from her mother, concerning shock and sugar. There was, of course, no sugar whatsoever in this uptown, uptight home, until Rosie turned up. Glenn regards it as utter poison, so Rosie hides the bowl in the cupboard with the cleaning cloths, somewhere Glenn would never go. Here and now, whilst Rosie feels wrung out, she shovels the sugar into the tea in three generous dollops, and proudly leaves the bowl out. So what?

She is about to leave the kitchen, but for some reason she turns at the door and comes back in, 'Why are you fighting to keep the boys?'

Kemble is startled, 'What do you mean, why?'

'You hardly give them the time of day, Kemble.'

He glares at her, willing her to shut the eff up. He has no idea how to handle this moment with the audacious Rosie, he doesn't ordinarily deal with defiance too well. It challenges his already tenuous relationship with his own self-esteem. He is rendered ineloquent.

'. . . And?' is all he can summon.

Rosie decides to be really honest, 'You're doing this to get at Natalie . . .'

Kemble downs his drink, and returns to his keyboard.

Rosie speaks soft and firm, 'You want your wife back.'

He attempts to continue ignoring her . . . but this is a step too far. He turns on her, 'I want them. I can't have her.' He pours himself a sixth ill-advised whisky, and continues pointedly, 'Do you have any kids?'

Rosie puts her cup down, 'No . . . no.' She finds it hurts too much to say any more. She looks longingly at the door, wishing she was back in her room and moves towards it, knowing that this is a good moment to retreat.

Kemble is beyond reasonable now. 'You reckon it's easy then, do you?' he spits out.

Rosie looks him directly in the eye, unafraid. 'I think you're a coward.'

Kemble grins an ugly grin, 'And you're so perfect, are you?'

'Well, I could stand up to my mother, thanks.'

This is the tipping point for the tipsy Kemble, who unleashes, 'Aw, go fuck yerself. I don't see your perfect relationship anywhere. And where's your perfect kid?'

Rosie is speechless, there is no answer to that. Kemble senses victory, it's an uneasy one, but nevertheless he feels like he's in the lead enough to launch, 'Then back off, bitch,' at her.

Rosie is disgusted at his offensive and desperate attempt to shut her up. 'Why don't you drop the big man act, you baby.'

'An act, is it?'

'Yep, Kemble, a big sad obvious act.'

Kemble is unnerved by her, by this, yet something in him is drawn to her insults. 'Yeah? Is it?' he burbles, incoherently.

Rosie has nothing to lose. 'A lost little boy, trying to please his mummy. I bet you lie in bed at night, and dream of how free you're going to feel the day she dies. You fantasize about that, don't you? Of who you can finally become then, don't you?'

There is silence, while Kemble wonders how she knows this. He can't explain or understand it, but he actually wants more of her insults, they are accurate, and have somehow woken him up.

Rosie doesn't see this, she is just on a roll, since she seems to be getting away with it and it's immensely liberating.

Kemble asks, 'D'you want to say any more?'

'Yep. OK thanks.' Rosie picks up the gauntlet, 'you are a self-pitying disaster zone. Completely toxic.'

Kemble says nothing. She is getting to him.

She continues, 'You're incapable of even one small bit of bravery. Either of your eight-year-old sons has more courage in their little finger than you have ever had . . .'

His eyes moisten. Rosie hesitates, feeling suddenly guilty that she has said too much. He's crumpling in front of her eyes.

'Sorry, Kemble. I didn't mean . . . to go that far . . . it's just . . . you are bloody maddening.'

'Well, here's the thing lady. I want more. More of that. Plenty more, if you please.'

Rosie is astonished by this strange reaction, she senses that it is all getting a bit odd and inappropriate.

He isn't giving up. 'If I asked you nicely? Could you be more nasty?'

'What?! No!'

'If I begged?'

'No, Kemble. Stop it. What's the matter with you?'

He knows what the matter is. 'We got to the part at the lawyers, where I should've kept my promise. I promised Nat. I couldn't do it. I'm a useless shit.'

'You're emotionally crippled, for sure . . .'

'Yep. That's it. Keep going . . .'

'Oh, give over, for God's sake! I'm not playing your weird games, Kemble, I'm telling you the truth as I see it.'

Rosie moves closer towards him, squares up to him. He says nothing. So she does. 'It's difficult, I'm sure, but you've got to step up, pal. Got to. And soon.'

Everything on Kemble's face tells her that he is on the edge. He doesn't know how to be in this situation, he rarely confronts anything, least of all himself.

'Christ, I know it's hard, but really Kemble, you have no option if you want what's right for those lads. Now is the time to dig deep . . .'

In the giddy midst of his inebriation, and possibly because of it, Kemble knows that what she says is right. But the one little shred of misplaced ego he has left keeps him trapped within his lies. He doesn't want her to know it all, he wants to be able to keep his secret because he hasn't even told it to himself yet. Not properly.

Natalie guessed. She told him that their marriage was no longer possible, and that he wouldn't be able to have an authentic happy life until he worked things out for himself, that she thought it was why he drank so much and threw his weight around so randomly. That it was at the centre of all his trouble, at the centre of him. And now Rosie is hovering dangerously close to the real Kemble, and he feels cornered, defensive. It takes him back to being a teenager, and all the macho crap he invented about himself, mostly to impress his parents, mostly his mother. He is their only child. A boy. A man. Who would surely grow to be every bit the man his father is . . .

Kemble stands up, 'I know what you want me to do. What everybody wants me to do . . .'

'So do it, Kemble,' she says, 'man up.'

'Yeah,' he agrees, 'man up. Grow a pair . . . of these,' and with that, he grabs her hand, and thrusts it onto his balls. Rosie is startled, but stands her ground and doesn't flinch. She does the opposite, she holds his gaze. Very quietly she says, 'How dare you? Dream on, mate,' and she gives them a quick hefty squeeze til he winces. Then she releases him and walks off briskly, breathing hard and heading for the sanctuary of her room. Get away, get away.

The teetering Kemble is left standing alone with his embarrassment and shame, the two comrades he is most familiar with. So familiar, in fact, that he actively seeks them out as regular company he can rely on. He always forgets, though, that those two destructive reprobates are part of a mighty alliance, a triumvirate that includes their sinister old crony, anger . . . and when *he* now joins the gang, Kemble explodes inside, and chases up the corridor after her.

Before Rosie even has time to realize it he is thundering up behind her, an angry bull. He grabs her, and they fall to the floor together.

'Kemble, what the fuck are you doing?' she blurts as he fumbles about, clumsily pulling at her dressing gown. She squirms herself around until she is facing him, with Kemble on top of her.

'I'll show you, I'll show all of you . . .'

He pins her arms to the floor either side of her shoulders, his face is close to hers and their laboured breath is mingling, a clash of whisky and tea.

'What do you want to show me?!' she pants at him.

He falters. 'I'm a man. I'm . . . just a man. That's it.'

'I know that, Kemble.'

He lets go of her wrists and sits up, still straddling her. She sees in his desperate eyes that anger is leaving, and drunken confusion is replacing it. Kemble is an oaf in every way, lumbering around making all the wrong decisions and hating

202

himself. Her gown has fallen open and her breasts are exposed. Kemble can't take his eyes from them. But he hesitates. Why is he so bewildered? Is it the drink?

Rosie's glad he's so lost, it gives her a chance to escape. She pushes him off her and he falls away easily, and slumps against the wall. A big pathetic sack of potatoes. She clambers up, pulling her gown around her, and walks the few paces to her room, where she gently closes the door behind her.

What the hell has just happened?! Does she need to lock the door? No, she doesn't feel afraid. Does she need to leave the apartment immediately? No, because she doesn't feel compromised. He is the one who will feel a fool, not her. What a sorry, sorry excuse for a man he is. It's as if he's been used up, there's no point to him. Rosie pities him. How awful it must be to be him. To be privileged, empty, failed Kemble, chained to a massive inadequacy package like that, ready to throw himself over the side and let it drag him down to the depths, so far that he believes he will never surface again. All the time Rosie is thinking about him, she is trying to self-soothe by grabbing at the lovely Persian carpet with her toes. Feels a little bit better. Oh dear. What a ruddy weird mess.

Rosie has been sitting, thinking like this, in the gloom, for an hour or more, when there is a soft, uncertain knock on her door. So soft that she's not even sure it is a knock. She listens. It comes again. She takes a deep breath, and goes to the door. She opens it a tiny bit, and through the narrow slit, she sees

Kemble in a big white fluffy dressing gown. His hair is wet, and he smells of soap.

'I'm so sorry,' he says quietly, 'so sorry.'

She opens the door a bit more. 'I'm not loaded anymore,' he continues, 'this is me, cold shower, not so drunk, being as real as I know how. I'm sorry.'

Rosie can tell that eating this huge portion of humble pie is taking some stamina and no small amount of courage.

'Can I come in for a minute?' he asks politely. Rosie's instinct tells her that, despite everything this evening, she is safe with this broken, feeble fellow. She prays she's got it right when she opens the door fully, and steps back to allow him in. It flits across her mind that if this were happening to any good friend of hers, she would be strongly advising against it. Yet here she is, letting it happen. 'Just for the record, Kemble, you don't frighten me.'

He sits down on her sofa, and straight away, she notices that he is fidgety and fighting back tears. He coughs to steady his thoughts and to see the extreme emotion off.

'Why the hell can't I do the right thing? It's so ... clear ... what's right.'

'Think it's a toss up between what you're prepared to risk,' she says.

'What do you mean?' he says.

'Well, if you do the right thing, you risk losing the respect of your mother. If you do the wrong thing, you risk losing the respect of your kids.'

'I've never had the respect of my mother. No-one has that except for Dad. No-one. Never will.'

'So why are you chasing it then? If it's so impossible to have?'

'Dunno . . . always wanted it. Always.'

'Has it ever occurred to you that she might have decided, somehow, to never give it to you, on purpose? So that she can feel . . . sort of . . . important? Maybe that's how she needs to have her power. It's a bit messed up. A lot messed up. But the messed-upness is hers, not yours, frankly. Leave it be. Let her get on with it. You've got a job to do.'

'Yeah. I have . . . What?'

'Being a dad, for God's sake! Those lads, all three of them, are bloody *longing* for you. Just like you're longing for Glenn. But unlike her, you *can* give it to them. Can't you? Give 'em buckets of it, of you. That's all they want, Kemble. They don't need a perfect dad. Just a regular, interested, flawed wanker like you. They're waiting for you to get involved, and make the right decisions. That's all. It's easy. Achievable. Don't be like her, withholding it all. Don't be that, you know how much it hurts. Why would you do that to them? Don't let them feel they aren't worth it, or that you're dangerous for them in some way. They *are*, and you're *not*. Fact.'

In this moment, something shifts in Kemble. Rosie has thrown him a lifeline. He can see there's a way out, and the dawning relief of it, the beginning of acceptance, is overwhelming. He smiles weakly at her, and she smiles kindly back, and says, 'You have no idea how privileged you are.'

'I know. Jeez.'

'No, no. I'm not talking about stuff, material stuff, I mean that you get to be a parent. It's ... big ... y'know ... don't bugger it up ...' She nearly loses her composure. She doesn't want to be doing this in front of him, in front of anyone, but her emotional immunity is low, and has been all evening. 'You're so lucky. Some people really ... need you. You matter to them. It'd be a sin to squander that ... love. That's all.' She looks at him, she means it, bone deep.

Kemble knows it, maybe for the first time. Unequivocally. He feels huge compassion for her generosity and for her sincerity. He doesn't witness this often. His eyes fill with tears and he starts to softly sob. This is someone crying for the first time in ages. Rosie puts her hand to his face to wipe away his sadness and, simultaneously, he does the same to her. He moves closer to her and pulls her against him to hold her in his arms. Rosie's face is against the downy dressing gown. She closes her eyes and allows herself to be held. Two complicated, hidden people sharing their hurt, both of whom ordinarily do almost anything to avoid it, now both clinging to the wreckage, grateful for the honesty. She can hear his fast heartbeat through the cloth, and she can feel his body shaking as he submits to his sorrow. She holds him tight, like a koala holds a tree. She just wants to be there, and to not think. Cleaved together like this, the two of them pat and stroke and rock each other gently, until . . . eventually . . . they lull into sleep.

Somewhere in the thick of the night, Rosie is roused from her deep sticky slumber, and her lovely sensual dream, to find that sleepy Kemble is nuzzling into her neck. She feels his lips moving slowly over her face til he finds her mouth. It all happens in the treacle of half awake. The two of them wind around each other like ivy, as they kiss and inhale each other. Before they are alert enough to think, their most natural desires draw them together as they melt into sex. It is dozy and tender and easy, until Kemble suddenly ramps up his energy. Her gown comes off as he flips her over. She hears his breathing change, more urgent, and he is muttering low and animal. He kisses her back, and leans in to her ear from behind, she can hear him whispering, 'I'm not who I am. This isn't who I am,' as he pushes into her. He starts a steady long stroke, and groggy Rosie can't help liking it, he's strong and sure, and she is waking up fast now, as his rhythm increases. She is swept up in his grunts and she begins to realize he is in his own world. She turns her head to see his eyes are closed, and he is biting the air as he thrusts and jolts toward his orgasm. 'I . . . don't . . . want . . . this,' he gasps, 'Don't look at me.'

It's dawning on Rosie that this is not right for a thousand reasons when he suddenly ejaculates, panting 'Sorry, sorry, sorry.' He pulls away from her, and they both sit naked and hunched up, at either end of the sofa, separate and reeling from what just happened.

'Are you OK?' he asks.

'Yeah, OK. Sort of. Bloody hell, Kemble. I was asleep . . .'

'I know. Me too. Sorry. I just . . . want . . . oh God . . .'

'What, Kemble? What *do* you want?'

He hangs his head and puts his hand to his forehead. With his other hand, he reaches out to her, his lifeboat, and she takes it in hers. He pauses.

'I want . . .' he stutters. Will he say it? Will he finally put his secret out of him, and into the fresh air?

'I want to want women . . . but I don't . . . mostly . . . I . . . don't.'

And with that, Kemble's face collapses and he hides it from her, in unmitigated shame. Rosie lifts herself off her end of the sofa, and she goes to him. She pulls his hands away from his face so she can look him directly in the eye.

He is repeating, 'See? See who I am?' in hushed tones.

'I see you now, Kemble. I properly see you now. I get it. It's OK. Really, it's OK. It all makes sense.'

He speaks fast. 'Natalie knew, she told me to own it. She loved me, she said, but we couldn't stay married. She promised not to say anything til I get my head round it, til I'm ready.

And she hasn't. Even when she could've. I wish I didn't hurt her so badly. She deserves better.'

'Better than what?' says Rosie.

'Better than some ageing closet coward who can't face his own truth, and made her life a misery.'

'That's not the bit she deserves better than. She deserves better than a dishonest man too afraid to tell his family the truth, who drinks to dull the pain and absents himself from his most important commitments.'

'Hmm, if I'm honest, Rosie, that hasn't made me feel any better . . .'

They share a laugh. At last. Thank God.

'Oh, Kemble. You silly bloke.' She kisses him.

'I know. I'm a jerk.'

'Yes. You are. A massive jerk.'

'More. More. More insults . . . keep 'em comin,' he half-jokes.

'Don't start all that again. This is it, babe. The start of your new chapter. It ain't going to be easy, but at least you know exactly what you have to do. You've got to mend all of this, piece by piece. Then you've got to live an honest, real life. You big gay!'

'Don't. I can't cope with that yet . . . I'm not 100 per cent gay anyway, I don't think . . . Oh shit . . . I don't know . . . I haven't . . . y'know . . . tried. That. Yet . . .'

'Well, get a move on pal, life goes on happening while you're hiding away.'

'I know.'

'And don't worry. I'm not taking it personally, but let's face it, I've just been majorly gayed.' She stands up and holds her arms out, proudly displaying her lovely chubby body to him, and sings, 'My milkshake brings all the boys to the yard ... Honey little did I realize you was chasin' those boys ...! C'mere, give us a hug. Then get lost. I need sleep ... and no more of this craziness. Christ. I'm knackered.'

He stands up and gathers her into his arms, both of them still naked. Whilst he holds her close, he whispers, 'Thank you, Rosie' in her ear.

'S'OK. It's going to be fine.'

As they break away from eachother, they instantly become a bit embarrassed and aware of their nudity, as if the lights are suddenly on. Which, in a way, they are.

Beehive

When the family return from their Boston visit, the apartment buzzes back into life again. The Queen Bee Glenn resumes her primary purpose, which is to exist, to appear to be in charge, and to be well-groomed. She is well-serviced by all the other bees who pay close attention to her every need, which in Glenn's case means leaving her be for the most part. They all know on some level that it's the joining-in she finds irksome, so they happily, willingly, relieve her of that burden. This means Glenn spends a good part of the day at her writing desk, penning thank-yous and invites and writing donation cheques for the many deserving charities and projects she is involved with. Sometimes she wonders if all this worthy effort will ever make her feel good? So far it has only served to make her feel charitable, which she experiences as a satisfying duty, and nothing more. She is fulfilling her quota of considerate.

She is being perceived as compassionate enough.

She is falling into line.

Correct.

The drones and worker bees go about their business. On the roof, Rosie and the twins are helping Teddy to plant up two beautiful young lime trees. The last of the gardening budget has been spent on them, but Teddy is determined to grow the fruit in abundance, to use in his Mojiteddies. It's hot, heavy work and all four of them are sweaty and dirty.

As they pat in the last of the nitrogen-rich fertilizer to the pots around the base of the sapling trees, Teddy announces, 'OK guys, nearly done. Good work. And y'know what? I'm gonna name these two little fellas, because that'll help us to remember to water them. So this one is Red and this one is . . . Deborah.'

'Eh? What?' exclaims Three, upset.

'Just checking if you were concentrating . . . he he, of course this one is Three.'

'Mine's the tallest,' says Red, boasting.

'Mine's got more leaves,' says Three, smugly.

'Now listen, chaps,' says Rosie, encouraging them to concentrate. 'What are the four most important things to remember about these beautiful trees? What do you need to do to keep them flourishing?'

'Um,' Three puts his hand up, a school habit. 'I know, water them regularly, like Teds said. But not too much.'

'Yep. Enough, but don't saturate. That's right. And . . . ?'

Teddy knows, and can't resist joining in like a fellow junior, 'Yeah, and fertilizer every three months.'

'Yep. And . . . ? Red . . . ?'

He screws his face up trying to remember. They've been talking about this all morning. 'Umm. Can't remember . . .' he says, bashing his head to jog his memory.

'S'OK,' reassures Rosie, 'try to think what we talked about, plants are like people really . . . we need water, we need food, we need . . .'

'Sunshine!' shouts Red, suddenly remembering.

'Yes,' Rosie agrees, 'sunshine's great for light and for warmth, isn't it? Plants and humans need both. I reckon. Yes, that's it.'

Teddy jabs her in the ribs, 'You've forgotten the other thing. All plants and humans need . . .'

'What? Have I? What?' she says, smiling.

'Drainage! Boys, if we might demonstrate to the lady . . . our very own pipe system . . . ?'

With that, Teddy walks to the other side of the roof, where the wall to the water tower is, and he unzips his flies, followed by the two boys who copy him.

'No! Boys. Stop! Really, stop!' she shouts at them through her chuckles. She shields her eyes and turns away as she realizes they are all indeed about to pee against the wall. 'Stop it! It's revolting! Ha ha ha . . .'

As Rosie turns, she sees Glenn standing in the doorway to

the roof. She has appeared wraith-like, at exactly the wrong moment. Of course.

'Commendable as these attributes may be, might I suggest . . .' her voice cuts through the air like a knife, and succeeds in cutting off the pee-flow of Teddy and Three instantly. Like taps. Off. Just like that. Sadly, Red drank a full can of forbidden Dr Pepper earlier, and now has the steady unrelenting stream of a small carthorse, which he is helpless to stop. Glenn continues despite this. 'Might I suggest . . . a little less irrigation and a tad more study wouldn't go amiss. This is really fairly base, Miss Kitto. Disappointing.' She turns and leaves. A loaded pause.

Rosie looks back at the boys. Teddy and Three are zipping themselves up, suitably admonished, but Red still can't stop. He is turned away but the noise is unmistakable, he is still gushing. Rosie is relieved and delighted to see that they are all stifling giggles, until Glenn is well out of earshot, when they let go and laugh their heads off, including the alarmingly prolific urinator himself. Thank goodness, she thinks, they no longer seem too scared of the Queen Bee. Perhaps they are learning, with practice, to dodge her sting?

And still, Red wees on . . . longer than any human should be able to . . . so Rosie says, 'Actually, a round of applause, I think for the world's longest pee. Gents, I give you Red Wilder-Bingham, and his remarkable hose!'

They clap and cheer, and Red attempts to tip his invisible

hat, and bow his acknowledgement, but ends up peeing on his shoes in the clumsy process, which propels them all into gales of unbridled, uncontrollable hilarity. Rosie has to hold her sides as she gets a stitch. Now this is the kind of pain she doesn't mind at all . . .

A few floors down in the beehive, Thomas is busy in his office, attempting the first few brushstrokes onto a small canvas he has bought and propped up on an easel. He has a 'Paint Your First Portrait' manual leaning on his desk, and his eyes dart between the book and the canvas. He has mixed up the oil paints onto a small wooden board, and he has five various-sized brushes waiting on the lip of the easel. He has selected a thin one to start with, and he tentatively mixes a red and a white to make the fleshy colour he wants to use for the woman's face he is going to paint. He jabs it onto the canvas, stands back, and immediately regrets his vigour. Now he quickly turns to the chapter in the manual, headed 'How to Correct Your Mistakes . . .'

Elsewhere in the beehive, worker bee Iva is sneaking into the storage cupboard at the back of the kitchen in order to skype her daughter before she goes to bed. Iva doesn't like to annoy Mrs W.B. by making private calls during work hours, but her home in Poland is six hours ahead of here, so it's very difficult to find a time that doesn't overlap. If she sneaks a little call in in the afternoon, she can sometimes hear how her daughter's day has been, and she can be like a normal mum, just catching up, lovely and ordinary, chit chat about school and friends, and the shoes her daughter wants, and how well she can dance like Beyoncé. Iva can be an effective, loving, close-at-hand mum, not a stranger who's four and a half thousand miles away. She crouches on the floor, dials the number, and soon, there's the face of her darling daughter two inches from her own. They kiss the phone cameras either end to say hello as they always do, but this time, the young girl seems restless. She babbles away excitedly that she hopes it's OK, but her friend Blanka has come round to see the new kitten, so she can't speak now, sorry Mum, is that OK? Of course it's OK, Iva tells her, go and be with your friend and we will speak tomorrow. Thanks Mum! . . . and blip, she's gone. Two minutes of her. Normal. Heartbreaking. Iva sighs, turns off her phone and returns to the kitchen, where she will cook supper for somebody else's children, so that her child will have a better future.

A few hours later in the den, Thomas stands by a huge wide-screen TV. He switches the remote and it springs to life. The Yankees are playing, and Granpop wants to watch it with his boys. The coffee table is piled high with potato chips, dips, corndogs and hot nachos. The floor is strewn with newspapers and magazines, and in the centre of the circle of mess, are Teddy and the twins on the big leather sofa. Red and Three are nursing sodas, while Thomas offers Teddy a cold beer to drink from the bottle. The windows are open, and there is the distant sound of the same pre-match TV coverage coming from other open windows, carried on the gentle breeze. The excitement is palpable. New York is watching.

The twins are having their very first experience of watching an important game with Thomas. Little do they realize just how loud and passionate it's about to get. They will witness an explosive Thomas they haven't seen before, as he unleashes his passion for the team he has been so loyal to for so long. And thus, their nascent dedication to the same tribe will be fostered and inherited starting right now. The band of brotherhood expands to include them. The clan gains momentum. Their shared blood unites them, their lineage denotes their mob, and together, they would and could form a barbarian horde against all detractors and rivals. They are the Wilder-Binghams. They will sing, they will grunt, they will shout, they will rage, they will celebrate, and they will cry together in the pursuit of their devotion to nine men in tight leggings wielding a bat and hurling a ball. The testosterone saturates the air.

Thomas settles in next to Teddy with his own beer, all ready for the game to start. As they watch the pre-match shenanigans and endless advertisements, a nervous Kemble appears and lingers in the doorway, wondering if he is welcome or not.

'Hey Dad,' say the twins.

'Hey guys', he replies.

Thomas looks up at his son and smiles a welcome. They have shared games together before, but quite a long time ago now. Teddy can't hide his annoyance with his father, so he chooses not to say a word. Kemble appears to have passed the son test, and failed the father test. Better than nothing. He takes a deep breath and steps a bit further into the room. Thomas has seen Teddy's subtle rejection, and he holds out a bottle of beer to Kemble. Kemble takes it, and remains standing by the door to drink it. He's not quite in the room yet, but this will do for now. He's watching the game with his father and with his sons. He is present, and he's part of the gang. Slowly, slowly catchee monkey.

Times Square

I n the service entrance doorway of McDonald's, with the bright lights of the electronic billboards flickering all around them, Rosie, Three and Red are fiddling about, getting the last bits of their costumes on. The whole point of this exercise is to make some cash, so Rosie has refused to spend money hiring costumes, and anyway, she explained to the boys that it was good to do a bit of sewing: they'd find it useful in the future. Three asked her exactly *when* they might find sewing a useful skill? Rosie faltered, then reminded them that they would *always* be glad to know how to take up trousers and sew on buttons. They utterly believed her, although she had to admit to herself that in all probability these youngsters would take after their tall father and taller grandfather, and will never have to take a single pair of trousers up in their lives. Buttons though, are different. Everyone should learn how to sew on a button. With any luck, a sizeable fortune, some slap-up dinners in expensive restaurants and consequently, an ever-expanding girth, then the twins may well have to replace plenty of pinged-off shirt and trouser buttons in their prosperous long lives.

Whatever the benefits, they have had a fairly stressful head-scratching time measuring out and cutting up some of Thomas's old shirts and trousers to make their outfits. The colours are right, stones and burgundies and muted earthy tones. Red wears a brown shirt and maroon trousers which are looser than he wants. He made his droopy hat from some old pantyhose of Granma's, stuffed with cotton wool, and he has a big belt of Granpop's round his middle. Three is wearing browny-orange leggings borrowed from Rosie, and for the shirt, he has adapted one of Granpop's pyjama tops. He cut and sewed the sleeves to be much smaller and he tucked the collar inside. He too, has a big belt round his middle, which is stuffed with a cushion to give him a paunch. He has covered a floppy wizard's hat from Halloween in cloth from a sludgy old tracksuit of Granpop's. Each of them attach a Christmas Santa beard to their ears, and put their slippers on, and they are ready. Rosie has had to be inventive, she has wrapped a yellow tablecloth around her middle to make a long skirt, and she has pulled apart a blue dress to put it back together as an upper bodice with puffy little sleeves. The high white collar at the back is made from a white shirt of Thomas's, with wires attached to make it stand up from the neck. She has scooped up her hair, and placed a big red bow slap bang in the middle on the top, bold as you like, pure Disney. She stands up straight and looks at the boys. Bless them, they have tried so hard. Frankly, they all look a bit shoddy, but Rosie secretly thinks they may make even more cash due to the convincingly maladjusted and rather pathetic collective appearance. They just might elicit the sympathy dollar.

'So remember lads, if anyone asks, we are Snow White's Older Redhead Sister, and the Two Forgotten Dwarfs . . . ?'

'Greedy,' Three says, patting his big tum.

'And Farty,' says Red, and he christens himself with a tiny, strained parp, to demonstrate.

Rosie says, 'Thank you for that. Very classy . . . Not! OK, here we go . . . try to look suitably impoverished . . .'

They wander out into the bustling crowds of Times Square and are immediately surrounded by various other panhandling costumed characters – a couple of Elmos, a Hello Kitty, two Minnie Mice, a Spider-Man, a Super Mario and three Statues of Liberty, all hustling aggressively for the attention of the tourists to have their photos taken, and receive tips in exchange for the privilege.

Rosie has a basket of apples on her arm and starts to draw attention to her motley crew by shouting 'Apples! Free apples! Poisoned apples!' which, on reflection, she thinks might not have been the *best* selling technique, but certainly does pull some focus.

One small child starts to cry and grabs her father's hand, sobbing, 'Daddy! I don't want a poison apple from that scary, ugly lady!' as they rush off.

'Shut up Rosie, you're frightening people,' Three mutters

'OK! OK!' Rosie agrees, and tries an American accent, and a sweeter line of squeaky-voiced persuasion, 'Hello folks, wanna take a picture with me and my two height-challenged chums?' Absolutely no-one responds. Either people push roughly past them, or give them an extra wide berth. Rosie whispers at the boys, 'You need to sing, that'll help . . .'

'What?! Sing what?'

'Sing the mine-digging song, you know the one . . . dig, dig, dig, that one . . .' she encourages them.

'Really?!' moans Three.

'Yes!'

Red pleads under his breath, 'Someone please kill me.'

'Hey people!' Rosie shouts brazenly, to anyone who will listen, 'Wanna hear my little guys sing their favourite tune?'

No-one does. People just stare, perplexed.

She starts them off, 'One, two, three, four . . . Heigh Ho! . . .'

The boys fall in reluctantly and give it a half-hearted go, 'We dig did dig dig dig dig dig dig dig the whole day through . . .' they sing.

'Louder,' she prompts.

'To dig dig dig dig dig dig dig is what we like to do . . .'

Their feeble attempt is fairly painful but the sound and sight of themselves sets them all off giggling helplessly, which makes the singing virtually impossible. After a few minutes, two Elmos and a Hello Kitty sidle over. The Elmos are very tall and not a little intimidating, and they stand directly in front of the twins, obscuring everyone's view of them. The twins are immediately uncomfortable.

In her high-pitched, best Snow White voice, Rosie says, 'Hey, Elmo, can you trot on, please, mind out.'

She is immediately confronted by a hostile Hello Kitty in a swingy neon pink dress, with her hands on her hips.

'Listen lady, you need to vacate,' Hello Kitty seethes quietly. 'This is our patch,' comes from inside the giant white head. Shockingly, the voice is that of a man. How incongruous is this monstrosity with her cutesy face and glittery pink bow?

Rosie responds loudly, 'How lovely to talk to you, Miss Hello Kitty, especially since you don't appear to have a mouth . . .' then she lowers her voice, 'but you do appear, remarkably, to have a dick.' She reaches out for the boys, and raises her voice again, 'I think you'll find, Miss Hello, that since the parading of lovely fun characters like us ALL here, is not licensed or regulated by the city in any way, EVERYONE is welcome to join in, WHEREVER they wish, so thank you for your interest, and now perhaps you would like to move along . . . ?'

Rosie waits a moment, sees that Miss Hello Kitty and the Elmos aren't going to move, and shuffles the boys a few metres further down the street. She nudges them to start singing again.

'I don't think so,' says Three. 'These Elmo guys are pretty serious, this isn't good.'

223

'Just trust me guys, OK? We're not going to be bullied off by those twats. Do what I say. Stand still. Hold tight. Look up. And sing . . . two, three, four . . .'

The boys start up again, this time a little louder. Within seconds, the Elmos and Kitty return, and this time they have brought reinforcements, in the shape of Minnie Mouse, Winnie the Pooh and Piglet. Rosie and the twins are surrounded.

'Keep singing, Greedy and Farty! Look up! We shall overcome!' Rosie urges them on.

The sinister circle of colourful grotesques closes in on them, and the evil Hello Kitty once more leans in, and in its raspy voice hisses, 'Move . . . NOW!'

The boys continue to sing, although by this time, they are so frightened that they forget the words, and attempt to make some up in panic, 'Heigh ho, heigh ho, it's home that we should go! With a . . . bum bum bum and . . . a tum tiddle tum, let's go, crap, let's go.'

Rosie stands firm, and still in her whiney Snow White voice, she loudly says, 'Oh Minnie, Kitty and Pooh, you're being so mean! If you continue to terrorize me and my little men in this fashion . . .'

'Shush!' says Kitty, 'Shut up,' fearing that punters might hear.

Rosie continues, 'then I'm afraid we will simply HAVE to call for the POLICE! POLICE!' she shouts.

Kitty waves her hands wildly and growls, 'Shut the fuck up, lady. OK. Listen. We do a deal, OK?' The giant weird white kitten looks around shiftily to check no public or cops are listening or approaching, 'You're scarin' people off. If we give you this – it pulls out a hundred-dollar bill from its bright pink dress pocket – you disappear and you don't never come back. Capish?'

For a brief, victorious moment, Rosie looks Hello Kitty directly in the big, shiny dead button eyes, and is tempted to kick her in the Kitty gonads, until she feels a tug on her skirt from a trembling Three cowering next to her, still attempting to sing, bless him.

'Capish,' she snarls, snatching the money, then she turns to the twins. 'Slowly and surely now, with your heads up, lads, follow me, and sing out! Heigh ho . . . !' With this, Rosie marches off like a mother duck with her two little ducklings following behind, keeping in step and singing proudly until they are around the first corner, out of sight. Then, the boys rip off their beards and clutch each other in equal measures of victory and relief. They all cling together and Rosie brandishes the money.

'We did it! Not quite the way we imagined, but we did it! Listen, we made enough money to buy the last plant. That's what we came to do. And I'll tell you something, chaps, it may not have been your talent that earned this dosh, but it most certainly was your immense courage! Well bloody done! And y'know what, there's enough left over to treat ourselves to sundaes! Phew! What flavour are you going to have, Red?'

'Chocolate.'

'Three?'

'Strawberry. What about you?'

'I'm going to have double gin and tonic flavour . . . c'mon!' Rosie says.

With that, all three Disney rejects dive down into the subway station, and head for the plant shop around the corner from where they live, where the boys have already spied a beautiful big white rose bush they know Granma Glenn will love.

One Month Later

Up on the roof, the garden has flourished. The New York City summer is yet to begin and the more temperate May sunshine is tickling the flowering plants awake. Granma Glenn's rose bush is showing off a cluster of gorgeous creamy flowers, with glossy light green leaves. Rosie accompanies the twins whilst they cut a couple of stalks to take to her at the lunch table. It's their idea that if they take some cut flowers to her, she might want to come back up to the roof sometime, to see what they've done. How quickly they are learning to coax her without directly asking her. This is how Granpop Thomas has operated her for years, and his is the most successful technique, so of course, they ape it. Three is looking at the label from the plant shop, still attached to one of the thicker branches of the rosebush, describing its horticultural genealogy. It's referred to as a 'bush floribunda-korbin' and underneath, it states that this is an 'Iceberg Rose.' The irony isn't wasted on Rosie, who chuckles quietly to herself.

Kemble is up there too in his sloppy Saturday leisure gear, chopping a handful of basil with Red to take to Iva for sprinkling on their soup. He has even helped to replant a patch of watercress. Red drowned the first lot after re-watering it when Three had already done so. An elementary and useful mistake. Kemble bought the watercress in tiny pots and nurtured it on his bedroom window ledge until it was ready to bring up here and join the more mature plants. He appears to be flourishing at approximately the same rate. Pretty soon, Rosie thinks, he might well be entirely grown up. He really must hurry, because Teddy is hurtling into adulthood at the rate of knots and Kemble needs to leapfrog over him and reinstate himself, as the astute, protective parent Teddy needs him to be. Watching him lovingly assist Red, Rosie fills up with hope. Perhaps the sunshine is thawing this family a little bit?

Rosie has been doing a lot of quiet thinking in the last month, trying to be honest with herself about why everything crazy that's happened, has happened. Why she was so available for it, and why she didn't stop it? She hasn't had any more alone time with Thomas, but he is repeatedly, secretly, asking her if they can. She must find a way to talk to him, to explain why, despite their desires, she knows full well that it's better for them to put the brakes on. He constantly tries to catch her eye, and she constantly finds ways to be looking elsewhere. She must sort it. Must.

Tomorrow.

Red and Three place the small glass vase with the two vanilla-scented blooms in front of Granma Glenn at lunch, and for the briefest moment, she is speechless. The beauty is there for all to see, utterly tangible. The outside has come in, and Glenn can't deny how lovely it is. Neither would she, because she's not a monster, she's just a frozen fossil. The twins tip their hopeful faces towards her, waiting for a response.

'Well, well, well,' she begins, 'how splendid is this? Grown especially for me, you say?' She smells the flowers, 'What a pleasant, fresh aroma. Thank you, boys.'

'And Rosie, she dug it in,' says the ever-honourable Three.

'I see,' replies Glenn, 'well then, yes . . . thank you . . . Miss Kitto.'

It may be begrudged, reluctant, and leave a taste of vinegar in her mouth, but Glenn has done it, she has thanked Rosie, and that effort is noted. This isn't easy for Glenn, there's a good deal more joy in the room than her control gauge can comfortably manage.

Thomas smiles at Glenn and leans over to pat her hand for reassurance, as Iva doles out the soup. He knows more about Glenn's complicated internal struggle than anyone else, and he is the person who notices when her better nature prevails. Glenn has her full court assembled for lunch and should really be content enough to sit back and enjoy the view.

Rosie looks around the table and takes a deep breath when it occurs to her that she has come to learn more about all three of the adult men sitting here than she ever could have imagined, and here she is, sitting snugly in the midst of them, the only one in the total know. How precarious is her position? She could feel powerful if she were an entirely different person altogether. She doesn't. She feels privileged.

And strangely vulnerable . . . ?

There is Thomas, assured and benevolent, thankful to her and trusting her with the security of his marriage. A man who fears the sunset of his life, their sex has been his tonic, a kind of latter hurrah, a celebration, a rapture, easy and fun.

There is Kemble, a crumpled man, still partly hidden by his own shame, but slowly emerging. He shared his difficult secret, and believes she will keep his counsel, and he is right to have that faith. She will. He is safe. A man who fears this middle-aged, noon part of his life, a man for whom the sex was a kind of remedy, an acceptance. It was a happy mistake, which reminded him of what he truthfully knows about himself.

There is Teddy, the anxious novice, keen as mustard and hungry to know. He was in a wobbly no-man's-land of experience until she tenderly took his hand and . . . nudged him to a more confident place. A young man fearful in the dawn of his experience, who feels lucky to have found himself under the auspices of her bounty.

There they are. The secret three. And who is she? How did

she come to be so bold? Where is her heart in all of this? Has she, as she truly believes, got it neatly tucked away all nice and sound, so that none of these astonishing experiences can hurt? Is she right to feel delightfully bewildered by it all, or is that just rash and irresponsible? Right now, she can hardly contain all her thoughts, and she doesn't even really want to. She wants to relish her time here, and feel everything she can. Be the impulsive her.

Rosie is giddy with all the reflections tumbling around in her mind, and somehow, even forgets to eat her tomato soup. She has nibbled at her bread and had a few sips, but she is so preoccupied that she doesn't desire any more, and she pushes the plate away, half-eaten.

Kemble has had no such problem. He has heartily scoffed the lot. 'That's me,' he says, wiping his mouth with his napkin.

'Don't be silly, Kemble,' says Glenn, 'That's such a small bowl, eat some more.'

Kemble wonders if his mother even knows how easily she belittles him. It's become sheer habit, and utterly acceptable to her. More dangerously, it seems to be pretty acceptable to everyone else too. He looks around the table to see who might have noticed Glenn's little stab at control. No-one is in the slightest bit interested, except Rosie, who holds his gaze. Christ, he thinks, it's so clearly customary for his mother to treat him as if he were four years old that even his own sons don't notice it any more. The unacceptable has become normal.

He really mustn't allow it. Rosie's supportive presence spurs him on.

Quietly but firmly, he says, 'But I'm not hungry.'

Glenn stares at him. This would ordinarily work, and be enough to intimidate him into submission.

Kemble is not prepared to even enter the arena. 'I'm not hungry.'

To which Glenn merely sips her coffee and says nothing. All is calm, all is dignified. A small battle is won nice and quietly, but make no mistake, Glenn registers the shift.

Rosie is helping Iva to clear up after lunch, after the family have all dispersed. Kemble has taken the twins out, and given the rare opportunity of an unexpected afternoon off, Rosie is intrigued to realize that her number one desire is to sleep, which is not at all typical. She walks to the swanky fridge and pours herself a large glass of chilled water, which she glugs down.

'Iva,' she asks, 'is there a medicine cabinet? I feel a bit drained. I think I've got a bug. Need to knock it on the head before the boys get it.'

Iva looks at Rosie. She considers, then goes to a cupboard in the corner and opens it. She reaches up to get some paracetamol.

232

'Here,' she says, 'but between you and me, what you need, we don't have.'

'Excuse me?' Rosie is popping a couple of tablets out of the blister pack.

'You are pregnant, I think,' says Iva.

Rosie is stunned. She turns to stare at Iva, wide-eyed. Then, with a disbelieving laugh she says, 'Yeah. Right.'

Iva stares back at Rosie, straight-faced, unblinking. There is a heavy, heavy, heavy pause whilst the two are eye-locked together. Rosie slowly puts the paracetamol down on the table.

Within ten minutes, Rosie has bombed down to the nearest pharmacy, and with her legs wobbly under her she asks, in a shaky voice she's never heard before, even though it is her own, for a pregnancy-test kit. As she rushes back to the apartment, with the kit in her handbag, and her head in a whirl, she ducks in to the Church of the Heavenly Rest opposite, above where the boys go to school.

There is a big wedding in full swing, and the aroma of newly cut flowers instantly overwhelms her. She feels slightly nauseous. An usher approaches her, and asks in hushed tones, which side of the family she is part of, so that he can direct the latecomer to her seat in the very full church. She indicates that she will be discreet and sit at the back and slips into the last

233

pew, next to and behind a row of middle-aged couples in suits, posh frocks and huge, frothy fascinators.

Rosie has come in for five minutes of solace, but is sucked into the surreal other world of someone else's big day. She looks around to see if she can escape, but the ruddy ushers are standing between her and the big back door, so for the moment, she is stuck. Still, she thinks, she can try to sit calmly and gather herself, even though she is unwittingly part of this occasion. She closes her eyes and bows her head to concentrate and as she does so she is increasingly aware of the overpowering scent of the woman next to her, a sort of potent lupin smell. This is added to by the strong musky aftershave from the man directly in front, and the woman next to him, whose perfume of choice would appear to be warm pungent cat's piss. Rosie takes deep breaths to steady herself but, of course, this means she is inhaling deeper, so further odours are assaulting her nostrils. She opens her eyes and looks up to the beautiful vaulted ceiling. In the background the priest is wittering on about love and commitment and future and blah and blah and blah. Just a few minutes hence, she will find out whether or not her life is about to change out of all recognition, for ever. What the hell is going on? How should she be thinking about it? The normally centred Rosie is a feather in the wind, she has no idea how to be at this moment. All at once, her mind is churning different possible options at her. She tries to quieten it all down, so that she can listen to her own heart and clear her head.

All she can hear herself wishing is:

'Please don't let it be . . .'

followed straight away by:

'Please do let it be . . .'

And, as she sits there in the giant church whilst other people are making their giant promises, she comes to realize that this decision is actually already made, and that she can do nothing to change it.

'So maybe . . . let it be . . .'

And before she has any time to think about that startling simple truth, the organ blasts into life, propelling them all to stand and sing

'All things bright and beautiful . . .

'All creatures great and small . . .'

Oh God, a small creature might be growing inside her . . . right now maybe . . . inside her actual belly . . . where soup is slurping about at this precise moment . . . greasy orange Iva soup, that seems to not want to settle, it wants to get out, prompted by all the intense stenches coming from everyone nearby which are turning her stomach, which starts to rumble like a wakening volcano. Just as Rosie realizes it's too late, the soupy spew spouts out of her like a geyser, projectile vomiting forwards, spilling all over the whiffy couple in front, drenching their posh clothes in orange goo.

'Oh my God, I'm . . . so . . . sorry . . .' she utters, as they turn around to see the telltale last drops dripping from her lips. She grabs her purse and in shock and horror, she runs for the door.

Twenty minutes later, Rosie is locked in her bathroom sitting on the side of the tub with Iva right next to her as they closely watch the tiny window on the white stick of the pregnancy test. Will the second blue line show up? Will it cross the first blue line already in evidence, making it all true? Making it fact? Rosie counts away the last minute.

Fifty-seven

Fifty-eight

Fifty-nine . . .

Fifty-nine . . .

Fifty-nine . . . come on!

There it is. The second blue line.

FUCK.

Iva says, 'See? Pregnant!'

Rosie is hypnotized by it. She can't take her eyes from it. Her face is a mixture of emotions. First, there's doubt, 'Are these things always accurate?'

Then hope. Iva nods.

Now guilt replaces the hope.

Then gradually, like a cloud going in front of the sun . . . disbelief.

Then Rosie laughs, the kind of laugh you do when you've been very drunk and silly the night before. An excusing, self-conscious laugh. She says, 'I really can't be. I've been trying for years. And my age . . . ?'

'Believe me, kochanie, I been pregnant. I know you are.'

'We'll do the test again. Yes, that's what we'll do,' says Rosie, and with that, they leave the bathroom and go straight to the kitchen where she glugs down several pints of water.

Later on, as night is falling, Iva is pouring coffee whilst yet another pregnancy test is developing on the table in front of them. Rosie nervously gabbles on, 'I got to thirty-six, quite happy without a kid. I've always thought that I didn't need to mark my presence here by making another one of me. Of us. I didn't feel like I needed to live my life vicariously through a little person. I was very happy living it for myself, and for him. And I really thought all that biological clock stuff was bollocks. Until it suddenly wasn't. It happened, bam, like that. My nipples started to hurt every time I held a baby. And I realized that time really does run out, and as soon as you notice that, it runs even quicker, like you've tipped up the bottle of time and it's spilling everywhere, faster than you can scoop it up. I suppose I panicked a bit. Today is over by tomorrow. I asked myself, 'Are you really not going to do this?"'

Whilst she is talking, Iva is timing the test. Rosie continues in full flow, 'I convinced him it was what we both wanted. He was happy enough to stay as we were. He did it for me. He's lovely like that, a proper kind man. He works on the railways, did I tell you? He's a signalman. Quite solitary. Lots of early morning and late shifts. He's a vital cog, he says. He's my vital cog . . . was . . .'

Rosie drifts into weightless memory for a little moment. Iva touches her hand tenderly and she quickly recovers.

'So we started trying, and every month . . . nothing. Suddenly, you're checking mucus, weeing on sticks and obsessing over every blip in your cycle. It's like being told your legs are going to fall off soon; it makes you desperately want to go for a walk. And sex becomes sex. Making love is out the window. Doctors, tests, then we realize we're broken. It's not going to happen naturally, so it's IVF time. We have a timetable, instead of a relationship. Inject this, donate that, watch the follicles, scan the egg. So difficult to organize around his shifts. And then, just as your hope is at its thinnest, the docs say "stop". No more. It's over. They assign you a counsellor. So you can talk about letting go,' her voice fades a bit.

Iva asks, 'So you let go?'

'Yea. Let go of it all. Of everything. Everything. I . . . couldn't go back to it being just me and him. Too . . . hurts . . . too much. So I put the Absence Switch on, and scarpered . . .'

'What is "Absence Switch"?' says Iva.

'Oh, it's what he does at work if he has to leave the signal box. You'd think it would all be electronic wouldn't you? Not in the rural stations, like lots in Cornwall, they still have an actual bloke. If he has to leave, and no-one else comes, that's what they do, put the Absence Switch on, then no train traffic can pass through. Shuts it down. Goes dead. For safety.'

Iva picks up the test and looks at it. She picks up the first test in the other hand and turns them both to show Rosie. They match, both positive. Rosie sits motionless as Iva puts her arms around her, and pulls Rosie into the most necessary hug she has ever had.

'What am I going to do?' Rosie says.

Iva pulls her stool up closer to Rosie. 'Zofia,' whispers Iva.

'Eh?' says Rosie.

'My daughter's name. You trust me. So I trust you.'

'Oh, Iva.' Rosie's voice is trembly, 'thanks.'

'S'OK. Just telling you that even though you have the important choice, you will never regret a child. Is where your real heart will beat. I wonder if I make right choice to leave. I wonder every day, I miss her so much. I don't see her ready for first date, or help with school exam, or grow garden. BUT, I grow her future. Not long now.'

'That's right. Time, you see, ticks away so quickly,' says Rosie.

'Make no mistake. Under this uniform, is mother. More important than anything else . . .' Iva continues, 'So, which one is the father?'

Rosie attempts to look puzzled. She has no idea what to do with her face.

Iva says, 'You have sleep with all the men in this family, yes?'

Rosie almost chokes on her water. How does she *know*? She considers continuing the pretence, but Iva has trusted her. She can't lie. She doesn't want to.

'Somehow . . . yes,' says Rosie in a small voice, hardly able to look at Iva.

'If you touch the little boys, I go to police.'

Rosie splutters a laugh.

Mercifully, Iva joins in, before she continues the cross examinations, 'So which one did this?'

'How the cock should I know? Your minkie doesn't light up when you conceive . . .'

Unheard and unbeknown by Iva and Rosie, Glenn pads down the darkened hallway. She hears voices coming from the kitchen. She stops to listen, and hears Iva say, 'Please say you will keep it' and Rosie say, 'Look, I've wanted to be pregnant so very much, of course I will keep it. No question.'

Iva – 'You got eighteen years of sick stains, worry, guilt, anger. And biggest best love you ever had. You gonna go home?'

A pause for thinking.

Rosie – 'I walked away from all that. Ran rather . . . not sure . . . if I can go back.'

Glenn leans into the crack in the door to closer watch the two women in the kitchen.

Iva says, 'So, maybe you do it here, on your own?'

Rosie says, 'I suppose I will. You have.'

They look at each other, there's nothing to say, and everything to think.

Then, suddenly, Rosie laughs long and loud,

'Oh my actual God. I'm having a baby!'

The two women fall together and wrap their loving arms around each other.

The Big Breakfast

However formal and sometimes stilted they can be, Sunday breakfast is still the favourite meal in the Wilder-Bingham household for everyone who lives there, even Glenn, who was up very early this morning, itching to get breakfast started.

Today is a banquet where bagels are the featured delicacy, and every imaginable accompaniment is in evidence in great abundance. The side table is heaving with platters of smoked salmon gravadlax, chopped liver, bacon, cream cheese and lots of curious pickles. Iva has made a huge fresh fruit salad at Glenn's insistence. Glenn is the only one eating it, of course.

Kemble is helping Red to cut and toast his bagel with the very sharp knife. Thomas removes the cartoon section of his fat Sunday paper, and hands it over to Three. Then he leans towards Teddy, and whispers in his ear something that elicits from Teddy, 'No way! Granpops, you old dog!'

'Shhh, keep it down, folks will get jealous . . .' says Thomas, twinkling away like a naughty boy hiding a catapult in his trousers.

'What is it, Pop?' asks Kemble.

Rosie looks up from her plate, she is working out how to make it look like she's eating, when in truth, she feels pretty grim. She's curious to know what this mystery is that Thomas is teasing with, and in a tiny way, she has a distant alarm bell ringing. Something about him hiding secrets and laughing makes her uneasy. Might he be careless?

As soon as he speaks though, she relaxes, although his announcement is pretty surprising,

'Well, OK, don't cry, guys. It's looking very likely that I am . . . in the fall . . . when it fits her schedule . . . thanks to a friend of a friend of her agent who I happen to know . . . going to have a drink with . . . hold yer fire, Granma . . . with . . . Nicole Kidman.'

There is a stunned silence.

Teddy splutters his cappuccino, 'Whaaat?! Really? No!'

'Who's Nicole Kidman?' ask the twins.

'Norma Jean in *Happy Feet*' Teddy quickly tags her for them, in their own sphere of reference.

'Seriously Pop?' says Kemble.

'Yep. It's gonna happen. So, deal with it, suckers . . . !' Thomas throws an extra knowing chuckle Rosie's way. She smiles. Yes, this was on his wish list, she remembers.

Glenn looks over to see Thomas's beaming face. It's a face she no longer feels she knows. He smiles back at her.

243

'What in the world is happening to you lately?' she says.

Thomas takes a pause, looks to the ceiling, and thinks. 'Wait a minute,' he says, 'Yep. I think . . . I'm pretty sure . . . Yes . . . I'm happy!'

Somehow that very word affects Glenn as if she has started an internal bleed, a slow drip of sadness. She can't even quite understand why it should make her feel like this. After all, this is Thomas, her beloved. Why should she take his happiness so badly and so personally? It could be that the one thing she knows for sure is that his happiness has absolutely nothing to do with her.

Everyone else is silently delighted by Thomas's cheeky comment, and Rosie is still grinning when Glenn glances at her, and identifies a suitable target for her frustration.

'Do you have something to say to us Miss Kitto?' she asks in a cut-glass tone. She is staring relentlessly at Rosie.

For a millisecond, Rosie is startled. How does she know? Then, as she gradually feels rumbled, Rosie's smile fades and she shakes her head.

Everyone around the table watches with great interest.

Glenn pushes her, 'I think you have. How long do you seriously intend to keep this secret?'

Even Red and Three stop munching and turn to watch this heated moment unfold. What's going on? Why is there such tension at bagel time?

Rosie sees Glenn is not going to back down. She is in the jaws of the Rottweiler. There will be no easy outcome here. Rosie looks in the faces of each of her darling fellows around the table, especially the littlest ones, and she lets out a huge sigh.

Without even pausing between mouthfuls of her fruit salad, Glenn casually announces, 'She's pregnant.'

Rosie slowly closes her eyes just to shut off the finality and starkness of those two words coming out of Glenn's mouth, where frankly, they don't belong. Strangely, she feels a whisper of relief in the shadow of her closed eyes.

Until she opens them again, and immediately sees that this information isn't going down well.

Thomas reaches out with one hand to steady his coffee cup. Teddy is blushing from his neck up, a bright red flush. Kemble's eyes are wide open with shock.

Only Red and Three jump up from their seats and race to her, very excited. They fling their arms around her neck, and kiss her cheeks and shriek, and their fuss only serves to emphasize everyone else's stillness.

Red – 'It's a baby! It's a baby!'

Three – 'Can I hold it when it's here?'

Red – 'Call it after me.'

Three – 'What if it's a girl?'

Red – 'If it's a girl, it's GOTTA be Hermione!'

Glenn slices through the celebration with her joy hatchet. 'I presume you will be leaving us?'

Rosie quietly answers, 'Yes,' lowering her head and hoping

245

all of this can pass with as little pain as possible. At least Glenn only seems to know that one rudimentary fact. Thank God.

Thomas puts down his coffee cup and takes a deep breath, but before he can speak the twins barrel in, shouting over each other, 'You can't go. What about the garden? Don't say that. Don't go Rosie. Please! Please! Please!' They are starting to get genuinely upset, and so Iva scoots them off to the kitchen, and safely out of earshot. As she passes Rosie, she gives her a quick flicker of solidarity.

When the twins are gone and the room is still, Thomas looks to be on the verge of speaking.

Rosie is shooting him as many 'shut up and stay schtum' vibes as she can, when she feels a hand on her arm. She turns to see it's Teddy, being supportive. She reaches her hand towards his, but he is already leaning forwards to stand up.

He starts to speak as he rises, 'If you want to stay . . . Rosie . . .' and although he is about to willingly do the most noble thing he's ever done in his young life, he is thwarted by the fact that his napkin is caught between his trousers and the tabletop, so he has to pause and interrupt himself while he fumbles free of it.

Rosie seizes the moment and also stands, as does Thomas, but it is Rosie who rushes to speak. 'OK, listen, no more of this. I am leaving the table now, because I have to sort this out . . . myself . . .' and she goes to leave.

Glenn looks at Teddy and Thomas standing, and she is puzzled.

Teddy throws the offending napkin down, and blurts out, 'It's mine! The baby . . . is mine.'

Rosie stops in her tracks and sees the words Thomas was clearly about to speak die on his lips. Glenn, unblinking, lets this awful news sink in. So too, do Thomas and Kemble. Thomas sinks down, back into his chair, whilst Kemble's eyes could not be wider.

Rosie wishes she could rip her skin off in shame.

Glenn regains her composure, and calmly folds her napkin, 'Edward, I want you to sit down.'

Teddy obeys, then immediately springs up again, 'No! It's my baby!'

Glenn turns her eyes ever so slowly to look right at him, 'You stupid boy. Has it not occurred to you that she has probably also slept with half the men in Manhattan?'

Rosie cringes, the cat is most certainly out of the bag. It seems to have turned on her and is scratching her eyes out. She puts her hands to her head in distress.

Thomas looks, and sees Rosie crumpling. He can't bear it. He takes a deep breath and joins the conversation, 'Well. I do indeed know of at least one other person . . .'

The tectonic plates that form the edifice of Glenn's hardened heart shift and crack. The fault line was always there, but this is a seismic shift. It breaks her. This can't be true. Can't be. She calmly, coldly turns her gaze to her husband, her face betraying nothing of the shock wave pulsing through every atom of her. Thomas stares back at her for a moment, to own his confession, but then, unusually, his gaze falters.

Teddy's jaw is slack with shock.

Then, very quietly at first, but growing slowly louder, Kemble starts to laugh. He can't help himself, he chuckles and then, as if surrendering, slowly raises his hand, in confession. He is also to be counted.

Thomas, Teddy and Glenn all gaze at Kemble's hand. He can't help it, he laughs again. He's nervous and this is crazy.

Teddy finally sits down as if he's been punched in the gut.

Glenn now turns her terrifying glower full beam on to Rosie, who is, as far as she is concerned, sent from Satan himself. Thomas, Kemble and Teddy all stare at her as well, as the magnitude of the situation sinks in. There is absolutely no sound in the room whatsoever. The world has stopped spinning and all life has frozen in time.

Rosie looks around the table from face to face, as they all process the shock. To Rosie, every single one of them is stark naked, including Glenn. Including herself. She has lobbed a grenade into the middle of the family, and exploded them all, revealing everyone to each other, raw as the day they were born.

Nobody can think what is right to say, and what is right to do.

As if on God's perfect cue, a shaft of sunlight bursts into the room as a cloud clears outside, and lands directly, beautifully, on Rosie. It's blinding, and she has to lift her hand to shield her eyes.

Then the door opens, and Iva breezes in to find herself slap bang in the middle of the Annunciation.

The scrape of chairs, and Rosie heads out to her room, Glenn heads to hers, Thomas to his office, Kemble to his bedroom and Teddy to his. Like ants they disperse, and like teenagers, all of them slam their doors tight shut.

Iva is left to clatter about in the kitchen, clearing up the detritus, as always.

The only room with the door open is the den, where the twins are on the PlayStation, loudly killing stuff. They want to stay out of the way of all the stressy adults.

The apartment is dark and closed off.

No buzzin' in the beehive today.

Sad Beehive

In each of their individual cells, the family are reeling.

Thomas is sitting on his sofa in his office, imagining that this is very possibly where he is going to sleep tonight. He pours himself a whisky. This is a fine mess. Exactly what he most feared has happened. Glenn is terribly hurt. He would do anything to change that right now, but it's all too late. He is in shock about Rosie, he thought he alone was significant to her. This changes all that. His ego is mighty bruised. Christ, the baby might be his . . .

Kemble sits at the desk in his room, drinking from a half bottle of vermouth he keeps in his briefcase. He was going to dump it after his conversation with Rosie, but he now feels that he might as well drink it to help him unpick the messy news he's just had. Why does he want to laugh? Something in the heart of him really doesn't mind finding out that his perfect father might not be quite so perfect after all. And that his mother might have to face some tricky truths at last. He recalls her face from a few minutes back. Oh the schadenfreude. It's kind of delicious. He would be able to properly appreciate it, if only he weren't so involved. Christ, the baby might be his . . .

Teddy is sitting on his bed in a room Glenn has resolutely kept like a twelve-year-old's with all of his childhood stuff from a lifetime visiting this apartment. She has even kept the furry dog-on-wheels Teddy learnt to walk with, and a clown jack-in-the-box they gave him for Christmas one year. He is pegged out two ways, pinned backwards to his childhood by all this stuff and the way Granma thinks of him, and pinned forwards into his future where he could very possibly soon be a father himself. Christ, the baby might be his . . .

In the den, the twins are playing on their PlayStation while they nurse low-level anxieties about Rosie leaving. Their worries are offset by the fact that absolutely nobody seems to be stopping them playing for hours. Goodies versus baddies, shooting and killing, and points for rewards.

Red asks Three, 'Why is Granma so angry with Rosie?'

Three answers, 'Coz she kissed a boy and got a baby.'

Red, 'She can kiss who she likes.'

Three, 'Yeah. It's not like she killed anyone.'

Red, 'Yeah,' as he murders Three's baddie character, 'Gotcha douchebag! Suck my balls!'

Three, 'Asswipe!'

Red, suddenly worried, 'Hey, I kissed Rosie last week, just here, on her face, I didn't give her that baby, did I?'

Three, 'No, you dickbrain. It has to be lips.'

Behind the tightly shut door of her bedroom, Glenn sits and gazes at her reflection in the mirror of her dressing table, just as she did on the day the wretched Kitto woman arrived. She looks at her reflection and wonders how a person with an intelligent face like this can so easily miss seeing signs of imminent trouble on a woman like Rosie? Maybe it was her sheer Englishness that duped Glenn into a false sense of propriety. Maybe she mistook her for Mary Poppins. Since when was Mary Poppins such a whore? Glenn lets her overriding fury about Rosie's predicament mask her outrage over who might be responsible. She just can't allow herself to really think about it since she can feel every ounce of her shaking with shock. Any tenuous last vestige of control over this family has just been right royally annihilated by the wrecking ball that is the truth. Glenn isn't ready to entirely confront that yet, and she's not sure she ever will be.

Look at her face. Not a sign of the devastation. Except, perhaps, in the eyes. Yes, she is blinking too much and when she looks right at them, she can see fear. DAMN. Stop that straight away, come on Glenn Wilder-Bingham, get a grip.

Even Rosie's door is unusually shut. She needs privacy for packing. The minute she left the breakfast table she started to frantically throw her stuff into suitcases, but now, deflated, she sits down on the bed, letting it all sink in. Everything has spiralled so quickly, all she can think of to do is to leave. Yet again, she needs to slam that Absence Switch on and flee. Yet again, it is all her fault. Where will she go this time though? Where do you go when you're already hugely apart from everything and everyone you really know. She realizes that although New York was her adventure, her new chance to reinvent herself, she has steadily started to belong here. Both in this city and in this family. Just for a moment there, she began to nest in and shape her life differently. And now . . . look what she's done. She has never felt such a fool, and she has never felt so untethered. She has stranded herself in a fast river of uncertainty.

Without any warning whatsoever, and certainly without a knock, the door opens so violently that it bangs in its hinges, and Glenn is suddenly in the room. She slams the door shut behind her.

Rosie immediately, instinctively, puts her hands to her stomach.

This is the real, raw Glenn, resolute, cold and hard. She steps towards Rosie. 'How much?'

'How much what?' says Rosie.

'To be rid of that,' says Glenn, and she points her finger at Rosie's belly. Rosie moves up the bed, keeping her hand protectively over her stomach. She is silenced for a moment as this further bombshell lands on her. Luckily, the explosion jolts her into an indignant reaction.

'Hear this, Glenn,' she starts, laying out her stall early on by dropping Mrs W.B.'s full moniker. 'I'm not getting rid of this. EVER. I am truly sorry for what happened, but no, I'm not going to do that. And you don't have any say in the matter.'

Glenn's eyes gleam with utter contempt, 'You will have nothing from us. No support. Nothing. No judge in his right mind will fail to see this for exactly, exactly, EXACTLY what it is, gold digging.'

It's as if Glenn is speaking a different language, so foreign is her accusation from the truth.

Rosie is adamant, 'I don't want anything from you. This is my baby.'

'I want it gone,' says Glenn.

Rosie nods. 'That's fine. Look, there's my suitcase. I am going. It *is* gone.'

'No, no, no. That's not good enough,' Glenn spits.

'Listen Glenn. I am keeping this baby. I have been trying for this for years. I genuinely believed I could never have a child.'

'So, I see, you come here and just take what you want? You burgle my family? You thought you couldn't have one, so it's alright to steal someone else's . . . life, to get it?'

With that, Glenn steps forwards and without a second thought she slaps Rosie hard around the face. One thwackingly accurate smack which instantly turns Rosie's cheek bright red and leaves a hand-shaped welt branded across it. Rosie is winded with the shock of it. The shock and the humiliation. She rubs her cheek and stares at Glenn, who is wide-eyed and lit up like a raging fire. Rosie can see throbbing taught veins standing out on her neck. This is full-on Glenn the dragon. Terrifying.

Rosie Kitto is not afraid. Not of people. Her parents taught her to be unbullyable when she was little, and she's never forgotten that lesson. She knows not to shrink, she knows to stand tall and inhabit every atom of her flesh, to the tips of her fingernails and to the ends of her curly red hair. She knows to breathe deep, and to remain calm. Look up. Look straight. She pauses. She inhales, and on the exhale, animal instinct interrupts. She strikes Glenn back, on the face.

Short, sharp, slam.

The blow tosses Glenn's head sideways, and Rosie hears the surprised air escape from her, whoof. Glenn regains her balance. How she hates Rosie. Quick as a witch, she reaches for Rosie's hair and grabs it until she pulls her down onto the bed. Glenn is so much older and lighter than Rosie, she ought to be frail, but she is fuelled by fury and spite, and Rosie is caught off guard.

Glenn splutters, 'Get out of my family, you bitch,' as Rosie struggles to stand back up.

Glenn is swinging at her again, so Rosie pulls her down on top of her. They scuffle on the bed, pushing and shoving, with Rosie blurting out 'Stop it! Stop it!' whenever she can find the breath. Glenn is a bony ball of spikey limbs, lashing out every which way. Eventually, Rosie has had enough, and in an effort to overpower her, she grabs at Glenn's thin hair, grasps it hard and jerks her head backwards. Glenn cries out in pain. Rosie is strong. And she is pregnant. She has everything to protect. In that moment, Rosie clambers away from Glenn, and she stands up, out of breath.

There is a pause while both women check each other out, and try to get their breath back.

Glenn sits up on the bed, but it's clear that this physical fight is over. She's tired. Mortally tired. Of everything.

Under her breath, but loud enough to hurt, she says, clean and clear,

'You cunt.'

After Rosie exits the room, Glenn replays the moment in her head a thousand times in ten seconds. How it sounded. How Rosie looked. How she, Glenn, triumphed. Some of the word is still in the room, pinging off the walls, but most of it landed right inside Rosie, where it was aimed. Good.

Then, for a brief, surprising minute Glenn weeps. She is wrenched, embarrassed by the sobs that engulf her. As quick as they come, and under orders of her iron will, they stop.

Rosie races up the darkened hallway to Thomas's office. The sun has gone behind the late afternoon clouds and the room is quite gloomy. Thomas is sitting in his big armchair, looking like a big empty thing of a man. It's the first time Rosie has thought of him as a sad sight, and it pains her to see, as her eyes adjust to the light.

'I didn't come here to hurt anyone, y'know', she says.

'I have to say, it doesn't look like that, kiddo.'

Rosie nods. He's right.

Thomas continues, 'Why then? Why did you come here?'

'To run away. Get out. Of a difficult situation.'

'Right. And now you've landed yourself slap bang in another one. And why me? Why did you pick me?'

Rosie hesitates while she tries to work out 'why' herself. She's not in the habit of stopping to think about that, she prefers not to, quite frankly, but now, here, she wants to be honest. Yes. Why?

It's suddenly startlingly obvious, so she says, 'Because you wanted me.'

'I see,' he ponders this. It doesn't sit well, 'And you sleep with *anyone* that wants you?'

Rosie slumps onto the sofa opposite him. Is that true? 'I think . . . I haven't felt worthy of being wanted in a long time. And somehow, with you, I went back to feeling bold again. The old me, happy in my skin. Lovely. It's my own fault, but I was a bit of a performing monkey, trying to cheer everyone up, including myself. When really I was some giant useless ovaries with a person wrapped around them. That's all I could think about. This bit that wouldn't, couldn't work. The broken bit.'

257

Thomas looks at her and feels a swell of kindness towards her. He loves her honesty. He doesn't hear it often. If ever.

'Me too,' he says, 'not the ovaries part, obviously, but the broken bit. Yep. I have certainly felt that. And pretended not to. That's my job here. Not to break.'

They both sit silently for a minute, thinking about this.

He says, 'But y'know what, I didn't really know what broken felt like, until today. This is "broken". And I've done it.'

Rosie leans forwards, she wants so much to go to him, to hold him and to reassure him this will all be OK, but she really can't. They just need to be here, broken together.

Thomas says, 'Look, I'm a father here . . . or maybe grand-father . . . or maybe even a great-grandfather. It's not so bad. And the kid won't ever need to know I'm broken, because I won't be to them. And anyway, I can change . . .'

Rosie hurriedly interrupts him, 'I'm going back to England . . .'

Thomas immediately stands up. This is urgent, 'No. Stay. Please stay Rosie. I'll teach it to play guitar badly . . . how about that?' He sits next to her on the sofa, looking her right in the eyes and truly meaning it. He puts his hand on hers.

Suddenly, the light bangs on. Bam. Glenn is stood in the doorway, with her hand on the switch.

'You appal me,' she says.

Thomas replies, 'Well, then be appalled.' There is a new hardness in his voice.

'I want her gone,' says Glenn, clearly.

'And I want her to stay.'

Rosie lowers her head. How is she in the middle of all this? Because she's a prime idiot, that's how.

Glenn cuts through it all. 'Then it's me who has to go.'

And she turns around.

And she leaves.

And he doesn't stop her.

That Night

In their vast, neat bedroom, Thomas is getting ready for bed. He hasn't ever gone to bed in this apartment without Glenn. Of course he has been away without her, but he has never been home without her. He marvels at how tidy the room is, even though she has rifled through drawers and taken three large suitcases of clothes and shoes and other stuff. She has removed herself without a sign of her leaving. That's Glenn. Stealthy, ordered, almost invisible.

Almost.

Of course, there are the remnant signs of her everywhere. The folded handkerchief on her dressing table, the spare lipstick in the tray next to it. He takes the top off the lipstick and rolls it up. Frosted Peach. It looks the same in the case as it does on her lips. She has worn this colour for ...... ever. He has kissed her lips with this colour on them. He has had this colour on his own lips afterwards. They have laughed about it. As he looks closely at the lipstick, he notices for the first time that it seems iridescent, has a sort of opal luster to it. Maybe that's why it gleams when it's on her lips. He wondered how they always look slightly wet. He likes that. Only now is he remembering how much he likes that.

In the bathroom, he brushes his teeth, and while he does, he looks over to her sink where her soap and her small sponge are. Her toothbrush isn't there. Not in its holder where it always is. He opens the cabinet above her sink, and sees that various items are gone. The cream in the red jar, the other cream in the blue tub, the hairbrush. Gone. He feels no sentimentality about it, he is simply noticing the difference. He doesn't actively miss her at all yet, because he is still stinging from how cruelly she handled everything, how curt she was with Rosie. He doesn't miss how brusque she can be.

He spits out the toothpaste foam, and he wanders back into the bedroom, where he drops his trousers and his underpants and sits as always, with his bare arse on the crisp bedlinen. It's satisfying. He looks out of the window and he can see the moon. Subconsciously, he starts to hum, and then half-sing, 'Say, it's only a paper moon, sailing over a cardboard sea . . . hmmm hmmm . . . if you believed in me . . . hmmm hmmm.' He finds it soothing to sing, he always does it. No reason not to now, just because it's different without her. All the more reason.

He takes off his shirt and his vest. Now he is naked except for his socks. Of course, no-one has laid out his pyjamas.

That's fine. He doesn't really want to wear them anyway, never has, he's certainly not going to now that he has the perfect opportunity to reject them. His clothes are in an untidy pile on the floor. So what? His socks are still on. So what? He's going to sleep in them. He tucks his legs up and pulls the duvet over himself, and he lies back onto the pillow. He reaches out and snaps the light off. As soon as he can't see, all of his other senses are instantly heightened. The apartment is all quiet, so there is no discernable sound save the constant traffic noise and occasional police siren from outside. Normal. He tastes the remnants of the toothpaste sloshing about in the back of his throat. Normal. He takes a deep breath in, and as he does the smell of Glenn from the other pillow permeates his head. Lilac. Normal. He rolls onto his side towards the centre of the bed. He reaches his hand out and smoothes the sheet where she would ordinarily be. As his big hand sweeps upwards, he pushes it up under the fragrant pillow and his fingers touch her nightdress which is folded there. He drags it down, so that it lies bunched up in the place where she would be. Not normal.

Where has she gone to?

After a while, Thomas rolls over onto his back. It occurs to him, in his restlessness, that Rosie is lying somewhere in this apartment, all alone. That his wife has gone. That the truth is out. That he would love to quietly walk down the corridor and slip in beside her. That Rosie's heart is beating under the same roof as his, close by. How he would love to go and find her, but he knows he mustn't.

It's just as well that he doesn't go looking for her, because he wouldn't find her in her room. She is in Red and Three's room, where they have insisted that she stays while they fall asleep. It's been a tempestuous and confusing day, and she wants to calm and reassure them. Somehow, all three of them have managed to squeeze into one of the beds, and she lies in the middle of them with her arms around both, whilst they squirrel into her armpits and gradually drop off to sleep as she quietly reminds them of their amazing superpowers,

'Superheroes, may I say thank you for your infinite empathy today, Red, and you Three, for your phenomenal mental strength and intuitive aptitude. Once again, your skills come to the fore . . . and . . . help to . . .'

There's no point in talking, they are both sound asleep. How lovely to fall asleep being praised. Rosie feels that's the least she can do, now that she's causing such a storm. As she lies there, her breathing chimes in with first Red and then Three, and within twenty minutes, all three of them are breathing deep together. Only she is awake. She finds this closeness very touching. These two little chaps have come to utterly trust her. Is she about to upturn their lives once again? The whole point of her being here was to stabilize them during this wobbly time with their parents. Has she now made it all worse? Should she stay or should she go? Is the decision hers to make at all?

As the boys fall deeper into their peaceful sleep, and start to sweat and dribble on her shoulder, Rosie eases her way out from between them. She lifts Three back into his bed, tucks them both in, and heads off to the kitchen.

By the night light above the cooker, Iva is wiping down the surfaces and preparing to finish up and take to her bed, when Rosie trudges in and flumphs down onto a chair at the table. She holds her head in her hands. Iva sighs deeply and puts two glasses on the table, one large wine glass, and one very small espresso glass tumbler. She then brings an open bottle of red wine from the larder.

Rosie sees the label, 'That's Thomas's St. Émilion. You can't drink that.'

Iva replies, 'I make the order. For twelve bottles. They send thirteen, is on special offer. No extra money. Mr W.B. don't know. He don't lose nothin'. Way I see it, is my commission! Is OK. I never take anything. Never. Honest Iva. True. Come on, one little glass won't hurt the little *dziecko*. Is good for your blood. Keep you strong.'

She pours the wine into both glasses, and they chink them together.

'*Nowe zycie*. New life,' says Iva.

'New life. Yes. For all of us,' says Rosie.

They drink a sip each.

'Should I just go Iva? Maybe I should just finish packing and go tonight?'

'You can't go. Leave me all alone as only woman. No thank you,' says Iva.

'What do you mean?' Rosie says.

'Mrs W.B. left. Couple hours ago. I help her with three big suitcase. In the elevator, in the taxi, gone.'

'Oh my God. She's gone already, so quickly! I thought that was just an idle threat to make Thomas worry . . . or something. God. She's gone.'

'Yep. Gone. She don't say goodbye to no-one.'

'Where has she gone?!'

'She don't say. Just . . .' Iva clicks her fingers, 'like that. Into the night. If you go too, will only be me left. No way. What about twins?'

'I know.' Rosie agrees, 'I know. But look at me. Really, look at me. I'm a ruddy mess. I'm eight times the size of an average female New Yorker, I upped and left my partner of lots of years just when he probably needed me the most. Now I'm a home-breaker three times over in the same apartment.'

'And . . .' Iva chimes in, 'you are rubbish cook, and you have crazy bad hair and big ugly feet as well . . .'

'OK. Steady on.' Rosie holds her hand up to no avail.

'Face up to it, English, is all your fault. People shouldn't go into something where they can't get out.'

'I can get out. I can get right out . . . and I will, soon, just watch me.'

'Or, or, or, you can stay and try to mend things,' Iva suggests.

'What? Mend things? I can't make this mess better, I can't.'

'Can,' says Iva.

'Can't,' says Rosie.

'Can.'

'Can't. Can't. Can't.' Rosie flicks two fingers up to Iva, a rigidly, resoundingly successful British rudeness. Iva responds in kind by returning the Polish version, a fuck-you gesture which takes her both arms to do, as she flexes her left arm and puts her right fist into the elbow to do a massive flip-off. Rosie picks up the gauntlet. She stands up, and wobbling and shaking her whole body she sucks her teeth and points with all ten fingers, making Iva roar with laughter.

'What in hell is that?!'

'I am telling you, quite conclusively, Iva, that you can go screw yourself, that I think you are stingy, that you smell rancid, and that I have violated your sister repeatedly. So there.'

'Thanks,' says Iva, pouring herself another glass of wine.

'Honestly though, I don't know where to start, I really don't,' Rosie says.

'How about at the very beginning?'

'I'm not Julie Andrews, and I am not Mary cocking Poppins.'

'No, you're not. I think *that* lady keep her legs closed.'

Rosie splutters a laugh. What next, she wonders?

Triumvirate

Fresh out of the shower, dressed and smelling of lemons from the soap Glenn makes sure is in every bathroom, Kemble ambles down the corridor, past the well-displayed, well-edited gallery of pictures. He wishes he didn't have to live here, somehow he feels as if he's still in school every minute he spends in this apartment, and these photos only serve to compound those feelings. They are a brazen exhibit of only the best elements of this fractured family. Who is this show for? It's not as if his parents have an endless parade of a social life, people visiting who might want to peruse the photos on their way to the bathroom during a rowdy-but-fun dinner party. He remembers an element of that from his young child-hood, but it hasn't happened for ages here. His mother, Miss Glenn Havisham, seems to have hermited herself away in this stifling place, and Thomas has toed the line, to keep the peace. Not that there's much peace today. His father rang through to his room on the internal phone and asked Kemble to come to his study. So, here he is, feeling more like he is about to enter the headmaster's office than ever.

As Kemble pushes the door open, his father is framed in the morning light of the window, and Teddy is sitting in the big armchair. The atmosphere is pretty tense, and Kemble has a sense of foreboding. This ain't going to be easy.

'Come in, son,' says Thomas.

'Oh no,' says Kemble.

'Yes,' Thomas says, 'We need to talk about the baby.'

Kemble even now rails against any suggestion his father makes, however benign or beneficial. It has become his habit to be surly and oppositional as a matter of course. 'Why exactly? I don't really want to.'

'I don't particularly want to either, Kemble, but we should.'

Teddy pipes up, 'Neither of you have to. I said I'd take care of it, OK?'

Thomas sighs. Kemble grunts sarcastically, 'Holy cow, if you only knew how stupid that sounds. You are eighteen!'

Teddy stands up and faces his father, 'Why don't you just butt out? Don't think you can go "Dad" on me now, after all this time for Chrissakes!'

Kemble laughs. An ugly, defensive laugh. 'We're a farce. You, me and him. We're a punchline. No-one will believe this crap, I'm not sure I do.'

Teddy stands firm, 'Neither of you had the right to do what you did. You're not free. Neither of you. Totally wrong.' He stops to consider whether he should say what he wants to say next. He opens his mouth to speak, then doesn't quite manage it as he looks into his father's disappointed, judgmental eyes. Then, summoning his courage, he decides to go ahead anyway,

'I've phoned college. I've deferred for a year.'

Kemble snorts some more disapproval and holds his hands in the air in surrender, 'You crazy asshole.'

Thomas turns from the window, 'That was a mistake, Teddy.'

Teddy is furious, 'What?! Because I don't treat fatherhood like a joke? Is that what you mean? Because I'm prepared to take some fuckin' responsibility . . . ?'

Thomas tries to mollify him, 'Listen, you don't know you're the father.'

Teddy is utterly indignant, 'That baby's mine. I so know it. I was the first . . .' he looks at his father and grandfather, gradually becoming less certain . . . 'I bet I was the first . . . was I the first?'

'Unless we look in our diaries, we won't know that,' says Thomas.

'OK, OK, that's what we should do then,' says Teddy, frantically searching around for one.

Kemble cuts through with, 'Well, if I'm honest, I don't want anything to do with it. I could fake some interest, but I'd rather be upfront. It's a huge mistake, whoever's it is, admit it.'

This is a step too far for Teddy, 'Yeah, everything about you being any kind of father is a mistake, that's for sure. She must be crazy to have gone anywhere near you. Did you drug her?'

Kemble laughs heartily. Too heartily. All of that landed on him like a blow.

Thomas, of course, has no idea what the idiotic laughter is covering up, so he looks disappointedly at Kemble, 'You will have to take some responsibility, son. The baby is either your brother, your son or your grandson . . .'

Teddy interrupts, 'or daughter . . .'

'Yes, of course, or daughter. So, whether you like it or not Kemble, you are equally culpable. As for me, I will definitely be supporting Rosie and the child.'

'How?!' Teddy shouts, incredulous, 'OK, you've got the money, yeah I get that, but you're too ancient, Granpops. You will be dead soon, and come on, surely it won't have been you anyway. Not from a one-night stand. Not with your worn-out old jizz.'

At the mention of a one-night stand, Thomas freezes.

They all stop and check each other's faces. After such injurious remarks, Thomas can't help allowing himself a little triumphant smile.

Unfortunately, Kemble who has always been forensic when it comes to rows, notices that giveaway smirk, 'Ah. I see. So Dad was a *regular* caller. He was her fuck buddy. This just gets better . . .'

Teddy explodes, 'Don't you dare call her that! Rosie is wonderful, you know she is. She's a person!'

'Yeah' replies Kemble, 'A person who puts out plenty, plenty, dude.'

This is just too much for the sensitive Teddy, who lunges at his crude father. Thomas has to wade in to try and stop the attack. Quick as a wink, Thomas shoves Teddy to the floor, and with a couple of swift manoeuvres, he niftily pins him to the carpet in a side control hold, which try as he might, Teddy cannot wriggle out of. Thomas has done it. Instinctively, he has grappled a young man to submission in the scarf hold called Osaekomi-waze. It worked. The old judo worked.

'OK! OK!' comes the strangulated cry of the choking Teddy, 'get off, Granpop!'

Thomas releases his hold and rolls off the lad, breathing heavily. Kemble helps his father to stand up and says, 'Steady there, pops. Wow, still got some of the judo juice from way back when, eh?'

Thomas huffs through his breathlessness, 'Not strength, not age. Skill. Think the last time I seriously did that was with you when you were about . . . what? . . .'

'Sixteen. In Martha's Vineyard. I cheeked, Mom.'

'You did.'

'I didn't do it again.'

'No. Not til now.'

Thomas leaves that sting in the air and stands with his

hands on his hips. He looks at his grandson, 'Get up, Teddy, it's just pride keeping you on the floor. That's done now. We've got more important things to consider . . .'

Kemble says, 'Where is Mom?'

Thomas replies, 'Gone.'

The three men stand in a triangle, silently and awkwardly acknowledging how very lost they all are.

Whispers

Rosie and the twins are on the 6 train heading south to Grand Central Terminal at 42nd Street. The boys sit opposite her, happily chuntering away, looking at little toys from their pockets. Rosie's eye is taken by a beautiful dark-skinned young woman further up the carriage who is clearly, proudly pregnant. Various people including the twins have offered their seats to her, but she has politely declined. Why, Rosie wonders? Perhaps she wants to stretch her back? Rosie can't take her eyes from the woman's lovely round belly which protrudes from her coat. As the train rocks along, Rosie imagines that baby also being rocked in its watery hammock, and while she pictures it, she has a wave of realization that there's a baby, albeit much smaller, in her belly too. Also being rocked along in the subway. It occurs to her that she is responsible for three young lives today, not just the boys, and in a few months' time, her belly will be big like that too. Not that it isn't always big, but it will be big in a different way from now on.

She tries to envisage how her baby looks right this second. She's not exactly sure how pregnant she is, but she thinks it must be about six weeks or so. What is a six-week foetus like? A fish? A snail? A scary hobgoblin? How big is it? The size of a dime? A humbug? A lentil? Does it have a head, or legs or arms yet? Or is it more tadpoley? Does it have webbed extremities, waiting to turn into limbs? What if it doesn't grow properly? What if the webbed stumps stay that way? What if it's eyes never materialize? Or its brain grows on the outside? Or if it's not a baby but something altogether strange, like a sea creature, a bottom feeder, as yet undiscovered, with pale waxy skin and fins and gills where the nose and mouth should be? What if it has eight rows of backward-facing teeth and decides to eat its way out of her . . . ?!

It's at this heightened moment of inner terror that Rosie is brought straight back down to earth by a sound she knows well and is currently living to regret.

Three has decided to issue a challenge by saying the word 'penis' louder than he ever should. Rosie started the game weeks ago when the three of them were forced to go to a dull exhibition of medieval art, curated by an acquaintance of Glenn's. Glenn of course, didn't want to go, but sent the twins with Rosie, assuring them it would be culturally interesting. It might well have been, but it truly wasn't. Once the boys had identified a few swords and dogs and dragons, it was all over. It took fifteen minutes for them to lose interest, but the private

274

viewing was a couple of hours, so to try and beat the tedium, Rosie invented this game that Three is starting again now. The idea is to exclaim a rude word, until the loudest and bravest is the winner. The boys elected to use the word 'penis'. Rosie agreed it was an excellent choice since the likelihood of embarrassment was huge. It amused the three of them greatly at the exhibition, and now Three resumes the fun, this time on a crowded train.

'Penis,' he says, clearly but not too loud. This is the point at which Rosie judders out of her tortured baby imaginings. Oh Lord, she is going to have to pick up the gauntlet. She waits a few seconds. Only the man next to Three really heard him, and he quite possibly believes Three has some kind of verbal tic.

Now it's her turn, here goes. 'Penis!' she exclaims, and a couple of people nearby look up to see whether they really heard what they thought they did. The middle-aged man next to her definitely *did* hear, so he gets up and moves away. Rosie looks around, unperturbed, as if butter wouldn't melt in her mouth, as if that so wasn't her. Blameless. Red and Three are creased up with laughter, especially at her supreme nonchalance. Now it's Red's turn, and Red is a boy who won't be beaten. He gathers himself. He waits until the atmosphere has settled, a minute or so. Rosie watches him closely, all the while attempting not to be caught watching. It's crucial for the game that they aren't linked. She sees him gather his nerve, lose it, gather it again. The battle seems endless and difficult, as he struggles to muster his courage. He really wants to do it, but he is quite shy. Will he? Won't he? Eventually, Rosie sees the tipping point – a change happens in his eyes as he decides to dare, he takes a deep breath and valiantly, he shouts at the top of his voice,

'Penis!'

Now the whole carriage take notice, and Red can't hide his crimson-faced guilt. Luckily, this is just the moment they have to disembark, so all three run for the door amid plenty of tuts and disapproval. Rosie looks back over her shoulder, and is delighted to see the pregnant lady laughing her head off. Good, thinks Rosie, she's one of us, she'll make a great mum.

As they run and run, all three of them are holding hands and guffawing loudly. Something about the silly game tickles them all equally. The freedom to be utterly reckless and puerile is lovely. They live with so many rules and restrictions at home, they live with Glenn, for God's sake. At least, they did . . .

'Good work, Red, you're a lionheart sir!' cries Rosie.

She leads the boys through the magnificent huge central concourse of the station. It's bustling and loud. She knows exactly where she's heading and the happy lads follow her down a wide ramp towards the frontage of an Oyster Bar and Restaurant at the bottom. When they get there they are standing in a low vaulted area which is entirely tiled. The wide, parabolic sweep of the shiny curved ceiling gives them the feeling of being in a marble crypt, fairly oppressive, but very beautiful. The multitude of tiny tiles are small and either green or stone-coloured and there are broad arches indicating various exits, and the way to the toilets. The boys are confused.

Red – 'Are we going to eat in there?'

Three – 'I don't think I like oysters, sorry'.

Rosie assures them, 'Nope, we aren't eating there, I just wanted you to stand here for a moment, and listen. What do you hear?'

Three – 'Just people. On phones n' stuff . . .'

Red – 'And shoes . . . feet . . . walking.'

Rosie – 'Yep. Good. But there's more to hear, so Red, you go over to that corner column over there, Three, you stay at this one, and I will go to that one. We'll be at three corners of this same roof, OK? Only a few metres apart, so don't worry. I want you to turn in toward the wall, where the corners meet, backs to me, OK?'

Red – 'Er.'

Three – 'OK.'

Red – 'OK. Why?'

Rosie – 'You'll see . . . go on.'

They are wary, but the little lads do as they are directed, go to the allotted stations, and turn their noses to the wall like obedient dunces.

Rosie whispers into her corner, 'Hello men of the Wilder-Bingham tribe.'

She turns around to see their reactions. Both whip their

heads around, mouths agog, they are amazed how clearly they heard her. This is a perfect whispering gallery, the architecture and the ceramics possess the most remarkable acoustic property, and they can hear her as clear as a bell, even though they are at some distance. Her whispers have miraculously followed the curve of the low domed ceiling, straight to their ears. They turn their faces back to the wall and respond.

Red whispers, 'Hello, Rosie.'

Three whispers, 'Three to Rosie. Wow, this is, like, so amazing!'

Rosie whispers, 'Isn't it? Listen carefully. I want to say sorry to you both. I've been a bit of a twit because I let this baby happen, just when I should have been looking after you two.'

Red – 'Dad said you kissed everyone, even him. Is that true?'

Rosie – 'Yes. It is. I was stupid.'

Three – 'Not everyone. Not Iva or Granma, or us . . .'

Rosie – 'No.'

Red – 'Who was the best kisser?'

Three – 'Shuttup Red! Can we meet the baby when it pops out? It can help with the garden . . . are you staying to finish the garden . . . ?' he asks, tentatively, with a little wobble in his hushed voice.

Before Rosie can answer, another voice from the fourth, remaining, corner joins the party line of whisperers, 'Time to come home, my little men . . .'

The boys know instantly. It's Natalie. It's their mom! They turn simultaneously, spot her and run to her.

Rosie hangs back to let the three of them have their happy reunion.

'We're going home with Mom!'

'It's Mom!'

The boys shout to Rosie, beckoning her over. Rosie walks towards the excited group, and Natalie reaches out to embrace her too, which takes Rosie by surprise. She is so intensely embarrassed by what a fool she's been, she expects plenty of negative judgement, but this is not the case with Natalie, who murmurs in her ear as they hug, 'I'm not going to pretend this isn't a weird situation. After all, I may be directly related to . . . this new little person . . . Christ! . . . *Quel scandale*! But look, it's happened, and now you need to take care of yourself, OK?'

'Thanks, Natalie.' Rosie feels herself welling up.

'No,' Natalie replies, 'thank you for looking after my gorgeous boys, although, maybe you looked after Teds a bit . . . too well?!'

Oh God. I . . . don't know . . . what . . .' Rosie says, turning red.

'Doesn't matter. Truly. Doesn't. He adores you. Just . . . wants you to be OK, y'know,' says Natalie.

Red interrupts, 'Our stuff is still at Granma's' and Three adds, 'Granma's not there!' which is clearly news to Natalie, who glances to Rosie for confirmation.

'Yep. Gone. Not sure where. Lots to sort out' says Rosie, telling Natalie in adult code as much as she can in front of the

279

twins, and then she turns to them. 'I will pack up your stuff and get it all to your mum's, don't worry. You guys go home, have a lovely time, and don't kill each other.'

'Can we come and do the garden still?' asks Three, genuinely concerned.

'Yes! There's heaps to do.'

'Of course,' Rosie reassures them once she gets the nod from Natalie that it's fine, 'C'mere and give us a hug, you hooligans!'

The three of them go into a huddle, and Red says emphatically, 'No kissing, OK?'

'OK, gotcha,' agrees Rosie.

'Tell Dad bye,' says Three.

'OK,' says Rosie.

'Tell him see you soon'

'OK. *Au revoir.*'

As Red and Three walk off towards a different exit with their mother, Rosie watches feeling equally sad and happy. It's right that Natalie has them back with her, especially now that Glenn is no longer around to enforce the cruel separation, but she knows she will miss them very very much. Just as they dip out of sight and disappear into the crowd, she hears a distant cry of,

'Penis!'

She may have some explaining to do to Natalie.

Rosie turns and heads for a home with an increasingly diminishing number of folk in it.

Too Late

Glenn's rented apartment is a surprise. She stayed at The Waldorf for two days and that's as much as she could manage. To be in one's own city and to be in a hotel is all wrong, unless of course, you're having an affair, like Thomas did. All the time she sat in her sterile suite on the eighth floor she was reminded: That's. What. He. Did. She even wondered if he had done it there, in a hotel they knew well? Did he maybe do it in that very room? Glenn knows these terrible imaginings are preposterous, but she can't help it, her mind is invaded and it exhausts her.

So, she has contacted a rental realtor and now here she is, having chosen the least suitable, most crazy stupid option he offered. There were no reasons to opt for this. Then again, there were no reasons not to. That's where Glenn's head is at the moment, in a no man's land of muddle. All sense of anchorage and order are absent. Only chaos and shock occupy her.

So here she is, in a loft apartment on Mercer Street in SoHo, three floors above swanky designer boho shops. There are bare floorboards and giant floor-to-ceiling windows. Thankfully for Glenn, there are also matching shutters, so she needn't suffer too much brutal light. The apartment is furnished with stark modern furniture, clean lines, bright colours, uncomfortable. The art on the walls matches the rugs, the cushions and the open-kitchen cabinet doors, all bright red and Rothkoesque. This is young, hip living. Sadly, Glenn doesn't have the young hips to match it, but . . . here she is. She astonished herself when she said yes. Nevertheless, she made a bed up, did a shop at the grocery store around the corner, and now she awaits the arrival of Kemble, with a bottle of Pinot Grigio chilling, and olives in a shiny red dish on the shiny red kitsch kitchen counter.

The buzzer goes and she answers it, letting him in herself. There is no porter service here. She waits for him to climb the four floors, there is no elevator here. When she went shopping earlier, she had to take two rest-stops to manage the stairs. No matter, it'll do her good. She finds herself excited to see him. She hasn't seen anyone from her family for a week now. Thomas has left a voicemail asking after her, but she decides to ignore it for now, she's not ready for him. Kemble, however, is a different prospect. He represents a tiny fragment of something she can still possibly control, so she has summoned him. As she waits for him to climb the stairs, she realizes that actually, she really *wants* to see him. Perhaps he will help to alleviate the awful unbelonging she feels in the pit of her belly. He does, after all, belong to her, and she to him, wherever the hell she might be living.

He knocks on the door and she lets him in. With no kiss, no hug, and eyes averted, he enters her new place, and stands in the centre of the large main room, looking around, 'Woo. Nice pad, Ma. Different.'

'Yes. It's . . . what I need presently,' she says, and pours him a glass of wine. Kemble perches himself, as she does, uneasily on a breakfast bar stool, half on, half off.

'How could you, Kemble?' Glenn's vitriol takes her by surprise. She has revealed her injuries far too quickly. This wasn't the civilized scenario she'd prepared for. But she can't help herself. It's just so raw.

'You're the one with the high moral standards, Ma. The rest of us are merely human beings. Who get stuff wrong sometimes . . . make mistakes.'

A pause. Glenn tries to gauge Kemble's courage. She wants him to catch her hurt, but he seems resilient.

'I'm stopping it all. The kids have gone back to stay with Natalie,' Kemble finally says.

Thump. This is a direct blow to Glenn's heart.

'No, you are not! They belong with you.'

Kemble is nodding, but not agreeing one bit, 'It's not what I want, Ma. Actually, it's not what I've ever wanted, if I'm truthful. I've instructed the lawyers.'

This is too much for Glenn, who feels as if someone has just severed the chain of her anchor into her family. She slams down her wine glass dangerously, close to bursting.

'Those boys belong with this family!' she blurts out, half spoilt child, half dictator,

Kemble climbs off his uncomfortable stool, and confronts her, 'There is no "this family", Mother. Look around. Listen, I want my kids to like me, not resent me, or pity me . . . like I do *you*.'

Thump.

'I don't want your pity.' She stares at him, furious.

He stares back. He isn't afraid, and Glenn can clearly see that. 'Like I said, I've told the lawyers. I just thought you should know.' Kemble puts his wine glass down carefully, as if it's the winning chess piece.

Glenn watches him. She is on the back foot, stumped.

'Ma?' he says.

No response.

Kemble shrugs his shoulders and moves towards the door. Just when he is almost out of it, he hears her make a small, thin sound.

He turns, 'What did you say?'

She speaks it again, very very quietly, 'I'm lonely, Kemble,' she says. It's a tremendously hard thing for her to say. A confession.

'Can you help me?' she continues, faltering. It appears that she needs him, for the first time ever. He doesn't know how to feel, it's so unfamiliar.

'I wouldn't know how, Mother.'

He closes the door behind him with a quiet clunk.

Glenn sags. She stings all over.

Love Me Do

Rosie sits in the armchair in her room. It's the only place in the apartment now where she truly feels permission to be. Other than the roof garden, this is her sanctuary. It's small and still, hidden away as it is behind the kitchen. Everywhere else feels a little bit like trespassing without the twins around. They were her reason to be here after all. It's not that anyone is making her feel unwelcome. The only person who did that was Glenn, and she is gone. Quite the opposite, the men are constantly requesting that she be anywhere she wants to. Although they are all still reeling, they are supportive. But she needs a small space to be in, right now. Curled up in the chair, she unconsciously mirrors the tinier version curled up inside her. She is listening to Lennon and thinking about family and home. Ordinarily she would avoid this emotional pitfall, but today, on her own in her room, she wants to wallow in nostalgia, she wants the comfort of memory. She listens to old Beatles tunes. 'Love Me Do' is next. She loves it. It connects her to her father, and as is so often the case with favourite songs, the lyrics, the 'someone', suddenly takes on acres of new, relevant meaning,

Yes, someone like you, little surprise bump. You are going to get so loved. How and where, she doesn't quite know yet, but she does know that all she can do is her best and she will certainly do that. Other than this new family, who were strangers to her a few months ago, she hasn't yet told anyone about what's happening. All her contact with home is via text, so she doesn't feel she has actively lied by not mentioning it, she has simply omitted to tell them. It's not exactly fibbing, but it's not great. The minute family and friends find out, they will be lobbying for her to come home immediately, or even clambering on aircraft to get to the US straight away. She wants to let it all cook for the right amount of time, at the right temperature until she and the baby are ready. Instinctively she knows that, in every way, both physically and mentally, this is a process, and she needs to trust it, now more than ever. The overriding impulse she is obeying is procrastination. She will tell them. Just not now.

There is a knock at the door, and she uncurls herself to answer it. It's Thomas. 'May I come in?'

'Yes, of course.'

He flumps his big frame down on the sofa. 'Look, Rosie,' he reaches out, and takes her hand, 'I really don't like you sitting in here, locking yourself away. This is your home just as much as anyone else's . . .'

287

He looks into her eyes so earnestly, and Rosie has an instant profound understanding of something very important. In this room, in this apartment, in this moment, she sees herself reflected in his eyes, and she knows – without doubt – that he is now regarding her as a kind of troubled daughter. He clearly doesn't look at her like a lover anymore.

Is it simply that they are in this apartment where their love for each other could never and should never and will never happen? No, Rosie thinks, it's not the geography that has forged this change, it's everything else.

She and Thomas are two people in a predicament. They love and like each other very much, but the impetuous and reckless element of their sparky affair has evaporated entirely. That was the steam that bubbled and excited and bubbled away, and now they are left with the sediment of it, the real tangible consequence. It's OK, because what remains is nothing short of miraculous, but the fact is that the sexual attraction between them is vapour, and it's . . . gone.

Just like that. Vanished.

Rosie is relieved to know it, and to see so surely that he knows it too. All of this realization has dawned on her in a matter of seconds and Thomas is still talking to her,

'. . . please please come and be around us all. You are in this family, in every way, now.'

'Thank you, Thomas, that means a lot to me. And . . . thanks for making it . . . y'know . . . alright. Are you OK?'

'I think so, yes. Got plenty of stuff kicking around in this ol' head. Not quite sure what's going to happen, or how to be, but I'm hanging on to the things I know for sure.'

'Which are?'

'Well, I'm going to be here for my family, that's one thing. I'm going to support any decisions you make, and I'll be here for that little bean in there, whatever shape and form you want me in . . . father, friend . . . your choice.'

Rosie squeezes his hand.

'And there's one big thing I know for sure,' he continues, 'I need my wife. I need to fix it. I love her, always have, always will.'

'I know,' says Rosie. And she does. They are quiet together for a minute. It's not awkward, because they are both sitting firmly in the centre of the truth and the responsibility, which is what each of them need to do.

'Hey, come on now, come and see what's going on with Teddy,' says Thomas, puncturing the moment, 'it's sort of awesome.'

Rosie allows him to pull her out of her cocoon, and they walk through the kitchen and up the corridor towards the sound of loud music coming from the library. The tune is familiar, although difficult to place initially because it's so stop and start. Thomas pushes open the door, and Rosie sees a sight that lifts her heart.

The yellow daffodil sofas are pushed back, and the big room

has been temporarily transformed into a rehearsal space for Teddy's band, 'The Hell No's', who have set up their microphones and speakers. They are plugged in and already practising the tune Rosie recognizes to be a cover of 'You Are My Sunshine'. Rosie and Thomas sit down on one of the displaced sofas to listen.

The band is five people, four are old classmate chums of Teddy's who have been in various versions of bands together since they were fourteen. Preppy boys, over-groomed in pastel shirts and tight trousers with floppy hair and stubborn acne. Rosie recognizes that these are the friends he often speaks of, but there's a new addition. A girl. A dewey-skinned dark-haired peach of a cheeky girl, with a mini-skirt and leather ankle boots and a chunky bob and black tights and lots of friendship bracelets and startling blue eyes and thick eyeliner and bright red lips and a smile as wide as the Brooklyn Bridge and perfect perfect teeth. A shiny, interesting gorgeous girl, whose very proximity to Teddy is making him blush. The sister of one of the boys, she is the singer they've been looking for. Teddy harmonizes with her, and revels in the little smile presents she gives him throughout the song.

Teddy plays lead guitar, and Rosie is surprised by his confidence and ability. He is properly good. He even has a bit of the necessary swagger like his idol, Jim Morrison, if Jim Morrison had ever been a preppy boy. The sound is loud and full, they are all accomplished, and Rosie sits back to listen to beautiful live music in the Wilder-Bingham library, the first room she ever entered here.

Oh, please let that girl like Teddy, and please let Teddy have the chops to show her who he really is, Rosie thinks. Thomas is humming along and smiles at Rosie, glad that at least the Teddy part of his family is working. Hell yes, The Hell No's are bloody marvellous, and Rosie is overwhelmed by the notion that there is strongly beating life in the very heart of this home, and that means real hope for the chance to fix it. Yep, they might just cope . . .

This is further confirmed when she notices the door opens and Kemble peeps in. Is he an unwelcome interloper? He's always wary of what kind of reception Teddy might give him. Deservedly so. But on this occasion, Teddy is so swept up in the music he forgets to frown, and so it seems that Kemble is received in with no problem. He takes his time, as always, to inch his way into the room, but the music itself is the magnet, along with his fathomless pride in his eldest boy. Look at how assured and content Teddy is! What Kemble wouldn't give for a tenth of that kind of happy. How grateful he feels to be part of such a beautiful boy.

Beckoned eagerly by his father, he slides in next to Rosie on the sofa, the three of them strangely connected, sitting in a row, being the audience and loving it all.

Solo

It's two p.m., and Thomas Wilder-Bingham is sitting still in his study. He did a morning's work at his downtown office, but he was restless and tired, so has come home. His daily texts to Glenn are going unanswered. It's been months now. He doesn't even know where she is, not really. He knows she is in SoHo somewhere. He knows she is basically alright. He knows this via Iva, who is regularly delivering Glenn's mail to her but who has sworn to keep the address to herself, as has Kemble. Thomas has decided to strictly adhere to all of Glenn's requests, however little he likes it. He knows her well enough to know that she will harbour her fury for some time yet, before she will consent to even the beginnings of reconciliation. She is stubborn about the trivial stuff, she is certainly going to be extra stubborn about this most cataclysmic of crimes. He is the perpetrator. He is guilty. He must take whatever she dishes out, if he truly wants to mend with her. It's OK, he reassures himself, he can wait. He has time.

And then . . . the truth slams home. He doesn't.

He doesn't really have time.

He's old. He doesn't like to think of it, but that's the truth. Unless they can sort this out soon, there will be precious little good healthy time for him to prove his apology to her. And anyway, what IS his honest apology? The last thing he must do is be fake now, so to be begging for forgiveness for something he just can't truthfully be sorry about would be worse than ever. His regret is for her hurt, not for his slice of delight and certainly not for the consequence, Rosie's pregnancy. Yes, he was selfish, yes, he was greedy, yes, he was secretive, but never for a moment did he consider that his actions would uproot his family or hurt his wife. Maybe that is in fact his greatest offence, being dumb. Even so, finding some light in his darkness was, for him, life-saving. It wasn't until Rosie shone a warm beam into his murkiest shadows did Thomas realize just how gloomy he was. On that day, the day of Bill Sharpe's funeral, Thomas confronted his dread of the quickening of time, and realized that he must live the rest of his life with meaning and with joy. He really should have told Glenn this, but how? That in itself would have been hurtful, to tell her just how sad he was, she would have doubtless taken it personally. OR worse, and more likely, she would have rejected it all as utter nonsense. Glenn lives in a world where rejection is the norm. She rejects life. Regularly. Thomas has come to accept her rejection in many ways. While he has regarded it as part of her own protection, and part of her personality, there's no doubt that the sharp spikes of her constant rebuffs, however dexterous or smart they might be, have punctured him on so many occasions. He has been stung so often, the toxins have overwhelmed his system. Maybe her stings are now actually killing her. Is the Queen Bee alone in the hive, dying? On many *more* occasions he has had to witness the same shards tear into others, as a thousand unkindnesses. Only her grandchildren are spared the pepper of her. Everyone else has been stung at one time or another, and he finds her hard to defend.

He sits in his chair with all of this tossing around in his head, like loose furniture in an upturned boat. On his bookcase there are various photos, including one in particular of the young Glenn on their Kodachrome honeymoon in 1956, in a lifeguard-red bathing suit, smiling brightly at him as he takes the photo of his Beauty. He knows in his gut, for sure, that smile was real and warm and just for him, because he remembers the love they made together in the dunes just minutes before he took it. She loves him so completely in this photo, she has given herself to him so willingly and he has breathed her in, every last stunning gasp of her.

And she had wanted him. When was the last time this was really true? More years ago than he can bear to remember. They've done a whole life together, and made all these other lives along the way. Has their love trickled away all the while so imperceptibly slowly that he hasn't noticed the river ran dry while he's still trying to swim in it? Are they just beached? Is that why he has made it alright in his head to gulp Rosie down? Was he parched? Has she helped to keep him alive?

Then, his eye catches the tiny frame which contains the stubs of two tickets for Ella Fitzgerald's concert at Carnegie Hall in 1991. It was his birthday present from Glenn that year, a chance to see his favourite singer perform for the final time. Unforgettable. Even now he could feel sad about that last encore. He wept all the way home that night, and Glenn comforted him and teased him, calling him a 'soft and silly fellow', and all the while she had her arm through his, and he loved it, crying extra tears purposely to get extra squeezes. This was the Glenn who knew him so well. His Glenn.

Thomas walks over to the easel. He has been painstakingly adding brushstrokes every day to the portrait he's painting. He looks at it up close, to see if the paint is dry, and then he sits further back to better judge if he has captured a true likeness. It's a head and shoulders. Yes, actually, it looks very like her. This is the Glenn of today, but he has softened everything about her face. Especially the eyes. They are more like the young loving happy eyes in the Kodachrome picture. The eyes that explain how very much she loves him. He has painted the strong, caring Glenn he once knew her to be and prays she will be again, if he can reach her.

*

Downtown, Glenn Wilder-Bingham is doing a very good impression of a functioning, coping adult. Unfortunately there's no-one to witness it. However, she is proud of the fact that, should anyone drop by – which of course they most certainly won't – she appears to be perfectly alright thank you. She is up, washed, dressed, hair done, make-up on, neat, tidy, ordered, tidy, neat. She made coffee over an hour ago, and hasn't moved from her seat on the uncomfortable modern sofa since. She isn't reading a book or a magazine or a newspaper. She is sitting as still as a statue, grasping the coffee and staring at the early autumn light pouring in through the crack in the shutters. The shaft that has pierced the dimness of this glum place is mesmerizing. She has watched it creep across the floor as the sun moves, and she sees it glint on every little knot and groove and grain in the dark wood. She notices the dust particles dancing in the beam, but she feels neither fascination at their busy little jig nor annoyance that the dust is there in the first place. She feels nothing. It's as if her emotional batteries have been removed. As if she has taken Valium. She is numb.

When Kemble told her that he pitied her, her lights were finally punched out. Something left her. Asking for anything, especially for help, would be in desperation, *had* been a last resort for this proud woman. She never imagined it would mean nothing if she did have to. Her emergency services have not turned up. Apparently, there *is* no cavalry unless you pay for it. This is a total shock to her. She has always believed that family are tight, that they would come through for her if needed, fiery hot and ready for action. She has forgotten that if you don't stoke the fire, it goes out.

So Glenn sits here, suspended in time, wondering if she matters.

Thomas has been making efforts to contact her, but even he is trying less and less. He has overlooked her, hasn't he, and by so doing, he has robbed her of her power. She is not on her perch any longer. Initially, she thought that moving into this little apartment might give her a lofty position from which to direct operations at a distance. But it would seem that nobody whatsoever is actually missing her. Has removing herself backfired? No homage is being paid, no grovelling done, no abject apologies made. If only she could have some of that, even a little bit, from anyone, she might use it as a foundation upon which to build her pride back up again. It's impossible to grant forgiveness if no-one will even turn up. You can't get an emotional purchase on a no-show.

Glenn realizes, in a very deep place somewhere near her locked heart, that everything she knows how to do inevitably has to change. It's simply not working. She has ground to a halt. She has no idea how to be anymore.

In the meantime, she will sit here, studying the floor and trying not to scream. She will twirl the expensive rings on her liver-spotted thin old twiglet fingers and watch if the light catches fire in the diamonds. She will wait to see if she can feel anything about even that, whether beauty itself can still move her. She will sit and be, as precious time ticks by. Only her skin is holding her together. All else inside is jelly and air.

Little does Glenn Wilder-Bingham know, but the cavalry *has* arrived and is standing on the street outside, looking up at her window. Rosie Kitto so wants to ring the doorbell of the fourth floor apartment. She very nearly does, but she finally decides against it, not her business, and she walks away, leaving the jelly woman very wobbly, very alone, and very stuck.

Deal

Natalie opens the door to her house to find Kemble on the doorstep, clean shaven and well put together in his work suit.

She is wary, 'Oh. Hi. The boys are at school . . .'

'I didn't come to see them, that's Saturday, I came to see you. It's over, Nat. The boys stay with you,' and with that, he hands her a big envelope of official papers. She takes them, and with her jaw slightly dropped, she pulls out the papers and checks through them.

She stifles a low-down sob of relief, and says, 'I'm sorry it had to be like this. Truly.'

'Don't be. It's my fault.'

Natalie smiles a sad smile, and Kemble does too. He looks up the road, to avoid her seeing the brimming water in his eyes.

He says, 'I was angry that you wanted out. But I know it was impossible for you to stay. Once you knew . . . of course you knew, because you know me better than anyone. Better than I know myself.'

Natalie reaches out and touches Kemble's arm. Kemble has missed this touch, and he slightly sinks into it.

He says, 'Thanks for keeping schtum. I will find a way to tell the boys, I need to explain . . .'

'Yes. You do. And they will get it. Y'know, Kem, I always thought we were strong,' she says, and withdraws her hand. Kemble wishes it could stay there forever.

'Me too. But it was only you who was strong.' He can't say any more. He takes her hand, brushes it against his cheek, and kisses it. Kemble is saying goodbye. They stand like this for a moment.

'Does Glenn know about this?' Natalie asks, tentatively, indicating the papers.

'I told her. And Nat, I'm transferring to the Paris office in the New Year. I'll be here for . . . y'know . . . the baby's birth . . . but then . . .'

Natalie is concerned, puzzled.

Kemble continues, 'I've rented an apartment in the Marais. It's only for a couple of years. There's plenty of room for the boys when they visit, which I would like to be a lot. All three of them, and you could come too. Why not? You are what I know about France.'

Natalie says, 'It's a long way from home. And your mother . . .'

'Exactly. Maybe I can honestly be who I should be there . . . I hope.'

Natalie smiles and Kemble sees that she thinks this could be a good move. He loves to see her smile, it's been a while. And he loves to be the reason she is smiling. He loves her face. He loves her. He loves that she is such an honourable person and such a good mother. He feels so much less than her.

'Do you want to come in?' she asks.

Kemble looks past her into the house, his old life. In some ways, it's where he most wants to be, but it's not his life anymore, so he shakes his head.

Five minutes later, Kemble rounds the corner from his beloved old home and heads into what was his favourite haunt, the best coffee shop in Brooklyn. Just as he puts his hand on the door, he hears a voice behind him.

'Dad,' Teddy puffs.

'Hey,' says Kemble.

'Mom told me what just happened . . .'

'Want coffee?'

'No . . .'

'Sorry. I forgot, you hate coffee. Want juice?'

And with that small remembering, Teddy starts to feel unforgotten and a little bit known again by his father. 'Yeh, OK,' and they go in together and sit by the window on bench seats with a formica table between them.

'So you're sneakin off again, then?' Teddy says, aware that his question is loaded.

'I'm not sneakin' anywhere, Ted, it's a great opportunity and I'd be a fool not to take it.'

'But you've got kids. Who live here.'

'Yes. Kids. Who I need to support, so I need to work, and the best work for me currently is in Europe. They value my skills there Teds. Did you know I have skills? I'm a half-decent lawyer. Look, I fucked up here. I need to get out from under your granpop's wing. Move. Start again. It's *Paris,* Ted, you'll love it. There'll be a room for you. The Marais. Where you always ask to go, to get that peasanty-sausage thing you love in that bistro . . . ?'

'Brasserie Ma Bourgogne. It's Beaujolais Sausage. I thought it made me drunk.'

'Haha yes. How old were you?'

'Dunno, maybe eight? Like the boys are now . . .'

'Yeh. And the owner let you have cherry liqueur.'

'Mmm, my introduction to serious drinking.'

'Those Frogs. They love their booze and their food and their kids.'

'Look at Mom.'

'Yes, Ted, look at her. Beautiful. Mom's family will be a ten minute walk from me. It's only for two years. You'll come. A lot, I hope, and you'll bring the twins. Or sometimes not, you'll come on your own. Or . . . maybe . . . bring your girlfriend . . . ?'

Teddy snaps a look at his dad, 'What girlfriend? What do you mean? Who do you mean?!'

'Cool it, son. I mean, whichever girlfriend you might want to bring. Whatever. Whoever, that's all. Hey, you're a tad touchy. Is there someone I should know about . . . ?' Kemble smiles at him.

'No,' Teddy shuts it down pronto, he wishes no further discussion on that topic.

'OK, OK. I get it.'

A pause.

'I think you've been a total shit to Mom,' Teddy braves it.

'OK.' Kemble concedes quietly.

'In fact, for me, Dad, you ratsuck sweaty fat ass balls . . .'

Kemble is dumbstruck 'How did you know?'

'Eh?'

'Well . . . because I kinda do . . . Teds . . . that's part of the problem . . .'

'What the fuck are you saying?'

'Well. I didn't quite imagine telling you like this. And I don't really have anything definite to say. All I know is that, for a long time now . . . I kinda . . . don't want women.'

'What? Sorry, I don't get it. What about Mom? What about *Rosie*?'

'Teds, I love your mom. Always have, always will. And as for Rosie, I've been asking myself that. I think it was like a . . . umm . . . a last try. In case I was wrong. I wanted to be wrong. Because, believe me, this isn't the easiest thing to own. It's not who I've been. Or maybe it is who I've been, but not been able

303

to be . . . sorry . . . not making much sense . . . not the easiest thing to understand, or to tell your granma . . . or anyone . . . or *you*.'

Teddy is completely stunned. He sits looking at the man who used to be his dad until two minutes ago. Now, who is he?

Teddy says, 'So . . . you're gay . . . ?'

At which point, the ultra camp waiter who is placing their drinks in front of them, says to Teddy,

'Honey, we're all a little bit gay. Deal with it. And snaps for you, handsome . . .' He clicks his fingers like applause, 'You're totes adorbs. And yes please, I would like a big tip . . . if you get me. Ha ha ha,' and off he flounces.

Kemble and Teddy are stunned. Kemble breaks the silence when he says, 'I'm not that gay,' and both of them laugh together, comfortably.

'Oh my God, Dad, does Mom know?'

'Yes. She kind of told *me*, actually. She knew things weren't right. I was drifting and not wanting to think about it, and boozing so that I didn't . . .'

'Yeh, we saw that part'

'Yeh, sorry. I didn't want it to be true. But in the end . . .'

'Is there . . . someone?'

'Didn't I just ask you that?' says Kemble, smiling, 'No. There isn't. Yet. If ever. I don't know how to be . . . this. I'm a learner, Teds.'

'Me too,' says Teddy.

They sit and drink and think.

Teddy is the first to speak. 'It's weird, but y'know what, it's OK. It's really OK. In fact it's kind of easier, because stuff sort of makes sense. I thought you . . . hated Mom or something, or us, or me. I thought it might be me . . .'

'Christ, Teds. No. It's not you, son. It's me. All the difficult stuff is always me. Ask your granma!'

'Shit, does she know?!' Teddy can't imagine that scenario.

'Nope. Might not . . . bother . . . with that.'

'Do it Dad. Butch up. Granpop will be OK and he'll handle her. Tell her. Don't be a wuss.'

Kemble looks into the eyes of his lovely boy, who speaks the truth. 'Maybe. Let's see. It's tempting to just run and keep running from that one . . .'

'I don't think you're running away this time though, Dad. You're running towards something, aren't you?'

'Yes, Teds. That's right. So right.'

'Got to hand it to ya. You've got balls,' says Teddy.

A pause.

'Are mine ratsuck sweaty fat ass ones?' says Kemble.

Teddy smiles. 'Yep. Sorry 'bout that.'

'No prob, man, no prob. Listen, Teds, here's the thing. If you seriously don't think I should go to Paris, I won't. Just like that. I won't. It's your choice. I mean it. You decide, and I will go with whatever you say.'

'Really?' Teddy is suspicious.

'Really.' Kemble means it.

Teddy takes a minute to think. He relishes having the power. For the first time in a long time, Kemble has made a clever decision.

'Yes,' says Teddy, at last. 'You should go, the temptation of that French sausage is too great.'

They both simultaneously hear properly what Teddy has just said . . . and then they convulse with laughter. Kemble attempts to be heard through his mangled snorts, 'Thanks for that, son. You got it in one! Ha Ha ha . . .'

Everyone in the diner notices the father and son doubling up in helpless laughter at the table by the window. The father and son who clearly adore each other.

As the laughter subsides a bit, Kemble speaks through his happy tears, 'Help me to tell the twins?'

Teddy nods.

Mary Mary

As the year wanes so the roof garden grows and changes, and the same goes for everyone visiting it. High up and part of the Manhattan skyline, and now part of their lives, each person who lives in the Wilder-Bingham apartment uses it in different ways.

Rosie is often up here alone, tending the various beds, reading or dancing with her earphones on. She has much more solitary time now the twins live back at home. She tries to take the time to read her gardening books whilst she is actually sitting in the garden, so that she can judge what needs to happen next in terms of planting, and so that she can identify the weeds from the plants and so on. Sometimes, she is overwhelmed by just how giant a subject gardening is, and by all the differing advice she reads. When this happens she lies down under a thick blanket and spreads herself out like a beached starfish. As she stretches, she breathes deep and looks up into the clouds. When she is flat like this, she can see the sky with no interruption, and she can dream. She is increasingly aware of her swelling belly and the unfamiliar little movements she can feel inside. Her daydreams are full of the baby and everything about it, and while she daydreams she invariably floats off into sleep. Her conscious thinking mingles with her dreams, and the garden nurtures all of it. When she rouses from these treacley pregnant-lady-naps she wakes to the hints of autumn roses and lavender all around her. Sometimes, for a fleeting hazy few moments, she thinks she's home.

The twins often come up here too. Sometimes with Natalie, sometimes without. They are changing as well, so quickly that Rosie is convinced that if they stood stock still for fifteen minutes, and she watched only them, she would witness them growing in front of her very eyes. She would hear bones stretching, and see skin expanding, and feel their hair growing thicker and longer in her hands. Mini Hulks. They love to cultivate the areas they planted or made. Three tops up the water in the bowl inside his Noguchi pebble circle, and Red prunes and weeds around his herbs. While Rosie watches them concentrating on the garden, it occurs to her that Glenn, still in sad purdah, is missing out on so much. If the stalemate doesn't end soon, she may not recognize her grandsons by Christmas.

Even Kemble visits the roof garden, usually with the boys, but sometimes on his own, to check on his watercress. Occasionally, he cuts a bunch and puts it straight into his mouth, crunching away while he looks out over the city and makes muffled eating phone calls arranging his move to Europe. He sat here with Natalie one evening while the boys were busy weeding with Rosie, and they sat in deck chairs, side by side, and they held hands like good friends. No war. And the boys saw it, and they loved it.

Iva was supposed to go home for a three-week holiday but Rosie persuaded Thomas to let her go for two months' paid compassionate leave if she promised to cover for her, so the apartment is messy, and windows and doors are wide open and cushions are unplumped and dishes are out of place ... but no-one really cares. They are all spending more time up here on the roof anyway, so it doesn't matter.

Teddy has brought the shiny girl up here and made her a persuasive Mojiteddy using the fresh mint. He lives in hope it may have the same disinhibiting effect on her that it did on Rosie, but so far, they are still just friendly. He wonders how much she likes him, but he doesn't let his doubt stop him from asking her up here again, and he makes sure the fairy lights are always on for her, and tea lights twinkle around where he invites her to sit. Rosie promises him the shiny girl will like that. He wants her to feel safe with him. He waits and wonders. Her name is Izzy.

Thomas brings his guitar up here, and practises in the nippy open air. He can nearly do a nearly passable rendition of

'Johnny B.Goode' now. It's competent enough to play to the others without feeling too embarrassed, so he has, and they have all clapped and cheered. Which is fine . . .

BUT.

Really, he wants Glenn to hear it. She is the one whose approval matters the most. She is who matters the most. She. Who is gone. Where is she? Months and months have passed by. He still sends her texts each week. Polite enquiries as to her wellbeing, and gentle reminders that he cares. Nothing too pushy, nothing too passionate. He doesn't want to scare her off. Well, look, he's already done that. He doesn't want to give her reason to stay away. He wants her forgiveness, but only when she is ready, otherwise it won't be real and it won't last.

He sits on the roof and rehearses the things he will say if he gets the chance. He doesn't want to get it wrong. He wants to be able to tell the truth, and for her to know that's what it is. He can't retract what he's done, both of them will have to accept it and find a new way to be if they've got a hope in hell. What he knows for sure is that he'd like a chance at that. Nothing is quite right without her. He's not right without her. At first, he thought it was just habit, that missing her was like missing anything that happens daily.

Like missing coffee.

But that's just it.

That's the small stuff.

And it's always the small stuff that makes the big. She is

both. She is all the small stuff, the everyday, the familiar, the ordinary, the usual. But all those seemingly trivial regular things make up a whole big beating heart of a life. And it's a life he wants. Not exactly like it was, that won't ever quite work anymore, but a better, kinder life, with Glenn in it, at the centre, as the loving woman he first married, the person he trusts she really is, somewhere in there. He believes it, and he wants it so much that he has written it all down in a letter to her.

Since Iva is away, Rosie has agreed to deliver the stack of mail that has grown considerably over the passing few weeks to Glenn's address. She intends to push it through the door and leave. Thomas hands Rosie his letter to add to it. It's already autumn, and he doesn't want Winter to arrive without Glenn knowing what's in his heart.

Ice and Water

I t's mid-afternoon, and Rosie stands by the entrance to Glenn's building. There is the mailbox. In her hand is the bundle of mail from the apartment. On the very top is Thomas's letter. It would be simple to drop them off and go, but she is rooted to the spot. She left here once before, and regretted it. Something in her knows she is inevitably going to ring the buzzer, so come on, Rosie, do it. She stalls, looks longingly back up the street to where everything is easier than here. She imagines being in a cab and back at the apartment, tucked up nice and cosy in her room, eating a Krispy Kreme doughnut and watching reruns of *Judge Judy*, just being Rosie. Instead, she's the other part of her, she's the Rosie who is pregnant by someone in this woman's family, and whose last experience of Glenn was awful for both of them.

Has she the courage to ring the bell?

Has she?

Come on, Rosie.

Remember how you promised yourself you'd live?

YES.

Rosie reaches for the buzzer marked 'G. Wilder-B', Fourth Floor.

She presses it. She wants to run, like a naughty kid up to mischief. But her feet are set in moral concrete and she remains, her heart beating, her breath shallow. 'Please don't be in,' she thinks. That would give her a legitimate reason to scuttle away, if she could know she tried. Please. Please.

'Yes?' comes Glenn's brittle voice, further thinned by the intercom. Rosie leans into the microphone on the wall panel,

'It's Rosie.'

Silence.

'May I come up?' says Rosie.

Silence.

The door release buzzer sounds. Rosie pushes the huge metal door open and goes in and up the four flights, puffing all the way as she carries the extra weight. When she gets to Glenn's front door, she finds it open already, so steps inside and closes the door behind her. Rosie is surprised by the modern loft and how stark it is. It's hard to place Glenn in this environment. Yet, here she is.

She is standing in the middle of the large room with the shutters closed and only one standard lamp illuminating the space, along with the odd rogue shaft of light that bursts through the ill-fitting shutters. Unlike her very first meeting with Glenn, Rosie resists the urge to break the tension with a wisecrack, but she is certainly thinking vampire-related thoughts she has to suppress. Glenn's pale appearance doesn't help.

As Rosie's eyes adjust to the light she sees Glenn properly, and is shocked by how much weight her old adversary has lost in these few months. Already a thin woman, Glenn has dwindled to a whisper of a person, on the verge of emaciation. Her face is a skeleton version of the one Rosie knows, and her smart clothes hang loosely from her shoulders and scraggy neck. Glenn's eyes are latched on to Rosie's and they are haunted. Rosie has not seen this look on Glenn's face ever before. Perhaps because of how drawn her sunken features are, her eyes bulge and seem to plead. The two women take each other in.

The blossoming, fecund, shiny-haired, younger Rosie, full of new life, cheerful in her ever-tightening bright green coat and red brogues. The very epitome of abundant kindness and mischief. The perpetrator.

The shrunken, withering, expensively highlighted steel-grey-haired much-older Glenn, eaten away by stubbornness and her own acerbic innards. Head to toe cashmere and pearls. The very epitome of suppressed fury and pitiful tragedy. The victim.

Glenn speaks first, 'Don't think for a breath that I forgive you. I don't. You are an assassin,' she says in hushed tones.

'Please, Glenn, stop right there. I am not available for your bullying any more, so don't even bother. Seriously.'

'You are living in my home, with my men. I am . . . here.'

'Yes. So it would seem. And this is your choice. Everyone wants you back up there.'

'Everyone? What do you know of "everyone"? Who are you?'

'I am no-one of any consequence.'

'Do let me spare you the burden of your martyrdom, dear. Believe me, you are all consequence. Look at you,' she indicates Rosie's sizeable tum.

Rosie feels hugely defensive, and decides, on behalf of precisely what's contained there, that it might be best to retreat from the angry viper as soon as possible, and to regard this as a valiant try that failed. 'Here is your post. And there's a letter from Thomas . . .' She hands the pile to Glenn.

'Mr Wilder-Bingham' says Glenn, but Rosie has no time for this nonsense . . .

'Thomas,' she repeats emphatically, and backs carefully towards the door, mindful of the last time she and Glenn 'had words' and how physical it all became.

'That name is not for your lips . . .' spits Glenn.

'OK, OK. Let's just leave it there . . .' Rosie turns to go.

Then, she hears a flumph behind her. For the tiniest moment she considers not looking back, but of course she does.

Glenn has collapsed on the floor.

'Oh my god!' Rosie exclaims, and rushes toward her.

'Get away from me! Go on! Get out!' Glenn shouts at her, flicking her spindly arm.

The letters are scattered all around her on the floor, and Glenn has fallen straight down like a factory chimney, folding inwards on herself, into a neat pile of beige designer clothing containing a crumpled sliver of a woman. The wicked witch of the East Side.

Glenn looks up at Rosie, her woeful face full of shame and humiliation. 'Leave me!' she cries.

'Shut up, Glenn, put your arm around my neck, come on,' says Rosie as she gathers the tiny weak body into her arms. Rosie doesn't even stop to consider that she shouldn't really be lifting like this in her condition. It doesn't matter in the least, because there's nothing *to* Glenn. It's as if Rosie is carrying a pile of sticks, she is so light. Only now does Rosie realize just how seriously shriveled Glenn is. She's hardly there.

Rosie places the handful of bones that are Glenn Wilder-Bingham on the uncomfortable sofa, and props her up with the hideous red cushions. 'Are you hurt?' says Rosie, already feeling very carefully along the length of all her limbs to see if there are any breaks. It's intimate, but Rosie doesn't care, she needs to check.

'Stop it,' Glenn says weakly, but Rosie knows that what she's really saying is 'Don't stop it.' Rosie pushes on and gently presses and touches every part of Glenn's body, growing increasingly worried at how little there is of it. She opens the top of her blouse, and she removes Glenn's shoes, then when she's sure there are no breaks or cuts, she drapes a throw over her, and feels her forehead for a temperature. Nothing is out of the ordinary there. Rosie goes into the kitchen, reaches onto a shelf for a glass tumbler, and opens the fridge. To find there, exactly what she is looking for. A large bottle of good water . . . And only that.

There is nothing else in the fridge.

Rosie opens all the cupboards and doors to see where Glenn's food is. There is none. Rosie pours a glass of water and brings it back to the spectre on the couch, who sips it with her eyes closed. She can't bear to look at Rosie, and she can't bear to be looked at.

'What's going on, Glenn?' says Rosie.

Glenn doesn't answer and keeps her eyes tightly shut. Rosie persists, 'Please talk to me.'

Still nothing. Glenn pretends Rosie is simply not there, she utterly ignores her.

'I'm not leaving this spot until you talk to me and I can be sure you are OK. Do you hear me?' says Rosie.

With that, they sit in silence, Glenn feet up on the couch, Rosie opposite in the awful modern armchair.

They sit.

They sit.

While minutes and hours tick by, while the autumn light outside begins to fade, while the radiators tick. Glenn occasionally sips her water, until it's gone, but otherwise they just sit.

317

Eventually, the light has gone completely and the room turns cold. It's been about three hours. Rosie is astounded by Glenn's tenacity, and stubbornness. She is a peeved child living in the body of a seventy-eight-year-old, getting colder by the minute. Rosie realizes that Glenn is prepared to die of hypothermia to prove a point.

Rosie is not, so she breaks the big heavy silence, 'Where is the switch for the heating?'

'In the service room,' Glenn croaks, her voice dry after so long dumb.

Rosie gets up and searches around for the service room. When she finds it, she turns the heating on, and hears the boiler roar into life. She takes a deep breath and heads back to resume the sulk-off. This could be a long night.

Rosie sits back down in the same chair, and settles.

Suddenly, Glenn speaks, 'This is the most company I've had in weeks,' she says.

Rosie goes to speak, but Glenn quietens her. 'Shhh. Listen. I didn't mind at first. I liked it. No effort required. It was what I always look for, just me, no clatter, no people. And I waited. Of course he sent texts. Daily to begin with. How are you? I am here. That sort of thing. Polite. Then it was weekly. Now not so much . . .'

'He doesn't want to push it . . .' Rosie starts to say, but Glenn hushes her again,

'Just . . . hark . . . !'

Rosie sits back, admonished and startled by how old fashioned Glenn is. It's a reminder of a bygone era.

'I am still waiting. Waiting to hear anything that makes it possible to go back. I am waiting for an apology. I fear I may wait forever. Meanwhile, I will endure these endless goddam hours, and I will remember how this came to be. How it was that I married him because everyone said how good we were together, and because for the first time there was a good kind man who seemed to care. He saw something in me. I thought he was faking it. Because there was nothing to see. Not pretty enough. Not clever enough. Not remarkable in any way. Merely suitable. Even as early on as our honeymoon I realized that he is not the fake, I am. He is someone. Big and handsome. Loves life. Squeezes out every last drop. Loves it. Knows how to love. He is the one. I am only attached to him. No other purpose. Oh yes, I made a son, but nothing else. My parents had a marriage like that, got bored and in the end, they just about tolerated each other. I expected the same. Get bored with him, tolerate him.

But I couldn't, because I wanted Thomas, wanted him always. I love him, but I have nothing to offer and that nothing gets less and less as the years eat me up. I knew he tired of me ages ago. Because even I tired of me. I have realized these last few months sitting here in this god-awful loft that I am a disappointment with no purpose whatsoever, a pathetic creature who believes that being loyal is the right reason to be alive.

Loyal and ornery. That's me. Sounds like an excellent firm of solicitors. Loyalty means nothing now. I was at least part of someone else. I'm not anymore. So, I'm not really even here. I am disappearing. Which, frankly, would make it much simpler for everyone. Fact. There.'

Rosie looks at Glenn in the half light and realizes that this is no idle threat. Glenn has clearly made a decision to starve herself. To death. Her unworthiness is in charge, instructing her to destroy herself. Whatever the face was that Glenn is used to gluing on to her real one has crumbled off, plaster-like, entirely, and this is at last the real Glenn, the unpalatable Glenn that Glenn herself cannot abide. So much so, that she would rather not exist.

For Rosie, this is a precious opportunity and one she doesn't want to get wrong. She wants to reach inside Glenn and touch the right places, but it may be too late.

'Did you know,' starts Rosie, praying that she will say something that might resonate, 'that it is possible, in life, to change your mind? I only say this because I know it to be true. You can decide, for instance, to come in out of the rain. You can decide to call pain, fear instead. To call broken, unmended. To call anger, force. You can be different if you really want to, believe me, you can release yourself from these bloody awful terrors. In fact I am amazed that someone as powerful as you has allowed yourself to be so directed by them. What's going on there? Why are you not noticing what properly matters? What matters, Miss Glenn, is the innocent, is those three boys. Is Teddy. Is Red. Is Three. The ones who look up to you, who accept you. Who, yep let's bloody just say it, who love you. And I know that they really do. They look so much for your approval, your support. Who the hell are you to withhold it? If you just . . . disappear, they will all wonder if they weren't good enough for you to stay. You couldn't do that to them, could you? Let them feel like no-one cares? You surely couldn't inflict on them the same shitty stuff you feel about yourself? Could you? And Glenn, what about if you turned it all around, and *you* did some of the apologizing? What about that?!'

Glenn turns to look at her. Rosie fears she has gone too far. After all, it's probably Rosie who should be apologizing for all the upset she's caused, but she decides to finish what she has to say,

'Just for once, Glenn, please say yes instead of no. There.'

In this moment, at the mention of her grandchildren, something happens inside the older woman. It's as if Rosie is the water poured onto the ice that is Glenn. There is an initial shock, but the thawing is immediate. Rosie senses it, and carries on, 'Y'know, Glenn, it's weird but we have a lot in common, you and I, and I never thought I would ever say that. We are both a bit unknowable, both sort of untold stories. Both quite hidden. Just because I'm loud doesn't mean I'm sure about anything. I'm not. At least I wasn't. I've run away from stuff. And I've hurt people along the way. I know that. But right now, because of this,' she points at her belly, 'I am finally sure of something. I've got my purpose. Thank you, God. Or whoever ... actually ...' Rosie realizes something, 'Thank you, Glenn.'

Rosie reaches out her hand to the frail old woman, who looks at it, but doesn't reciprocate.

She scrutinizies Rosie intensely. 'I reach for him in the night,' Glenn says.

Rose picks up Thomas's letter from the floor, and hands it to her.

'You read it to me' says Glenn.

'Sure?' says Rosie.

'Sure.'

Rosie turns on the overhead light, carefully opens the envelope, and removes the single sheet. Then hesitates.

'Read it' says Glenn, firmly. So Rosie does,

'Wife.

This is husband.

Foolish, ashamed husband.

I am so sorry for hurting you.

I love you.

I don't know how to be without you.

Please please come home.

We need to fix it.'

Glenn listens, and she takes the letter from Rosie and holds it close. Then, silently, Glenn weeps some of the melted ice as hot tears. She covers her wet eyes with her right hand, and she reaches out to Rosie with her left.

'Help me. Don't let him see me like this. Feed me,' says Glenn quietly, through soft sobs.

Rosie gently takes the offered hand.

'I will' says Rosie.

The Date

In a shadowy corner of the appointed swanky downtown hotel Thomas Wilder-Bingham sits, nursing a whisky and fidgeting in his seat. It's five past seven. She is late. That's OK, it's her prerogative. In fact, he should expect it. However much he reassures himself, he is still looking at his watch every thirty seconds to check. He can't remember the last time he was this anxious. He checks his flies. Yep. He checks his shirt isn't gaping over his expanding belly. Yep. He straightens his best maroon tie. He checks he isn't sweating by swiping the napkin that's under his drink, across his forehead. He tries to settle. He can't. He checks his breath into his cupped hand. He hasn't done that since he was a teenager. He's all jitter. Now it's nine minutes past. Where is she? Perhaps this was a bad idea. Maybe she has bottled out?

Just as he starts to seriously doubt the wisdom of this whole enterprise, she appears by the bar and heads straight toward him, twinkling and smiling all the way. He wishes he could halt time and freeze this moment or at least see it in slow motion, so that it could last longer.

In the gorgeous flesh, Nicole Kidman is so much more than he imagined, and what he imagined was pretty stunning. Tall, elegant, alabaster skin, pale red hair, dark red lips, an unequivocal beauty.

'Thomas?' she asks as she approaches him. He can't believe his name is on her luscious lips.

'Indeedy,' he replies, and immediately cringes at how fake and over jocular that sounds. What an idiot.

'Lovely to meet you. Sorry I'm late, it's all a bit hectic . . .' He immediately warms to how friendly and real and Australian she is.

'No. Seriously. No. I don't mind waiting . . . all night if needs be . . .' Shut up, Thomas! How has he managed to sound both needy and reprimanding all at once? Get a grip, man, and be normal, like her. Breathe and be normal, come on!

'And sorry about this ridiculous dress' – indicating the strapless bejewelled sky-blue chiffon floor-length number she's wearing. Typically male, Thomas hasn't even noticed, so beguiled by her is he – 'but I'm just off to the premiere of this film I did last year. That's why I'm in New York. Home again tomorrow . . .'

'Right, yes, home, to . . . Australia?'

'No, I live in Nashville.'

'Tennesee, yee ha!' Thomas can't believe quite how much of

a cretin he's become in the last three minutes. He really must shut the eff up. He decides quickly that the only way to redeem himself is to tell it like it is. So he begins, 'OK Miss Kidman, may I call you Nicole?' She nods. 'Nicole,' he continues, 'first of all, I want to say thank you for agreeing to meet me, I know that George asked you as a favour . . .'

'I love George, and he spoke so highly of you,' she says.

'Well, I did threaten to kill off his entire family unless he made this happen . . .'

At this, Nicole laughs, freely and easily. Thomas can't believe it. He's made Nicole Kidman laugh! Could he love her any more? No, he couldn't.

'But nevertheless,' he goes on, 'it's extremely generous of you, and I just want you to know that I asked for this meeting because, y'see, I'm eighty-three and I have decided to cherry-pick little moments of joy to have, in whatever few years I have left. Some are little things, like wearing bright socks, or dancing a waltz, and some are gigantic things like this, meeting you. And you've made a long-held dream happen. So thank you.'

'Delighted I'm on your bucket list, sir, very flattered,' she says, and she smiles at him. As he sees himself reflected in her eyes, he knows that she regards him as a harmless sweet old man. Not for a moment does she think of him as a charming and smooth lothario, an international playboy and man of mystery. Somewhere in his silly fantasy about her, he thought that might have been a possibility. It isn't. Of course it isn't.

It's better than that. Two strangers are meeting for a fabulous fleeting moment. Just that. Just that.

Then, she says, 'Y'know Thomas, I admire you for eking out every last bit of fun you can have. We're not here for long. I know that. I wish my dad had got to eighty-three.'

'Oh, I'm sorry, I didn't know.'

'No, it's OK, just . . . makes you realize how precious the time is. And how important family is, eh?'

'Yes, indeed,' he says, and knows it. More than ever.

'Well, I have to race, I'm afraid, they have a car waiting for me outside . . .' she says.

'Of course, of course . . .'

'But truthfully, Thomas, I'd rather stay here with you, and shoot the breeze anyday.'

'Bless you,' he says, looking at this beautiful kind woman. She's not exactly begging him to stay, but it's near as, dammit. Job done.

'But just before I go, can I ask to see what socks you're wearing?'

Thomas laughs, and lifts his trouser legs to reveal snazzy bright-purple socks.

'Impressive,' she says, 'keep it up, Thomas, don't lose sight of the good stuff. And . . . in the interest of that bucket list?' He looks puzzled.

'Might I be granted a quick waltz before I go?'

Thomas can't believe his ears so he gets up from his seat,

trying to ignore his achy joints, takes Nicole Kidman in his arms and there, in the bar, they dance a few glorious, unforgettable steps. She kisses him on the cheek, and whispers in his ear, 'Bye,' and then she rushes off towards an impatient-looking PR lady, who is wildly beckoning her at the door. She turns, waves, and she's gone.

He is still waving ten seconds after she is out of sight, and he suddenly realizes that other people are watching this, slack-jawed in amazement, and boy, does he enjoy that.

He sits back down, and smugly polishes off the rest of his whisky, and chuckles to himself. He can't wait to tell Glenn about this.

Ah. Glenn. Yes.

Glenn is his reality. This was the fantasy which he was lucky enough to experience in the flesh, for five crazy minutes. And that's the point, he realizes, all this frivolity is like candy, he can have some occasionally, and he likes it, but Glenn is his bread. He needs her to live. Alone with his truth in the corner of the bar, Thomas Wilder-Bingham is lonelier than ever.

Meanwhile, on the other side of town, Rosie Kitto is feeding Glenn Wilder-Bingham chicken soup. Literally spooning it into her mouth.

And Glenn is allowing it, and every now and then, she says 'thank you' to Rosie.

And Rosie says 'It is alright.'

'It is alright.'

'It is alright.'

And Glenn is beginning to believe her.

Whisky

Later that same night, and gently sozzled, Thomas sits in the messy kitchen back at the apartment, with his grandson Teddy. He is teaching Teddy about the finer points of the best Scotch.

Teddy says, '... but I don't particularly want hairs on my chest, Granpops, seriously ...'

'Come on, Teds, just a wee dram of what they call Wall Street Wine. Won't do you any harm. And we are celebrating, buddy, celebrating the beauty of women, you shoulda seen her Teds. Exquisite. Nothin' like a dame. And if a dame were a drink, she'd be whisky. And in my humble opinion, which ain't all that humble if I'm honest, this, m'boy, is the best of them all. Glenfiddich, single malt, eighteen years old. Same age as you.'

'Not for long. And I have drunk whisky before ...'

'Not like this, you haven't. This is crafted by Scots and angels combined, and you can taste the mountains and the lochs in it, this is whisky with no 'e' Teds. W. H. I. S. K.Y. Scots say the time taken adding the 'e' is time away from drinking the nectar. Here . . .'

Thomas pours an inch of the orangey yellow liquid into a tumbler, and Teddy goes to drink it.

'Nah ah ah,' Thomas quickly intercepts, 'not so quick, Mr Hastypants, first of all, "the eye", – we look at it. Hold it up to the light, and ponder the years it took to brew. It's a sunset. A thousand sunsets. Then, "the nose"– we smell it. Move it around in the glass a bit, we could add a drop of water or an ice cube now to open it up, but, I think, maybe not yet. So put your nose in, and whaddya get?'

They both take a deep sniff, and Teddy can tell from the slight sting in his nose that this is going to bite. He's not sure exactly what he can smell, but he closes his eyes and goes with his instinct.

'Um, I think I smell . . . wood.'

'Yes! Yes, good man. That'll be the oak barrels it's aged in. Can you get a whiff of orchard fruit? Faintly sweet baked apple?'

'Hey, yeh, maybe.' Teddy isn't sure.

'Now, "the palate." Taste it. Just a sip.'

Thomas puts it to his lips first, then Teddy follows suit.

'It's rich, candy peel, and there's the apple again, cheeky fella. Roll it over your tongue before you swallow it, Teds,' says Thomas.

Teddy stifles a wince as the powerful alcohol hits the back

of his throat. He coughs a little bit, but he cannot detect a taste he can describe, which is ironic because in years to come, Teddy will always associate whisky with this moment, so the taste is key. For him, it's entirely sensory though, it's not about actual taste, it's about effect and memory. There is his grandfather, clearly transported to somewhere wonderful through the power of this strange amber spirit. He will remember that.

'And now, Teds, most importantly, "the finish", which is the aftertaste that lingers. For me, this determines the success, how many flavours will reveal themselves? How long do they stay? Do they change as the first flavour decays? What pushes through?'

Teddy stares at Thomas. What the hell is he yabbering on about? All Teds can feel is a ferocious alcoholic burn. He would prefer to call an ambulance than give a flowery analysis.

Thomas is still pontificating, 'And . . . exhale . . . there she blows . . . warm, distinguished, ah yes, a layer of . . . of . . . what? . . . salted toffee.' He breathes out slowly. Thomas is in his own heaven, 'Welcome to the world of whisky, boy. Long may you enjoy it. Here's to women in all their glorious, mysterious complexity.'

They chink their glasses. And sip. It burns Teddy again. Ow. He twiddles his glass in the ensuing silence.

'Pops?' says Teddy.

'Yep' says Thomas

'There's this girl . . .'

'There nearly always is. Are we talking about the cutie in the band?'

'Shit, man! How did you know?' Teddy is astonished, 'Yes, her name is Izzy. I really like her, but y'know, I don't want to . . . rush it. Like with Rosie, y'know . . . so . . . what do I do?'

'Do you think she likes you?' asks Thomas.

'Well, she kinda smiles a lot. How do I know? I've only ever been with . . . well . . . y'know . . .'

'Well, in my experience, if a girl likes you, she usually puts herself in the places where you'll find it impossible not to ask her out. That's what your granma did.'

This jolts Teddy. He has never stopped to think of Glenn as anything other than an old lady. She is always affectionate towards him, in her own prickly way, but he can't imagine her as anyone's object of lust, absolutely not. But Teddy knows that his grandfather is missing her terribly at the moment, being the wise boy he is, so, he shuts up and lets Thomas indulge in an intoxicated ramble.

'Your granma isn't . . . she never used to be like she is.'

Teddy takes a bigger sip of whisky. OW.

Thomas carries on, 'She used to be . . . so shy when I first knew her. The slightest thing would make her blush. Just like you.'

On cue, Teddy blushes, at his grandfather's uncanny insight, at its accuracy, concerning him. But this stuff about Glenn is a revelation.

333

'She finds the world hard, Teds, bit like you. I think that's why she has a soft spot for you. She can see under your skin.'

'No way. Yeh. Can she?' says Teddy, as he blushes again. He loves hearing that he and Glenn have something in common. He loves belonging.

'Yeh, she can. She's the person who would give you the low-down on Izzy, she's eagle-eyed when it comes to people.'

'But she's so . . . scary.'

'Not really, Teds, that's just the face she puts on to deal with our big difficult world. She's soft on the inside y'know. She used to . . . laugh and stroke my hair, and sing me to sleep sometimes.'

'Granma did?!'

'Yep. She did. I think it might be my fault that she changed so much. I let her down. She became Mrs Thomas Wilder-Bing-ham. Only. Glenn, the woman I married, a person in her own sweet right, just disappeared slowly, sorta . . . wilted, as the years passed. And I let that happen. I made way for it. Because it was my fault. And then along came Rosie . . .'

'You don't have to tell me that . . .' says Teddy, worried.

'No, I'm just saying we can all mess up, Teds, and I'm no exception. Seriously. Don't get me wrong, I loved that you looked up to me when you were a little guy, but now hey, you're a big tall man. Look across at me instead. We're the same, Teds, made of the same stuff. BUT. Listen, take my advice, don't try to be like me. Be you. Honestly, believe me, you are

334

SO worth being. You are really something. It's so clear. So clear.'

The burbling Thomas has another sip of whisky.

So does Teddy. Ow.

'Sorry, Pops, but you can't stop me admiring you. I just do and that's that. Deal with it.'

Thomas laughs at his grandson's chutzpah. How he loves this boy. He leans towards Teddy. 'Listen up chum. Let yourself off the hook with Rosie, OK? She doesn't want you feeling so responsible, neither do I, neither does anyone. We're all gonna look after her, you don't have to be the one, OK? You don't have to set fire to yourself to keep her warm. Seriously, Teds, go to college, kiss Izzy and be eighteen. Let the ol' man pick up the slack, yeh? Do me that favour eh? Be part of it, of course, but no heroics necessary. I know you. You'd sacrifice it all. And you mustn't, I mean it. Promise me.'

Teddy gets up and goes to his beloved grandfather, and they fall into a big boy bear hug with lots of back-slapping to make it more palatable for both of them. When they pull apart, Thomas pours more whisky into their glasses, much to Teddy's dismay,

He raises his glass. 'To Glenn Wilder-Bingham, the finest woman in Manhattan, wherever she may be. And may she come home soon . . .' They chink again, and Thomas takes a gulp this time, 'God that's delicious, Teds, isn't it? Robust, with a soft underbelly. Just like Glennie . . .'

335

Teddy sees the glisten in Thomas's eye, and decides to rescue the moment,

'Hey. Get your guitar. Let's slaughter the Beatles til they beg for mercy . . .'

Guggenheim

Rosie huffs and puffs to the corner of Fifth Avenue and East 89th St, trying to keep up with the fizzy twins. She moves at half the speed she used to, and the boys have little patience with her. They are excited about the arrival of the new baby, but they just can't believe how long it is taking to cook. Rosie has to draw pictures for them of exactly how it is developing inside her, and they are fascinated and disgusted in equal measure. As the winter creeps on, Rosie has to lay two A4-sized pieces of paper together on the floor, to be able to draw the outline of the actual size of the growing fetus. It's now about 17 inches long, and for the first time, it's too big to fit on one page. On their visits to 90th St, the twins are obsessed with knowing when it's eyes might open, or when it might be able to hear, and since both of those things are happening around now, they play music, they clap, they sing, they shine bright torches on to her bare belly and they tell the unborn baby,

'Don't worry, you won't be stuck in there for long!' and

'Someone's comin' to getcha dude, hang on in there!' They don't like how her navel sticks out, they refer to it as, 'Like, totally gross,' and they tease her about how often she has to stop for a pee. They call her the 'The Tap'. Her ankles and hands are fairly swollen and she finds herself tired and breathless whilst she transports the extra pounds around, and she can't believe that she actually waddles. Like a penguin.

Today is another adventure though, and she has brought them here to the Guggenheim Museum for the first time, she knows they will love it. As they enter, they have to undergo a security search, so the boys offer up their brightly coloured backpacks and Rosie willingly opens her big red handbag for the guard to furtle around in.

Unsure of exactly what exhibition is on currently, Rosie ushers the boys into the main hall of the phenomenal building. The outside is already a hit with Red and Three, since they consider it to look like either 'a giant spacecraft' or 'a huge curly white helmet that would fit on a massive zoid', so she knows she's on to a winner. These are the moments that make living in New York the dream she hoped it would be, stepping out into the vast, open space of the central atrium of the building. The atmosphere is nothing they have ever experienced before. Lofty and light.

Rosie wonders if Lennon and Yoko ever came to see anything here? Surely they must have . . . ?

The boys whisper, 'Wow' and 'Awesome', as they tilt their

heads up to see the sky through the big skylight, which has struts crossing it, giving it the appearance of a glass cobweb.

Rosie seizes the moment to explore their initial reactions.

'Guys, tell me the words that are popping up in your heads right now . . . ?'

Three: 'Big. White. Wheel.'

Red: 'Shell. Window. Sunshine.'

'Fantastic,' says Rosie, 'all those words are so . . . right.'

All three of them become aware of a small repetitive sound, so they seek out the source. Over to the side, there is a table, and two people, a young man and woman sit with a microphone between them, reading out a series of numbers in sequence,'

'Twelve thousand, four hundred and twenty two . . .' she says

'Twelve thousand, four hundred and twenty three . . .' he says, and on they go.

'What are they doing? asks Red.

'It must be part of the exhibition. Oh yes, look, it's written here,' Rosie looks at the leaflet she was given on her way in. 'On Kawara, is a Japanese conceptual artist who lived in New York . . . bla . . . bla . . . bla, oh, OK, I see, so his art is all about normal things he did every day, like who he saw, where he went, what he ate, and he made a record of it all, so these people are counting every single day out loud. Wow. It's weird, but I like the idea, don't you?'

'Yeh,' says Three, 'but I could do that.'

'Well then, you should, and maybe one day, you can have an

exhibit here with all your stuff? And we can all come to admire a big long line of all your different stinky socks . . .'

'Yeh,' says Red, agreeing that's no bad idea.

'Yeh,' says Three, knowing it is, and that she's kidding.

'So, my hearts, here we are right in the middle of this fantastic building. What do we always try to look for in any interesting space?'

The boys know this, it's par for the course on outings with Rosie, so they quickfire the words they know.

'Umm, colour, form, shape . . .' says Three.

'Yeh, umm, that word for clever, yeh, genius, umm . . . funny . . . not funny . . . what is it?' asks Red, then remembers, 'yeh humour . . . and . . . and . . .'

'I know, beauty' says Three.

'Beauty' repeats Rosie. 'I think that's my most important one. Although humour comes a pretty close second. Now, here's what's going to happen. I'm too babyfat to walk all the way up that curvy ramp, so I am going to sit here like a happy lump, and enjoy the view. You two are going to go up, up, having a look at the Japanese guy's work all the way, using your eyes and noticing everything so that you can tell me all about it when you get back down. Did you know you could see before you could speak? So, really look, look, look, OK? The ramp up is one long continual spiral, so just keep following it to the top up there. Once you get there, and you've done all your looking, and you're both ready, CAREFULLY – note that word please,

CAREFULLY – look over the wall to me sitting here and give me the thumbs up, OK? And when I give you the thumbs up back, you can commence Operation W.B. Shall we have a quick demo of the thumbs up, so there's no confusion? Here goes, you guys first . . .'

They both do it to her. She does it back.

'Right. We're ready. Off you go, and take your time, because I really want you to remember what you see so you can tell it all to me. Good luck, men, your country's proud of you.'

She slaps them both heartily on the back, and sends them off to start their exploration.

Rosie sits down on the nearest seat, which is in fact a low concrete wall, and she is grateful to take the weight off her feet. She sees the heads of the boys – one blondie red, one tomato-soup red, both unmistakable – as they gradually make their way up through the winding exhibition space. She allows herself time to drink it all in, and she acknowledges that moments like these, still and calm, are sublime. Even the normal, earthly timescale seems altered in a space so extraordinary, and while the unmarked time ticks by, she lets her heartbeat slow down. This must surely be good for the baby, the unruffled lack of rush. Rosie feels open and bright, the way she sometimes can in a church. Here, she allows all the subdued movement and chatter to pass her by. She likes it, it's cheerful and it's all around, but sitting, stopping and shutting up, are her way to an inner hush.

She breathes deeply, and closes her eyes for a moment, and when she shuts down that sense of sight, the others seem to perk up. She hears the muffled big quiet of people trudging around softly, showing respect for the artists' work. She smells the air from the chilly outside that has clung to the coats of people coming in and swooshing past her. She can still taste the remnants of the gum she disposed of in a bin two blocks away, and she's aware of how much she desires coffee, and how she's trying to have less. She can feel the coarse wool of her beloved green coat under her cold hands. She can feel the tightening of the coat around her swelling stomach. She moves her right hand up to flick her hair behind her ear and she feels the earring there with her fingers. Cherry earrings. Big and dangly. And so red. She can't see them, but she knows they are. She loves them. And then, she feels a turning from the baby, it could almost make her nauseous, but it's curious and miraculous, so she surrenders to it. The baby is taking its place, ready to be known, life waiting to live. Rosie slowly opens her eyes and she thinks, 'Yep, this is sort of it. The bliss I've been looking for. Someone else needs me, and they come first, and there's no denying it. I am going to be someone's mother, someone's everything. And they will be mine. Always.' Rosie Kitto is full of happiness. Full right up. She smiles and smiles.

The young man and woman are still at the desk, counting away the minutes, 'Twelve thousand, eight hundred and forty four . . .'

Rosie looks up. The boys are one floor below the top level, moving on up gradually. How lucky they are to have each other, their enduring need for love and security met so intimately. Rosie thinks about how being a twin has somehow helped both of these little chaps process all that's gone on around them. The distraction and the support for each by the other is key. They know and manage one another so well, fitting into each other seamlessly. Even when they differ, or disagree, they at least understand it about each other. She can't imagine being a twin.

A sudden shocking thought comes hurtling into her peace. OH GOD. What if she is carrying twins?! It's possible, it's in the genetics of the Wilder-Binghams. It could be. But wait ... no ... she has had scans. Expensive scans conducted by clever trained individuals in a reputable hospital, paid for by Thomas. No. She has an ultrasound image. There's one baby. She has seen it, with its little hand held up as if it's halting traffic, as if it's saying, 'hold it, I'll decide when, thank you.' She didn't ask to know the sex, it simply doesn't matter. And actually, it doesn't matter if it's twins either. In fact ...

Just as Rosie starts to fantasize about this possibility, she hears a whistle and looks up. There is Three, giving her the thumbs up over the wall. This is it. The moment all three of them have been talking about for the last couple of days. The boys have planned it meticulously, as if they are junior ninjas, and this is their secret mission. Rosie stands and moves to the centre of the circular hall, and she gives the thumbs up signal back.

At the very top of the building, the highest point of the ramp, the two intrepid eight-year-old adventurers cautiously look around to check that no guards are watching too closely. The coast is clear, the first guard is on the next level down, and is conveniently distracted by a girl in short shorts.

In a trice, the boys kneel down and, pressing the special invisible button on the side of their respective pairs of sneakers, the hidden wheels pop out under the heels. They stand up, lean back and before anyone can truly realize what's going on, off they both skate, gliding along in what appear to be normal sneakers. These sneakers are anything but normal, they are instruments of tremendous thrill, and both of the lads are adept at manoeuvring on them. Just as well, since they have plenty of dodging to do as they gather speed, flying downwards on the continuous sloping spiral ramp, faster and faster. Zoom, past the guard who only notices when it's too late.

'Hey! Stop! You kids!' he shouts, and everyone looks to see the boys zipping down the huge helter skelter.

'Come on, boys, go go go,' whispers Rosie under her breath as she spins round, watching them fly along on their downward race. Three is very slightly falling behind the more athletic Red, so Red reaches out his hand and they whizz down the last couple of levels linked together, whilst all the people in the building stand back to make a safe track for them to complete their wonderful ride. The onlookers start to clap as they tear by, and a few even help to hold the guards back. Zoom, zoom, zoom they go, round and round, with the wind in their hair and megawatt smiles. Very shortly they reach the bottom, by which time Rosie has waddled to the main exit and is holding open the door for the twins to shoot out, onto the sidewalk and away from any consequences. As they pass her, she shouts,

'Splendid work ninjas! Hooray!' and she puffs as she tries to catch up with them on the corner. They quickly flick their wheels back inside and all three of them resume ordinary walking towards 90th St, one block away, where they can celebrate and toast their superb victory.

Operation W.B. complete.

December

Iva places her suitcase in the hall, just inside the front door. Her shoes are soaking wet due to the short walk from the cab to the kerb outside through the slushy snow. She takes her coat and woolly hat off, and she stands still to listen out for anyone in the apartment. Nothing. It's unusual for there to be nobody home at all in the middle of the afternoon, so she takes a little exploratory walk and checks in each room. There is a definite change from the place she left. Curtains are pushed well back, letting tons more light in. Everything is brighter, messier, and more lived in. Doors are open, and the occasional tiny crack of an open window allows a cheeky cold breeze in and through. Cuttings are growing in pots on almost any spare surface, a few whole plants are inside for shelter against the winter frosts, and the kitchen worktops are covered in pots of herbs. This is now an apartment you might want to hang out in.

Iva notices, however, that the dishwasher is open, and half loaded. Clearly, whoever was doing that job was in a rush. She smiles, rolls up her sleeves, and sets about the stack of dirty dishes in the sink. Yep, they still need her here. Which is just as well, because fourteen hours ago, her heart broke as she walked away from her crying daughter yet again as she boarded the plane back to this place.

Three blocks away, Rosie is at an antenatal class. She is lying on her back on the floor, on a cushioned mat, with her feet flat on the mat and her knees raised up. She has a cushion under her head, and a professionally pink woman is walking around, weaving in between the twenty or so mats with other pregnant women on them, blethering on about breathing and breaking waters and stretch marks and how special and precious 'baby' is. Rosie is very large now, in her third trimester, and she has had a tolerance by-pass, it seems. Something about the droning midwife annoys her. It's the silly infantile language she uses, as if all the potential mothers are actually babies themselves. Rosie didn't really want to come, but was persuaded by the doctor. She reluctantly tries to make the best of it by smiling at the woman on the mat next to her, and she gets a very uncertain smile back. She notices that this woman is looking towards the top of Rosie's mat, which is where 'daddy' is supposed to sit and be supportive. The other lady's husband is dutifully stroking her head with his bony fingers. At the head of Rosie's mat sit Thomas and Kemble and Teddy. The nosy lady is confused, and gives Rosie a slightly disapproving sneer. Rosie isn't going to have this lofty nonsense, so she says, 'Yes. I'm VERY popular,' and that puts a stop to it. The Wilder-Bingham chaps look sheepish. Teddy goes bright red. Again.

As the night draws in back at home, Thomas suggests that they all get their coats on and take the twins up onto the snowy roof to decorate the biggest, hardiest plant for Christmas. He and Kemble use logs and firewood kindling soaked in gasoline to start a red-hot fire in a brazier, while Rosie sits wrapped up in three of Thomas's huge winter coats, directing the twins and Teddy, who are putting lights on the box-plant, along with lots of little hand-drawn Christmas figures the boys have made at school. On closer inspection, Rosie sees that the figures are all the people in the family. They have drawn everybody: Thomas, Glenn, Kemble, Natalie, Teddy, Rosie, Iva and, of course, themselves. They have laminated the little figures so that they can hang outdoors. They are for the most part quite accurate depictions of the family. They have drawn themselves as superheroes though, and Rosie seems to be an entire sphere, which is pretty authentic.

Iva brings a tray of steaming mugs of hot chocolate out onto

348

the roof, and with that, she brings the reassurance that she is back to buoy up the whole clan. They all stand in a circle around the red-hot brazier, sipping the warming drink, their faces burning and their backs freezing. Red and Three pretend the steam from the hot liquid is smoke, and they enjoy invisible cigarettes. Red offers one to his father, and Kemble willingly takes it and joins in, puffing the 'smoke' into the cold night sky.

Then, from utterly nowhere, Three suddenly says, 'Hey, Dad. Teds says you are a homosocksial, is that true?'

Kemble splutters his hot chocolate, and it fizzles on the brazier. 'Holy shitballs, Teds, thanks!'

'You said to help you tell them . . .'

'Yeh, but, jeez . . .'

'What is that, anyway?' says little Red.

Kemble is stumped. He feels all eyes on him, and he has no idea what he should say.

It's Thomas, standing next to Kemble, who breaks the silence, 'A homosexual, boys, is a free spirit,' and pats his son on the shoulder.

With that one small gesture, Kemble knows that his dad has his back, that there is no judgement, that perhaps he has suspected all along, and most importantly, that he is loved no matter what. Kemble is instantly ten tons lighter. He didn't realize how heavy he'd been.

'Hope I get to be a homosexual too,' says Three, and they all laugh, and relax a bit.

'The thing is, guys,' says Kemble, gathering his thoughts, 'you need to be whoever you really are, that's all. You two may be twins, but you are really different to each other, aren't you? You're unique, like Teddy is. So you need to notice all the stuff you're good at, all the stuff you are . . . and really be that. You don't have to be like me, be you. Whatever that may be.'

At this, Teddy looks across at his grandfather and they have a shared moment when they remember that Thomas gave his grandson this exact same advice just recently. So, the apple don't fall too far from the tree after all. How comforting. Teddy loves that it all chimes together. He also loves that he knew his granpop wouldn't make this difficult for his dad, he even told him so, and look, he was right. It's OK. It's really OK.

Kemble, Teddy and the boys surrender to the cold, admit defeat, and head indoors, mumbling about nachos and peanut-butter cups and other snacks they want to pillage the larder for. Thomas stays by the brazier to make sure it is safe to leave. Rosie and Iva stay with him.

'Well, wow, that Chaka'd my Khan!' says Rosie.

'Dear boy,' says Thomas.

'I knew this,' says Iva, 'always smells too good to be not gay, and has four tweezers.'

'I see' says Thomas, a bit bewildered.

The three of them stand for a moment, looking into the embers. All of them are thinking about Glenn, but no-one speaks of her.

Iva doesn't feel it's her place.

Rosie doesn't want to upset Thomas.

Thomas doesn't want to cry.

He coughs. Then, 'How was your time at home, Iva?'

'Yes. Good. Thank you Mr W.B. Was good to see my girl for long time. She grow so much. Coming a beautiful young woman.'

'Like her mum', says Rosie, slipping an arm around her.

They look again into the bright light of the dying fire. It's as if all the good ideas are in there.

'Iva,' says Thomas, 'I was just thinking, how about if your daughter came to spend Christmas with us here . . . ?' Iva looks at him. He means it, so she walks around the fire and throws her arms around him, and she doesn't feel cold any more.

Night

It's four a.m. An unholy time, the amber between very late and very early. The front door to the Wilder-Bingham apartment clicks gently and opens quietly. It's Glenn. She slips in stealthily. She is in her coat and stockinged feet, holding her shoes.

All is quiet, all is still. She stands motionless for a few seconds, drinking in the place she loves and misses the most. Then, in the darkness, she walks slowly down the hallway to the door of her old bedroom. As she pushes it open, her heart stops beating in anxious anticipation of finding something that will topple her. But no. There he is, big ol' daddy bear Thomas, fast asleep in their bed, sprawled over onto her side of it, and in his pyjamas. She watches him sleep. There is only the faintest half-light spilling in from the bathroom, but even in this, she can see he looks older than just a few months ago. Considerably older. Her darling man, breathing himself away.

She looks up and catches sight of herself in her dressing-table mirror, and sees that the same is true of her. Much older.

Older than a few months should rightly render her. She's whiter, more see-through than when she left here, because she has kept herself in the strict Gollum-dark ever since. Thankfully though, Thomas didn't see her a month ago, when she was at her dangerously thinnest. She at least has a layer of flesh on her brittle bones now, thanks to the endless supply of soup and noodles and spinach and chocolate milk and mashed potato Rosie has been grazing her on, all the while revealing an astonishing insight into Rosie's own comfort-eating habits. Something Glenn would like to address with her one day. But not now. Definitely not now.

Now matters more than ever, this very moment may decide so much about her future. She reaches over, and clicks the bedside light on. Thomas stirs and blinks awake, he is drowsy and ruffled like an old grizzly waking from hibernation. Slowly but surely he comes to, and realizes that she is there.

'What time is it?' he says, with a dry mouth.

'Do we still love each other, Tommy?' she says quietly, and in the big pause that follows, she hands him his glass of water from the bedside table, and he drinks.

He sits up properly and blinks at her. 'Yes. Most certainly. Well, I can only speak for myself, but . . . YES. Because I can only be as happy as you are, and because I . . . only know how to *be* when I'm part of you. That's gotta be love . . . isn't it?'

'Happy? I would like that very much. I haven't been for some time . . .'

'I know . . . I'm sorry . . .' he says.

'No, stop, it's up to me. I have to find it, I keep letting everything get in the way, and I've got used to thinking it's just out of my reach, like it'll be taken if I let it be here. Success is ringed by vultures, it'll be pecked at and ruined.'

'Glennie, you're confusing success and happiness.'

'It's nearly too late to get it right . . .' she says.

'No, no it's not. Because you really don't have to be perfect, my love, in fact I think it's a bit easier when there are a few mistakes along the way. We can all relate to failure, God knows, I certainly can. Don't quote me, but I think that's called being human. Isn't it?'

'Maybe . . .' she says.

'Why don't you try it for a while? Being human.'

Thomas knows this is challenging talk, he knows her like the back of his hand, and so also knows that she respects the tough line. She sits down on the bed. Looking at her there, in the night, in her coat, he feels so tenderly towards her, and he can see how very lost she is. The toppled queen. Yet there's something else, she seems softer, more open. He has an overwhelming desire to scoop her up and protect her. He remembers the young Glenn, and how he chose her above all others because she was different, not one of those uniformed ten-a-dime preppy debs. She was independent and prickly with a hint of wild. Look at her now. She has nearly killed herself trying to be like the others, yet what he especially loves about

354

her, is that she isn't. He needs her to know, so he says, 'I wish I could shrink your fear, Glennie, then you could just come home and be my wife, Kemble's mother and the boys' granma. The real true you. Not the one you try so hard to pretend to be. Christ, it's gotta be easier to let yourself off that hook. Just for the record, wife, zero fucks are given here about you being perfect, or any of us for that matter. We've got it wrong. So what?! Let's live, my darling, whatever best way we can, so long as it's together, eh? You know living? It's all the chaotic, messy stuff you do before dying. Whaddya say?'

She looks at him, 'I say sorry. That's what I say . . .'

'Hey, no . . .' Thomas tries to stop her,

'Shush, Tommy, listen. You know you're my king. I always wanted the best for you, and it was so hard to find out I wasn't the best. I did the deadliest thing, I weighed myself in the balance, and boy was I found wanting, so goddam disappointing, in every department. You were, you are, so very . . . beautiful. Always. More now even. You bastard. Yep, I knew you were going to be a hard dog to keep on the porch . . . I expected that . . .'

'Seriously Glenn. Do not make excuses for me. Please. I have made wrong decisions, not your fault. Me. Greedy me. All me. Not to do with you. I can't bear you would think that. It's more to do with panicking, time running out, y'know, we climb the stairs in this short life, up, up til now we're at the top of the house, that's us. High up. I have felt terror there, vertigo,

355

and I have been weak. And for that, I am so sorry. But I know now that I only have two choices: I can throw myself off or I can enjoy the view. And I want the latter. But I want to enjoy it with you. I can't do that unless you forgive me. Honestly forgive me, only that will do it. And I will know if it's not real, so don't try faking it.'

'Let's take it slow, and see . . .' she says, letting her blood run a bit warmer in her veins again. Thomas has returned her power to her, but this time, it fits her right, she can envisage a place, a position for her that is truthful. A sense of relief floods through her.

She continues, 'I've been lost, Tommy. I can't even walk properly, I'm just . . . constantly falling forward and then stepping just in time. It's no way to get anywhere.'

'Are you home now?' he asks, tentatively.

She pauses, then, 'I don't think so . . . yet . . .' she says.

'OK, OK. I'll wait. Just be right here, waiting. But, my little queen, would you at least take your coat off and lie down here with me for a while? Let me keep you warm? Just a few minutes?' he says, smiling, and holding the sheets back for her to climb in next to him.

'Sure you want to? Rosie says it's hard to cuddle a porcupine . . .'

They both laugh. Rosie. That girl. That trouble.

Glenn takes her coat off, and lays it neatly on the end of the bed, and she clambers in beside him. Immediately, her body knows his and she knows this is where she needs to be. And soon.

'That's it,' he says as he pulls her close, 'that's where my love belongs. What a phenomenally interesting woman you are. Thank you for coming here.'

And they lie together while she thaws.

'Don't ever die,' she whispers.

'Promise I won't,' he whispers back.

An hour or so later, as dawn is breaking outside, Glenn silently pads back along the corridor like a guilty mistress. She glances into Thomas's office, and sees there, the portrait of herself on the easel. She gasps. Yes, it's her, his wife.

As she tiptoes to the door, Iva appears from seemingly nowhere in a dressing gown and hands her a small plastic tub.

'Sausage in beer with cabbage. Will make you strong Mrs W.B.'

Glenn looks at her. In that moment Glenn couldn't be more grateful for the kindness.

'Thank you, Iva,' she says. With that, Glenn slips out of 21 East 90th St, with her head up and new hope.

They both know how much a consideration like this matters when you feel like you're a million miles away from what is really important.

New Day

Rosie Kitto is a big fat beached whale.

And she doesn't mind one bit, in fact she is playing it to the hilt, sitting in the corner of the kitchen, loudly directing operations from a large comfy chair on this bright winter morning. She is barking jokey orders at the twins,

'Get me waffles! Now! With blueberries! And peel the blueberries! Individually! Spit Spot!'

The boys are running about, answering to her every whim, her crazed slaves. Kemble, Thomas and Teddy join in the fun and add their raised voices to the orders, 'Juice! Here! Toast! Hurry! Eggs over easy! With a side of lobster thermidor! Now! Yesterday! With iced hot water!'

It's a busy, communal affair, with everyone chipping in, interrupting and messing about.

Iva is in the centre of the lovely chaos, supervising all the actual cooking. Sitting at the end of the counter, wide-eyed, amazed and tipping into occasional bewildered laughter is

Zofia, who arrived two days ago to spend the Christmas holiday with her mother in mad New York with all these mad people being mad. Iva explains in Polish to her that this family is crazy and not to worry, no one is shouting for real. Zofia has her hand to her mouth while she watches, delighted. She is a shy girl, the image of her mother, short and chunky with dark eyes and long dark hair brushed up into a neat, thick ponytail. She wears a home-made blouse her auntie sewed. She embroidered the collar with bright red thread in the shapes of birds and trees, and this lovingly made item of clothing sets the young girl apart as a foreigner, so unlike a cool fourteen-year-old native New Yorker. There is, refreshingly, no fashion to her whatsoever, except for her tell-tale cherished Beyoncé phone cover. Zofia is a bright-eyed innocent, and the twins love her. The only way they have communicated with her so far is to make her laugh, and once they discovered what a willing audience she is they doubled their efforts, which is part of their manic face-pulling clowning this morning.

The jollity is infectious, and the more Rosie laughs and laughs the more the twins show off.

In amongst the noise and the chatter and the yelling and the laughing, Rosie clutches her huge belly. She looks at Iva, the only one tuned to her from across the room. Could it be? It's a few days earlier than expected . . .

Then there's another pain.

And another.

Contractions.

This is it.

Now, the havoc changes into a new, different type of chaos as they all realize that this is the baby arriving, and everyone overhelps Rosie until Iva powers through and takes control.

At the same time, down in SoHo, Glenn is in her apartment, finishing her breakfast banana and watering the small bay tree Rosie planted for her to have indoors, alongside the basil and rosemary she is growing in pots from cuttings Rosie has taken from the roof garden. She has a little piece of home flourishing here, something to nurture and keep alive alongside herself.

As she lifts the small watering can, a shaft of sunlight nearly blinds her. She blinks and moves out of its way, but then, she has a thought and she steps back into it, closes her eyes, and stays there enjoying the warmth. She walks to the large window and folds back the shutters one by one, letting the golden winter sun flood into the huge room. She breathes it in, everso slightly fearful that she might just crumple to dust. But she doesn't.

She exhales and feels her heart expanding. How can light do this? It transforms everything. She turns her back to the big glass, and feels the heat spread from her shoulders to her bum. She sees how the light embraces everything in the room, and particularly how it falls onto the small painting she took from the apartment. She has it propped up on the mantelpiece. This portrait of Glenn Wilder-Bingham, lovingly painted by her husband. She adores it, and she notices how well it loves the light. There she is, staring back at her, the resurrected Glenn, the one with a purpose and a future and a family to keep together. The woman who doesn't want to just visit her life occasionally, the one who wants to properly live it. At that moment, her phone rings, with news from the hospital . . .

In the waiting room of Lennox Hill Hospital's maternity ward sit three potential fathers, the twins and Zofia. The men are anxious and pacing. The children are busy with crayons and colouring books. Even the older Zofia is enjoying the careful filling-in between the lines of the endless patterns in the battered dog-eared books.

'Will there be, like, loads of blood? 'Cause I might barf,' says Red.

'Shush son,' says Kemble.

'How does it get out?' asks Three.

'Shush,' says Thomas.

'How did it get in there?' says Red.

'Seriously dudes. Zip it. Or know violence,' says Teddy.

They hear the distant sound of a woman's strained cry. They all look up and remain, stock still, on alert, like meer-cats.

In the maternity suite, Rosie has chosen Iva as her birth-partner. Iva, the wisest and most composed person Rosie has ever known. Iva the faithful. Iva the great. This is who Rosie chooses to lay eyes on as she submits to the animalistic state she is into, the searing pain that threatens to gulp her up. Iva has done it before and knows what little whispers of comfort and encouragement to give her friend.

She reminds Rosie that, 'You not goin' to die. You just goin' to break for a little while. That baby fightin' hard. Come on, Miss Rosie, bet you sorry now that you such a slut . . .'

The doctor and midwives disguise their astonishment behind little giggles. But Iva's approach seems to be working. The puffing red-faced Rosie sets her jaw against each onslaught of contractions, as if England were invading Cornwall.

She girds herself with the rallying war cries of home, as she shouts at herself, 'Get on, maid! Oggy Oggy! Come on my 'ansome! Proper job!' between each of the crushing spasms. She pants and screams, loud and hearty, railing at nature.

Come on, Rosie.

This is what you've always wanted.

You can do it.

Mighty Rosie Kitto.

Who deserves this gift.

One last push, maid . . .

The nurse beckons the men into the room, and with the children trailing obediently behind, they all pad in quietly, keeping their voices to reverential hushed whispers.

Rosie is propped up with the lovingly wrapped-up wrinkly pink wonder in her arms. All they can see from the door are tiny fingers experimenting with the air. As they creep closer, they see the baby, eyes wide open and locked onto the mother's astonished beatific face. Mother and baby gaze at each other in stunned amazement. This is what giant love looks like. Two human beings, meeting for the first time, who will never let anyone or anything come between them. A bond even God couldn't break.

Teddy, Thomas and Kemble draw close.

'Who is this?' Thomas asks, hardly able to speak.

'This is Kensa. It's Cornish for first. She's the first girl in this family.'

'Kensa,' he repeats it. They all do, like an echo around the room, they try the name out loud.

'Kensa.'

'Kensa.'

'Kensa.'

'Yes,' Rosie says, 'Kensa Kitto. Say hello, boys.' The twins clamber up onto the bed next to her to get a better look.

'She looks like a monkey,' says Red.

'A pretty monkey,' says Three, making it better.

'That's your nose,' whispers Teddy to Kemble.

'And that's your chin,' says Thomas to Teddy.

'Hope she doesn't have my personality,' says Kemble.

'She's so wrinkly,' says Three.

'Yep. That will change. For about twenty years, somewhere in the middle of her life,' says Thomas, and then, 'she's . . . lovely.'

'Yeh,' says Teddy.

'Takes after her mom,' says Iva.

They all agree, and one by one, they all lean in and kiss Kensa.

Standing outside the door, watching this tender nativity through the glass, is Glenn. This could be everything she fears the most, but it isn't anymore, because this is the Glenn who opened the shutters, who is grateful to see the beauty of the scene, who longs to be a key part of it, who knows she has much to offer.

Who wants to love and be beloved.

This is she.

364

She pushes open the door, and as they all stand back and watch, she walks towards the bed.

'May I?' she asks.

'YES. YES. YES.' Says Rosie.

Glenn carefully lifts the baby into her arms, the first besides her mother to hold her, and with that one compassionate, gentle, gesture, the new life begins.

Acknowledgements

Carol Noble – for being brilliant, and joining me on the first leg of this adventure

Emma Kilcoyne – for never-ending encouragement and ferocious intelligence

Sue Hunter – for endless patience and typing

Debs Walker – for protection and scanning

Dave, Sammy, Emma and Mike – for keeping the home fires burning

Jono and Judith – for being true friends

Louise Moore – for keeping the faith

Jill, Liz, Huw and all at Michael Joseph – for hard work

Maureen Vincent – for anchorage

Robert Kirby – for foresight

Nicole Kidman – for being a mensch

Leigh, Liz, Jennifer and all my Spence buddies

All the kids I babysat in Manhattan

Ma and Pa Bignell – for pasties and support

Billie, Lils and Oly – for being my purpose

Nigel Carrivick – for excellent reading and kitten heels

The mighty B.F. – for reading aloud and for EVERYTHING else

Biggs – for all the endless love

Dolly – for bein' my faithful chum

If you loved

According to YES

and want to experience more
of Dawn's warm, funny writing,
then why not try her other novels

A Tiny Bit Marvellous

&

Oh Dear Silvia

For a taster of each,
just turn the page…

A Tiny Bit Marvellous

ONE

Dora (17 YRS)

My mother is, like, a totally confirmed A-list bloody cocking minging arsehole cretin cockhead of the highest order. Fact. In fact, I, of this moment, officially declare my entire doubt of the fact that she is in fact my actual real mother. She can't be. I can't have come from that wonk. Nothing in any tiny atom of my entire body bears any likeness to an iota of any bit of her. It's so, like, entirely unfair when people say we look alike because like, excuse me, but we properly <u>DON'T</u> thank you. And I should know. Because I look at her disgusting face 20/7 <u>and</u> excuse me, I do actually have a mirror thank you. Which I've looked in and so <u>NOT</u> seen her face, younger or otherwise, staring back at me. If I do ever see that hideousness, please drown me immediately in the nearest large collection of deep water. I would honestly be grateful for that act of random mercy.

At 5.45pm today she had the actual nerve to inform me that I will *not* apparently be having my belly button pierced after all, until my eighteenth birthday. She knows I booked it for this Saturday. She knows Lottie is having hers done. It was going to be our like together forever thing. Fuck my mother and all who sail in her. I hate her. She's fired.

TWO

Mo (49 YRS)

All things considered, that went rather well. Big pat on own back, Mo. I am definitely getting better at not letting her appalling language upset me. No one likes to be referred to as an 'evil slag', or 'hell whore', let's be honest, but I've suffered worse at the sharp end of her tongue, so ironically I'm grateful for these comparatively lesser lashings.

I am reminded of the trusty old David Walsh mantra I often recommend to my clients, 'When, in argument, you feel like taking the wind out of her sails, it is a better idea to take your sails out of her wind.' It certainly was no breezy zephyr I felt battering my aft as I purposely walked away, it was a Force 10 brute, but I am broad in the beam and made of suitably stern-ish stuff. As yet, unscuppered. If lilting a tad.

Yet again, no sign of Husband at the eye of the storm. He scuttled off to a safe port in the study to spend time with his ever-ready, ever-understanding lover, MAC. His endless muttered bleatings about female politics being a mystery are weak and wobbly to the point of jelly. Why does he constantly refuse to back me up at these critical moments? I have repeatedly explained the importance of consistency and continuity as far as the kids are concerned. We must present a united front. We should share my opinion at all times. I am, after all, the qualified child psychologist in this family. Other than fathering two children (total of six minutes' commitment to the project), I'm not aware of his training. However, have to give it to him, he is certainly a supremely skilled slinker-off-er when voices are raised, no one can better his retreating technique. He certainly gets the gold in *that* backwards race. Oh yes.

Then, he had the audacity to sit in Dora's bedroom with her for an hour whilst she apparently 'emptied out' and explained to him that she feels she and I are enemies and have been for years. I am not her enemy, I am her mother. Sometimes it's probably the same thing. It needs to be. I am <u>not</u> here to be her friend.

What *am* I here for actually? To be a guide, a judge, an inquisitor maybe? At the moment I am purely transport, bank and occasional punch bag.

Everso recently, it would have been me sitting next to her on that bed getting a wet shoulder complete with smeared mascara splats.

What a huge difference between fifteen and seventeen years of age. An entire personality flip has happened. Where has my sweet little goth gone? She of the smudgy eyes and red nylon dreadlocks and Tank Girl industrial boots and clamp-on nose-rings? It was so easy to love that one. That one was endearingly injured and tragic. Why have I been sent this Tango-skinned bleached-hair designer slave? I own a human

Cindy. Her insufferable rudeness grows with every waking moment. And quite a few sleeping moments I suspect. I'm sure she doesn't waste any dream time <u>NOT</u> hating me. Does hate have a cumulative effect? If so, Dora will be earning buckets of interest on her massive deposits of mum-hate. I just have to accept it, she loathes me.

Today's particular loathing is about refusing to let her have her belly button pierced. In this particular respect, I feel entirely vindicated. Was there ever an uglier mutilation? The very thought of it makes my unpierced and considerably larger stomach turn. Her choice of 'parlour' is that nasty dirty little dungeon opposite the carpet shop in the high street, 'Pangbourne Ink'. Obviously I've never ventured in, but I know the sister of the troll who owns it and she had chronic impetigo last year, so if Dora thinks I am sanctioning such a dreadful thing and in such a dirty place, she can think again.

Of course, soon she will be eighteen and if she chooses to maim herself *then*, she can pay for the privilege. I am not a medical doctor, but if something terrible were to happen to her belly button, an infection of some sort, wouldn't that seal her umbilical tubes? How would any potential grandchild of mine get its nourishment? She is risking any future child-bearing possibilities. Is there no end to her selfishness?

THREE

Oscar (16 YRS)

The suffering of the last hour has been unutterably awful. Both of the Battle harridans, the monstrous mater <u>and</u> the dreadful daughter, have been shrieking sufficiently enough to wake as yet undiscovered molluscs at the pit-bottom of the ocean's silty depths. I have mastered the art of ear-fugging – the application of twisted curls of wet kitchen paper administered to the inner ears. One would imagine this would provide a merciful relief. Yet still, their damnable harpy squawking prevails.

What unlovely wretches they prove themselves to be, abandoning all vestiges of class and style, allowing the vulgarity of their lower-middle-class shackles to triumph. How very very very disappointed I am in both of them. It is so extremely tiresome. I am exhausted from the disappointment. I must needs take to my bed. The confines of my room offer the succour and solitude I sorely need. Increasingly, I discover that the delights of the Nintendo III Dance Mat Challenge are my only worthy companion. There, at least, the red fires of my passion are sated. Farewell, dear diary, 'til anon.

AN EXTRACT FROM

Oh Dear Silvia

ONE

Ed

Wednesday 10am

He sits with a sense of being watched, although he himself is the watcher. Momentarily, the others have stepped outside so he is suddenly, shockingly, alone with her. It's odd for there to be no voices. No sound, save those of two human beings just being alive. He becomes acutely aware that for the first time in a very long time, he feels irrefutably more alive than her. She's always making sure you know she's chock-full o'life. She lives big and loud. Right to her fingertips. Her presently somewhat swollen fingertips. Look at them. Someone, perhaps a nurse, has tried to remove the coral-red varnish, but it is stubborn and has bled into her skin, revealing the nails beneath to be unbeautiful, nicotiney. Blotchy red fingers. Yellow nails.

She wouldn't like him to see such a personal thing, so he tries to stop looking . . . but of course he can't. He is transfixed by the unusual sighting. He feels her watching, and although she isn't and although he so wants to remain defiant, he looks away.

So. Here they both are again. Alone. They haven't been alone in a room for ... well, since they were married. What's that? About ... God ... What is it now? Five years? Something like that.

There she is. Breathing.

Here he is. Breathing.

That's it.

Pretty much like it was at the end of the marriage, really. Two people occupying the same air. Nothing else in common. Just oxygen. He remembers when sharing breath with her was exciting, intimate. He would lie close to her in the night, happily breathing in what she breathed out. The breath of life, their joint breath from their joint life.

This breathing now, though, is very different.

He hears his own. It's quick and halting. It fits with his heartbeat, which is anxiously fast and occasionally missing altogether, when he finds himself holding his breath whilst urgent frightening thoughts distract him.

Her breathing is entirely unfamiliar. It's regimented and deep. Her lungs are rhythmically resonating loudly around the room, chiming in with the bellow-like wheezing of the machine. She's being breathed for, through a huge ugly tube in her throat.

Because Silvia Shute, despite all the supposed life in her, is in a coma.